BOOMING

when Dan and his wolf-dog strode into the bar.
Silence fell. Tempers flared. Jerry Strann
had been spoiling for a brawl all day.

"Is this a damned kennel?" he taunted.
"Do I got to drink in a barnyard?
What's the dog doin' here?"

And he caught up the heavy little whiskey glass
and hurled it at the crouching dog.
It thudded heavily, but it brought no yelp
of pain; instead, a black thunderbolt leaped from
the corner and lunged down the room.

Strann raised his gun. "It's a habit of mine
to kill mad dogs when I see 'em."
And he smiled again.

Though his gun cleared leather before
the stranger stirred, the one shot fired
was not Strann's.

"Anyone else think this is a barnyard?"
asked Dan.

And Strann lay dead and still.

Books by Max Brand

Published by POCKET BOOKS

• Contents •

Contents

1 • The Scholar

AT the age of six Randall Byrne could name and bound every state in the Union and give the date of its admission; at nine he was conversant with Homeric Greek and Caesar; at twelve he read Aristophanes with perfect understanding of the allusions of the day and divided his leisure between Ovid and Horace; at fifteen, wearied by the simplicity of Old English and Thirteenth Century Italian, he dipped into the history of Philosophy and passed from that, naturally, into calculus and the higher mathematics; at eighteen he took an A.B. from Harvard and while idling away a pleasant summer with Hebrew and Sanscrit he delved lightly into biology and its kindred sciences, having reached the conclusion that Truth is greater than Goodness or Beauty, because it comprises both, and the whole is greater than any of its parts; at twenty-one he pocketed his Ph.D. and was touched with the fever of his first practical enthusiasm—surgery. At twenty-four he was an M.D. and a distinguished diagnostician, though he preferred work in his laboratory in his endeavor to resolve the elements into simpler forms; also he published at this time a work on anthropology whose circulation was limited to two hundred copies, and he received in return two hundred letters of congratulation from great men who had tried to read his book; at twenty-seven he collapsed one fine spring day on the floor of his laboratory. That afternoon he was carried into the presence of a great physician who was also a very vulgar man. The great physician felt his pulse and looked into his dim eyes.

"You have a hundred and twenty horsepower brain and a runabout body," said the great physician.

"I have come," answered Randall Byrne faintly, "for the solution of a problem, not for the statement thereof."

"I'm not through," said the great physician. "Among other things you are a damned fool."

Randall Byrne here rubbed his eyes.

"What steps do you suggest that I consider?" he queried.

The great physician spat noisily.

"Marry a farmer's daughter," he said brutally.

"But," said Randall Byrne vaguely.

"I am a busy man and you've wasted ten minutes of my time," said the great physician, turning back to his plate glass window. "My secretary will send you a bill for one thousand dollars. Good-day."

And therefore, ten days later, Randall Byrne sat in his room in the hotel at Elkhead.

He had just written (to his friend Swinnerton Loughburne, M.A., Ph.D., L.L.D.): "Incontrovertibly the introduction of the personal equation leads to lamentable inversions, and the perceptive faculties when contemplating phenomena through the lens of ego too often conceive an accidental connotation or manifest distortion to be actuality, for the physical (or personal) too often beclouds that power of inner vision which so unerringly penetrates to the inherent truths of incorporeity and the extramundane. Yet this problem, to your eyes, I fear, not essentially novel or peculiarly involute, holds for my contemplative faculties an extraordinary fascination, to wit: wherein does the mind, in itself a muscle, escape from the laws of the physical, and wherein and wherefore do the laws of the physical exercise so inexorable a jurisdiction over the processes of the mind, so that a disorder of the visual nerve actually distorts the asomatous and veils the pneumatoscopic?

"Your pardon, dear Loughburne, for these lapses from the general to the particular, but in a lighter moment of idleness, I pray you give some careless thought to a problem now painfully my own, though rooted inevitably so deeply in the dirt of the commonplace.

"But you have asked me in a letter of recent date for the particular physical aspects of my present environment, and though (as you so well know) it is my conviction that the physical fact is not and only the immaterial is, yet I shall gladly look about me—a thing I have not yet seen occasion to do—and describe to you the details of my present condition."

Accordingly, at this point Randall Byrne removed from his nose his thick glasses and holding them poised he stared through the window at the view without. He had quite changed his appearance by removing his spectacles, for the owlish touch was gone and he seemed at a stroke ten years younger. It was such a face as one is glad to examine in detail, lean, pale, the transparent skin stretched tightly over cheekbones, nose, and chin. That chin was built on good fighting lines, though somewhat overdelicate in substance and the mouth quite colorless, but oddly enough the upper lip had that habitual appearance of stiff compression which is characteristic of highly strung temperaments; it is a noticeable feature of nearly every great actor, for instance. The nose was straight and very thin and in a strong sidelight a tracery of the red blood showed through at the nostrils. The eyes were deeply buried and the lower lids bruised with purple—weak eyes that blinked at a change of light or a sudden thought—distant eyes which missed the design of wall paper and saw the trees growing on the mountains. The forehead was Byrne's most noticeable feature, pyramidal, swelling largely toward the top and divided in the center into two distinct lobes by a single marked furrow which gave his expression a hint of the wistful. Looking at that forehead one was strangely conscious of the brain beneath. There seemed no bony structure; the mind, undefended, was growing and pushing the confining walls further out.

And the fragility which the head suggested the body confirmed, for he was not framed to labor. The burden of the noble head had bowed the slender throat and crooked the shoulders, and when he moved his arm it seemed the arm of a skeleton too loosely clad. There was a different connotation in the hands, to be sure. They were thin—bones and sinews chiefly, with the violet of the veins showing along the backs; but they were active hands without tremor—hands ideal for the accurate scalpel, where a fractional error means death to the helpless.

After a moment of staring through the window the scholar wrote again: "The major portion of Elkhead lies

within plain sight of my window. I see a general mer-
chandise store, twenty-seven buildings of a comparatively
major and eleven of a minor significance, and five sa-
loons. The streets——"

The streets, however, were not described at that sitting, for at this juncture a heavy hand knocked and the
door of Randall Byrne's room was flung open by Hank
Dwight, proprietor of Elkhead's saloon—a versatile man,
expert behind the bar or in a blacksmith shop.

"Doc," said Hank Dwight, "you're wanted."

Randall Byrne placed his spectacles more firmly on his
nose to consider his host.

"What——" he began, but Hank Dwight had already
turned on his heel.

"Her name is Kate Cumberland. A little speed, doc.
She's in a hurry."

"If no other physician is available," protested Byrne,
following slowly down the stairs, "I suppose I must see
her."

"If they was another within ten miles, d'you s'pose I'd
call on you?" asked Hank Dwight.

So saying, he led the way out onto the veranda,
where the doctor was aware of a girl in a short riding
skirt who stood with one gloved hand on her hip while
the other slapped a quirt idly against her riding boots.

2 · Words and Bullets

"HERE'S a gent that calls himself a doc," said Hank
Dwight, by way of an introduction. "If you can use
him, Miss Cumberland, fly to it!"

And he left them alone.

Now the sun lay directly behind Kate Cumberland
and in order to look at her closely the doctor had to
shade his weak eyes and pucker his brows; for from beneath her wide sombrero there rolled a cloud of golden
hair as bright as the sunshine itself—a sad strain upon

the visual nerve of Doctor Randall Byrne. He repeated her name, bowed, and when he straightened, blinked again. As if she appreciated that strain upon his eyes she stepped closer, and entered the shadow.

"Doctor Hardin is not in town," she said, "and I have to bring a physician out to the ranch at once; my father is critically ill."

Randall Byrne rubbed his lean chin.

"I am not practicing at present," he said reluctantly. Then he saw that she was watching him closely, weighing him with her eyes, and it came to the mind of Randall Byrne that he was not a large man and might not incline the scale far from the horizontal.

"I am hardly equipped——" began Byrne.

"You will not need equipment," she interrupted. "His troubles lies in his nerves and the state of his mind."

A slight gleam lighted the eyes of the doctor.

"Ah," he murmured. "The mind?"

"Yes."

He rubbed his bloodless hands slowly together, and when he spoke his voice was sharp and quick and wholly impersonal. "Tell me the symptons!"

"Can't we talk those over on the way to the ranch? Even if we start now it will be dark before we arrive."

"But," protested the doctor, "I have not yet decided—this precipitancy——"

"Oh," she said, and flushed. He perceived that she was on the verge of turning away, but something withheld her. "There is no other physician within reach; my father is very ill. I only ask that you come as a diagnostician, doctor!"

"But a ride to your ranch," he said miserably. "I presume you refer to riding a horse?"

"Naturally."

"I am unfamiliar with that means of locomotion," said the doctor with serious eyes, "and in fact have not carried my acquaintance with the equine species beyond a purely experimental stage. Anatomically I have a superficial knowledge, but on the one occasion on which I sat in a saddle I observed that the docility of the horse is probably a poetic fallacy."

He rubbed his left shoulder thoughtfully and saw a

slight tremor at the corners of the girl's mouth. It caused his vision to clear and concentrate; he found that the lips were, in fact, in the very act of smiling. The face of the doctor brightened.

"You shall ride my own horse," said the girl. "She is perfectly gentle and has a very easy gait. I'm sure you'll have not the slightest trouble with her."

"And you?"

"I'll find something about town; it doesn't matter what."

"This," said the doctor, "is most remarkable. You choose your mounts at random?"

"But you will go?" she insisted.

"Ah, yes, the trip to the ranch!" groaned the doctor. "Let me see: the physical obstacles to such a trip while many are not altogether insuperable, I may say; in the meantime the moral urge which compels me toward the ranch seems to be of the first order." He sighed. "Is it not strange, Miss Cumberland, that man, though distinguished from the lower orders by mind, so often is controlled in his actions by ethical impulses which override the considerations of reason? An observation which leads us toward the conclusion that the passion for goodness is a principle hardly secondary to the passion for truth. Understand that I build the hypothesis only tentatively, with many reservations, among which——"

He broke off short. The smile was growing upon her lips.

"I will put together a few of my things," said the doctor, "and come down to you at once."

"Good!" said the girl, "I'll be waiting for you with two horses before you are ready."

He turned away, but had taken hardly a step before he turned, saying: "But why are you so sure that you will be ready before I——" but she was already down the steps from the veranda and stepping briskly down the street.

"There is an element of the unexplainable in woman," said the doctor, and resumed his way to his room. Once there, something prompted him to act with the greatest possible speed. He tossed his toilet articles and a few changes of linen into a small, flexible valise and ran down the stairs. He reached the veranda again, panting, and the girl was not in sight; a smile of triumph appeared on the grave, colorless lips of the doctor. "Feminine instinct, however, is not infallible," he observed to himself, and to one of the cowboys, lounging loosely in a chair nearby, he continued his train of thoughts aloud: "Though the verity of the feminine intuition has already been thrown in a shade of doubt by many thinkers, as you will undoubtedly agree."

The man thus addressed allowed his lower jaw to drop but after a moment he ejaculated: "Now what in hell d'you mean by that?"

The doctor had already turned away, intent upon his thoughts, but he now paused and again faced the cowboy. He said, frowning: "There is unnecessary violence in your remark, sir."

"Duck your glasses," said the worthy in question. "You ain't talkin' to a book, you're talking to a man."

"And in your attitude," went on the doctor, "there is an element of offense which if carried farther might be corrected by physical violence."

"I don't foller your words," said the cattleman, "but from the drift of your tune I gather you're a bit peeved; and if you are——"

His voice had risen to a ringing note as he proceeded and he now slipped from his chair and faced Randall Byrne, a big man, brown, hard-handed. The doctor crimsoned.

"Well?" he echoed, but in place of a deep ring his words were pitched in a high squeak of defiance.

He saw a large hand contract to a fist, but almost instantly the big man grinned, and his eyes went past Byrne.

"Oh, hell!" he grunted, and turned his back with a chuckle.

For an instant there was a mad impulse in the doctor to spring at this fellow but a wave of impotence overwhelmed him. He knew that he was white around the mouth, and there was a dryness in his throat.

"The excitement of imminent physical contest and personal danger," he diagnosed swiftly, "causing acceleration of the pulse and attendant weakness of the body—a state unworthy of the balanced intellect."

Having brought back his poise by this quick interposition of reason, he went his way down the long veranda. Against a pillar leaned another tall cattleman, also brown and lean and hard.

"May I inquire," he said, "if you have any information direct or casual concerning a family named Cumberland which possesses ranch property in this vicinity?"

"You may," said the cowpuncher, and continued to roll his cigarette.

"Well," said the doctor, "do you know anything about them?"

"Sure," said the other, and having finished his cigarette he introduced it between his lips. It seemed to occur to him instantly, however, that he was committing an inhospitable breach, for he produced his Durham and brown papers with a start and extended them toward the doctor.

"Smoke?" he asked.

"I use tobacco in no form," said the doctor.

The cowboy stared with such fixity that the match burned down to his fingertips and singed them before he had lighted his cigarette.

" 'S that a fact?" he queried when his astonishment found utterance. "What d'you do to kill time? Well, I been thinking about knocking off the stuff for a while. Mame gets sore at me for having my fingers all stained up with nicotine like this."

He extended his hand, the first and second fingers of which were painted a bright yellow.

"Soap won't take it off," he remarked.

"A popular but inexcusable error," said the doctor. "It is the tarry by-products of tobacco which cause that stain. Nicotine itself, of course, is a volatile alkaloid base of which there is only the merest trace in tobacco. It is one of the deadliest of nerve poisons and is quite colorless. There is enough of that stain upon your fingers— if it were nicotine—to kill a dozen men."

"The hell you say!"

"Nevertheless, it is an indubitable fact. A lump of

nicotine the size of the head of a pin placed on the tongue of a horse will kill the beast instantly."

The cowpuncher pushed back his hat and scratched his head.

"This is worth knowin'," he said, "but I'm some glad that Mame ain't heard it."

"Concerning the Cumberlands," said the doctor, "I——"

"Concerning the Cumberlands," repeated the cattleman, "it's best to leave 'em to their own concerns." And he started to turn away, but the thirst for knowledge was dry in the throat of the doctor.

"Do I understand," he insisted, "that there is some mystery connected with them?"

"From me," replied the other, "you understand nothin'." And he lumbered down the steps and away.

Be it understood that there was nothing of the gossip in Randall Byrne, but now he was pardonably excited and perceiving the tall form of Hank Dwight in the doorway he approached his host.

"Mr. Dwight," he said, "I am about to go to the Cumberland ranch. I gather that there is something of an unusual nature concerning them."

"There is," admitted Hank Dwight.

"Can you tell me what it is?"

"I can."

"Good!" said the doctor, and he almost smiled. "It is always well to know the background of a case which has to do with mental states. Now, just what do you know?"

"I know—" began the proprietor, and then paused and eyed his guest dubiously. "I know," he continued, "a story."

"Yes?"

"Yes, about a man and a hoss and a dog."

"The approach seems not quite obvious, but I shall be glad to hear it."

There was a pause.

"Words," said the host, at length, "is worse'n bullets. You never know what they'll hit."

"But the story?" persisted Randall Byrne.

"That story," said Hank Dwight, "I may tell to my son before I die."

"This sounds quite promising."

"But I'll tell nobody else."

"Really!"

"It's about a man and a hoss and a dog. The man ain't possible, the hoss ain't possible, the dog is a wolf."

He paused again and glowered on the doctor. He seemed to be drawn two ways, by his eagerness to tell a yarn and his dread of consequences.

"I know," he muttered, "because I've seen 'em all. I've seen"—he looked far, as though striking a silent bargain with himself concerning the sum of the story which might safely be told—"I've seen a hoss that understood a man's talk like you and me does—or better. I've heard a man whistle like a singing bird. Yep, that ain't no lie. You jest imagine a bald eagle that could lick anything between the earth and the sky and was able to sing— that's what that whistlin' was like. It made you glad to hear it, and it made you look to see if your gun was in good workin' shape. It wasn't very loud, but it traveled pretty far, like it was comin' from up above you."

"That's the way this strange man of the story whistles?" asked Byrne, leaning closer.

"Man of the story?" echoed the proprietor, with some warmth. "Friend, if he ain't real, then I'm a ghost. And they's them in Elkhead that's got the scars of his comin' and goin'."

"Ah, an outlaw? A gunfighter?" queried the doctor.

"Listen to me, son," observed the host, and to make his point he tapped the hollow chest of Byrne with a rigid forefinger, "around these parts you know jest as much as you see, and lots of times you don't even know that much. What you see is sometimes your business, but mostly it ain't." He concluded impressively: "Words is worse'n bullets!"

"Well," mused Byrne, "I can ask the girl these questions. It will be medically necessary."

"Ask the girl? Ask her?" echoed the host with a sort of horror. But he ended with a forced restraint: "That's *your* business."

3 · The Doctor Rides

HANK DWIGHT disappeared from the doorway and the doctor was called from his pondering by the voice of the girl. There was something about that voice which worried Byrne, for it was low and controlled and musical and it did not fit with the nasal harshness of the cattlemen. When she began to speak it was like the beginning of a song. He turned now and found her sitting a tall bay horse, and she led a red-roan mare beside her. When he went out she tossed her reins over the head of her horse and strapped his valise behind her saddle.

"You won't have any trouble with that mare," she assured him, when the time came for mounting. Yet when he approached gingerly he was received with flattened ears and a snort of anger. "Wait," she cried, "the left side, not the right!"

He felt the laughter in her voice, but when he looked he could see no trace of it in her face. He approached from the left side, setting his teeth.

"You observe," he said, "that I take your word at its full value," and placing his foot in the stirrup, he dragged himself gingerly up to the saddle. The mare stood like a rock. Adjusting himself, he wiped a sudden perspiration from his forehead.

"I quite believe," he remarked, "that the animal is of unusual intelligence. All may yet be well!"

"I'm sure of it," said the girl gravely. "Now we're off."

And the horses broke into a dog trot. Now the gait of the red roan mare was a dream of softness, and her flexible ankles gave a play of whole inches to break the jar of every step, the sure sign of the good saddle horse; but the horse has never been saddled whose trot is really a smooth pace. The hat of Doctor Byrne began to incline toward his right eye and his spectacles toward

17

his left ear. He felt a peculiar lightness in the stomach and heaviness in the heart.

"The t-t-t-trot," he ventured to his companion, "is a d-d-d-dam——"

"Dr. Byrne!" she cried.

"Whoa!" called Doctor Byrne, and drew mightily in upon the reins. The red mare stopped as a ball stops when it meets a stout wall; the doctor sprawled along her neck, clinging with arms and legs. He managed to clamber back into the saddle.

"There are vicious elements in the nature of this brute," he observed to the girl.

"I'm very sorry," she murmured. He cast a sidelong glance but found not the trace of a smile.

"The word upon which I——"

"Stopped?" she suggested.

"Stopped," he agreed, "was not, as you evidently assumed, an oath. On the contrary, I was merely remarking that the trot is a damaging gait, but through an interruped—er—articulation——"

His eyes dared her, but she was utterly grave. He perceived that there was, after all, a certain kinship between this woman of the mountain-desert and the man thereof. Their silences were filled with eloquence.

"We'll try a canter," she suggested, "and I think you'll find that easier."

So she gave the word, and her bay sprang into a lope from a standing start. The red mare did likewise, nearly flinging the doctor over the back of the saddle, but by the grace of God he clutched the pommel in time and was saved. The air caught at his face, they swept out of the town and onto a limitless level stretch.

"Sp-p-p-peed," gasped the doctor, "has never been a p-p-passion with me!"

He noted that she was not moving in the saddle. The horse was like the bottom of a wave swinging violently back and forth. She was the calm crest, swaying slightly and graciously with a motion as smooth as the flowing of water. And she spoke as evenly as if she were sitting in a rocking chair.

"You'll be used to it in a moment," she assured him. He learned, indeed, that if one pressed the stirrups as the shoulders of the horse swung down and leaned a trifle forward when the shoulders rose again, the motion ceased to be jarring; for she was truly a matchless creature and gaited like one of those fabulous horses of old, sired by the swift western wind. In a little time a certain pride went beating through the veins of the doctor, the air blew more deeply into his lungs, there was a different tang to the wind and a different feel to the sun— a peculiar richness of yellow warmth. And the small head of the horse and the short, sharp, pricking ears tossed continually; and now and then the mare threw her head a bit to one side and glanced back at him with what he felt to be a reassuring air. Life and strength and speed were gripped between his knees—he flashed a glance at the girl.

But she rode with face straight forward and there was that about her which made him turn his eyes suddenly away and look far off. It was a jagged country, for in the brief rainy season there came sudden and terrific downpours which lashed away the soil and scoured the face of the underlying rock, and in a single day might cut a deep arroyo where before had been smooth plain. This was the season of grass, but not the dark, rank green of rich soil and mild air—it was a yellowish green, a color at once tender and glowing. It spread everywhere across the plains about Elkhead, broken here and there by the projecting boulders which flashed in the sun. So a great battlefield might appear, pockmarked with shell-holes, and all the scars of war freshly cut upon its face. And in truth the mountain desert was like an arena ready to stage a conflict—a titanic arena with space for earth-giants to struggle—and there in the distance were the spectator mountains. High, lean-flanked mountains they were, not clad in forests, but rather bristling with a stubby growth of the few trees which might endure in precarious soil and bitter weather, but now they gathered the dignity of distance about them. The grass of the foothills was a faint green mist about their feet, cloaks of exquisite blue hung around the upper masses, but their heads were naked to the pale skies. And all day long, with deliberate alteration, the garb of the mountains changed. When the sudden morning came they leaped naked upon the eye, and then withdrew, muffling themselves in browns and blues until at nightfall they covered themselves to the eyes in thickly sheeted purple—Tyrian purple—and prepared for sleep with their heads among the stars.

Something of all this came to Doctor Randall Byrne as he rode, for it seemed to him that there was a similarity between these mountains and the girl beside him. She held that keen purity of the upper slopes under the sun, and though she had no artifice or careful wiles to make her strange, there was about her a natural dignity like the mystery of distance. There was a rhythm, too, about that line of peaks against the sky, and the girl had caught it; he watched her sway with the gallop of her horse and felt that though she was so close at hand she was a thousand miles from him. She concealed nothing, and yet he could no more see her naked soul than he could tear the veils of shadow from the mountains. Not that the doctor phrased his emotions in words. He was only conscious of a sense of awe and the necessity of silence.

A strange feeling for the doctor! He came from the region of the mind where that which is not spoken does not exist, and now this girl was carrying him swiftly away from hypotheses, doubts, and polysyllabic speech into the world—of what? The spirit? The doctor did not know. He only felt that he was about to step into the unknown, and it held for him the fascination of the suspended action of a statue. Let it not be thought that he calmly accepted the sheer necessity for silence. He fought against it, but no words came.

It was evening: the rolling hills about them were already dark; only the heads of the mountains took the day; and now they paused at the top of a rise and the girl pointed across the hollow. "There we are," she said. It was a tall clump of trees through which broke the outlines of a two-storied house larger than any the doctor had seen in the mountain-desert; and outside the trees lay long sheds, a great barn, and a widespread wilderness of corrals. It struck the doctor with its apparently limitless capacity for housing man and beast. Coming in contrast with the rock-strewn desolation of the plains, this was a great establishment; the doctor had ridden out with a waif of the desert and she had turned into a princess at a stroke. Then, for the first time since they left Elkhead, he remembered with a start that he was to care for a sick man in that house.

"You were to tell me," he said, "something about the sickness of your father—the background behind his condition. But we've both forgotten about it."

"I have been thinking how I could describe it, every moment of the ride," she answered. Then, as the gloom fell more thickly around them every moment, she swerved her horse over to the mare, as if it were necessary that she read the face of the doctor while she spoke.

"Six months ago," she said, "my father was robust and active in spite of his age. He was cheerful, busy, and optimistic. But he fell into a decline. It has not been a sudden sapping of his strength. If it were that I should not worry so much; I'd attribute it to disease. But every day something of vitality goes from him. He is fading almost from hour to hour, as slowly as the hour hand of a clock. You can't notice the change, but every twelve hours the hand makes a complete revolution. It's as if his blood were evaporating and nothing we can do will supply him with fresh strength."

"Is this attended by irritability?"

"He is perfectly calm and seems to have no care for what becomes of him."

"Has he lost interest in the things which formerly attracted and occupied him?"

"Yes, he minds nothing now. He has no care for the condition of the cattle, or for profit or loss in the sales. He has simply stepped out of every employment."

"Ah, a gradual diminution of the faculties of attention."

"In a way, yes. But also he is more alive than he has ever been. He seems to hear with uncanny distinctness, for instance."

The doctor frowned.

"I was inclined to attribute his decline to the operation of old age," he remarked, "but this is unusual. This —er—inner acuteness is accompanied by no particular interest in any one thing?"

As she did not reply for the moment he was about to

accept the silence for acquiescence, but then through the dimness he was arrested by the luster of her eyes, fixed, apparently, far beyond him.

"One thing," she said at length. "Yes, there is one thing in which he retains an interest."

The doctor nodded brightly.

"Good!" he said. "And that——?"

The silence fell again, but this time he was more roused and he fixed his eyes keenly upon her through the gloom. She was deeply troubled; one hand gripped the horn of her saddle strongly; her lips had parted; she was like one who endures inescapable pain. He could not tell whether it was the slight breeze which disturbed her blouse or the rapid panting of her breath.

"Of that," she said, "it is hard to speak—it is useless to speak!"

"Surely not!" protested the doctor. "The cause, my dear madame, though perhaps apparently remote from the immediate issue, is of the utmost significance in diagnosis."

She broke in rapidly: "This is all I can tell you: he is waiting for something which will never come. He has missed something from his life which will never come back into it. Then why should we discuss what it is that he has missed."

"To the critical mind," replied the doctor calmly, and he automatically adjusted his glasses closer to his eyes, "nothing is without significance."

"It is nearly dark!" she exclaimed hurriedly. "Let us ride on."

"First," he suggested, "I must tell you that before I left Elkhead I heard a hint of some remarkable story concerning a man and a horse and a dog. Is there anything——"

But it seemed that she did not hear. He heard a sharp, low exclamation which might have been addressed to her horse, and the next instant she was galloping swiftly down the slope. The doctor followed as fast as he could, jouncing in the saddle until he was quite out of breath.

4 · The Chain

THEY had hardly passed the front door of the house when they were met by a tall man with dark hair and dark, deep-set eyes. He was tanned to the bronze of an Indian, and he might have been termed handsome had not his features been so deeply cut and roughly finished. His black hair was quite long, and as the wind from the opened door stirred it, there was a touch of wildness about the fellow that made the heart of Randall Byrne jump. When this man saw the girl his face lighted, briefly; when his glance fell on Byrne the light went out.

"Couldn't get the doc, Kate?" he asked.

"Not Doctor Hardin," she answered, "and I've brought Doctor Byrne instead."

The tall man allowed his gaze to drift leisurely from head to foot of Randall Byrne.

Then: "H'ware you, doc?" he said, and extended a big hand. It occurred to Byrne that all these men of the mountain-desert were big; there was something intensely irritating about their mere physical size; they threw him continually on the defensive and he found himself making apologies to himself and summing up personal merits. In this case there was more direct reason for his anger. It was patent that the man did not weight the strange doctor against any serious thoughts.

"And this," she was saying, "is Mr. Daniels. Buck, is there any change?"

"Nothin' much," answered Buck Daniels. "Come along toward evening and he said he was feeling kind of cold. So I wrapped him up in a rug. Then he sat some as usual, one hand inside of the other, looking steady at nothing. But a while ago he began getting sort of nervous."

"What did he do?"

"Nothing. I just *felt* he was getting excited. The way you know when your hoss is going to shy."

"Do you want to go to your room first, doctor, or will you go in to see him now?"

"Now," decided the doctor, and followed her down the hall and through a door.

The room reminded the doctor more of a New England interior than of the mountain-desert. There was a round rag rug on the floor with every imaginable color woven into its texture, but blended with a rude design, reds toward the center and blue-grays toward the edges. There were chairs upholstered in green which looked mouse-colored where the highlights struck along the backs and the arms—shallow-seated chairs that made one's knees project foolishly high and far. Byrne saw a cabinet at one end of the room, filled with seashells and knicknacks, and above it was a memorial cross surrounded by a wreath inside a glass case. Most of the wall space thronged with engravings whose subjects ranged from Niagara Falls to Lady Hamilton. One entire end of the room was occupied by a painting of a neck-and-neck finish in a race, and the artist had conceived the blooded racers as creatures with tremendous round hips and mighty-muscled shoulders, while the legs tapered to a faun-like delicacy. These animals were spread-eagled in the most amazing fashion, their fore-hoofs reaching beyond their noses and their rear hoofs striking out beyond the tips of the tails. The jockey in the lead sat quite still, but he who was losing had his whip drawn and looked like an automatic doll—so pink were his cheeks. Beside the course, in attitudes of graceful ease, stood men in very tight trousers and very high stocks and ladies in dresses which pinched in at the waist and flowed out at the shoulders. They leaned upon canes or twirled parasols and they had their backs turned upon the racetrack as if they found their own negligent conversation far more exciting than the breathless, driving finish.

Under the terrific action and still more terrific quiescence of this picture lay the sick man, propped high on a couch and wrapped to the chest in a Navajo blanket.

"Dad," said Kate Cumberland, "Doctor Hardin was

not in town. I've brought out Doctor Byrne, a new-comer."

The invalid turned his white head slowly toward them, and his shaggy brows lifted and fell slightly—a passing shadow of annoyance. It was a very stern face, and framed in the long, white hair it seemed surrounded by an atmosphere of Arctic chill. He was thin, terribly thin—not the leanness of Byrne, but a grim emaciation which exaggerated the size of a tall forehead and made his eyes supernally bright. It was in the first glance of those eyes that Byrne recognized the restlessness of which Kate had spoken; and he felt almost as if it were an inner fire which had burned and still was wasting the body of Joseph Cumberland. To the attentions of the doctor the old man submitted with patient self-control, and Byrne found a pulse feeble, rapid, but steady. There was no temperature. In fact, the heat of the body was a trifle subnormal, considering that the heart was beating so rapidly.

Doctor Byrne started. Most of his work had been in laboratories, and the horror of death was not yet familiar, but old Joseph Cumberland was dying. It was not a matter of moments. Death might be a week or a month away, but die soon he inevitably must; for the doctor saw that the fire was still raging in the hollow breast of the cattleman, but there was no longer fuel to feed it.

He stared again, and more closely. Fire without fuel to feed it!

Doctor Byrne gave what seemed to be an infinitely muffled cry of exultation, so faint that it was hardly a whisper; then he leaned closer and pored over Joe Cumberland with a lighted eye. One might have thought that the doctor was gloating over the sick man.

Suddenly he straightened and began to pace up and down the room, muttering to himself. Kate Cumberland listened intently and she thought that what the man muttered so rapidly, over and over to himself, was: "Eureka! Eureka! I have found it!"

Found what? The triumph of mind over matter!

On that couch was a dead body. The flutter of that heart was not the strong beating of the normal organ;

the hands were cold; even the body was chilled; yet the man lived.

Or, rather, his brain lived, and compelled the shattered and outworn body to comply with its will. Doctor Byrne turned and stared again at the face of Cumberland. He felt as if he understood, now, the look which was concentrated so brightly on the vacant air. It was illumined by a steady and desperate defiance, for the old man was denying his body to the grave.

The scene changed for Randall Byrne. The girl disappeared. The walls of the room were broken away. The eyes of the world looked in upon him and the wise men of the world kept pace with him up and down the room, shaking their heads and saying: "It is not possible!"

But the fact lay there to contradict them.

Prometheus stole fire from heaven and paid it back to an eternal death. The old cattleman was refusing his payment. It was no state of coma in which he lay; it was no prolonged trance. He was vitally, vividly alive; he was concentrating with a bitter and exhausting vigor day and night, and fighting a battle the more terrible because it was fought in silence, a battle in which he could receive no aid, no reinforcement, a battle in which he could not win, but in which he might delay defeat.

Ay, the wise men would smile and shake their heads when he presented this case to their consideration, but he would make his account so accurate and particular and so well witnessed that they would have to admit the truth of all he said. And science, which proclaimed that matter was indestructible and that the mind was matter and that the brain needed nourishment like any other muscle—science would have to hang the head and wonder!

The eyes of the girl brought him to a halt in his pacing, and he stopped, confronting her. His excitement had transformed him. His nostrils were quivering, his eyes were pointed with light, his head was high, and he breathed fast. He was flushed as the Roman Conqueror. And his excitement tinged the girl, also, with color.

She offered to take him to his room as soon as he

wished to go. He was quite willing. He wanted to be alone, to think. But when he followed her she stopped him in the hall. Buck Daniels lumbered slowly after them in a clumsy attempt at sauntering.

"Well?" asked Kate Cumberland.

She had thrown a blue mantle over her shoulders when she entered the house, and the touch of boyish self-confidence which had been hers on the ride was gone. In its place there was something even more difficult for Randall Byrne to face. If there had been a garish brightness about her when he had first seen her, the brilliancy of a mirror playing in the sun against his feeble eyes, there was now a blending of pastel shades, for the hall was dimly illumined and the shadow tarnished her hair and her pallor was like cold stone; even her eyes were misted by fear.. Yet a vital sense of her nearness swept upon Byrne, and he felt as if he were surrounded—by a danger.

"Opinions," said the doctor, "based on so summary an examination are necessarily inexact, yet the value of a first impression is not negligible. The best I can say is that there is probably no immediate danger, but Mr. Cumberland is seriously ill. Furthermore, it is *not* old age."

He would not say all he thought; it was not yet time.

She winced and clasped her hands tightly together. She was like a child about to be punished for a crime it has not committed, and it came vaguely to the doctor that he might have broached his ill tidings more gently.

He added: "I must have further opportunities for observance before I give a detailed opinion and suggest a treatment."

Her glance wandered past him and at once the heavy step of Buck Daniels approached.

"At least," she murmured, "I am glad that you are frank. I don't want to have anything kept from me, please. Buck, will you take the doctor up to his room?" She managed a faint smile. "This is an old-fashioned house, Doctor Byrne, but I hope we can make you fairly comfortable. You'll ask for whatever you need?"

The doctor bowed, and was told that they would dine

in half an hour, then the girl went back toward the room in which Joe Cumberland lay. She walked slowly, with her head bent, and her posture seemed to Byrne the very picture of a burden-bearer. Then he followed Daniels up the stairs, led by the jingling of the spurs, great-rowelled spurs that might grip the side of a refractory horse like teeth.

A hall-light guided them, and from the hall Buck Daniels entered a room and fumbled above him until he had lighted a lamp which was suspended by two chains from the ceiling, a circular burner which cast a glow as keen as an electric globe. It brought out every detail of the old-fashioned room—the bare, painted floor; the bed, in itself a separate and important piece of architecture with its four tall posts, a relic of the times when beds were built, not simply made; and there was a chest of drawers with swelling, hospitable front, and a rectangular mirror above with its date in gilt paint on the upper edge. A rising wind shook the window and through some crack stirred the lace curtains; it was a very comfortable retreat, and the doctor became aware of aching muscles and a heavy brain when he glanced at the bed.

The same gust of wind which rattled the window-pane now pushed, as with invisible and ghostly hand, a door which opened on the side of the bedroom, and as it swung mysteriously and gradually wide the doctor found himself looking into an adjoining chamber. All he could see clearly was a corner on which struck the shaft of light from the lamp, and lying on the floor in that corner was something limp and brown. A snake, he surmised at first, but then he saw clearly that it was a chain of formidable proportions bolted against the wall at one end and terminating at the other in a huge steel collar. A chill started in the boots of the doctor and wriggled its uncomfortable way up to his head.

"Hell!" burst out Buck Daniels. "How'd *that* door get open?" He slammed it with violence. "She's been in there again, I guess," muttered the cowpuncher, as he stepped back, scowling.

"Who?" ventured the doctor.

Buck Daniels whirled on him.

"None of your——" he began hotly, but checked himself with choking suddenness and strode heavily from the room.

5 · The Waiting

THE doctor removed his coat with absent-minded slowness, and all the time that he was removing the dust and the stains of travel, he kept narrowing the eye of his mind to visualize more clearly that cumbersome chain which lay on the floor of the adjoining room. Now, the doctor was not of a curious or gossipy nature, but if someone had offered to tell him the story of that chain for a thousand dollars, the doctor at that moment would have thought the price ridiculously small.

Then the doctor went down to the dinner table prepared to keep one eye upon Buck Daniels and the other upon Kate Cumberland. But if he expected to learn through conversation at the table he was grievously disappointed, for Buck Daniels ate with an eye to strict business that allowed no chatter, and the girl sat with a forced smile and an absent eye. Now and again Buck would glance up at her, watch her for an instant, and then turn his attention back to his plate with a sort of gloomy resolution; there were not half a dozen words exchanged from the beginning to the end of the meal.

After that they went in to the invalid. He lay in the same position, his skinny hands crossed upon his breast, and his shaggy brows were drawn so low that the eyes were buried in profound shadow. They took positions in a loose semi-circle, all pointing toward the sick man, and it reminded Byrne with grim force of a picture he had seen of three wolves waiting for the bull moose to sink in the snows: they, also, were waiting for a death. It seemed, indeed, as if death must have already come; at least it could not make him more motionless than he

was. Against the dark wall his profile was etched by a
sharp highlight which was brightest of all on his forehead and his nose; while the lower portion of the face
was lost in comparative shadow.

So perfect and so detailed was the resemblance to
death, indeed, that the lips in the shadow smiled—fixedly.
It was not until Kate Cumberland shifted a lamp, throwing more light on her father, that Byrne saw that the
smile was in reality a forcible compression of the lips.
He understood, suddenly, that the silent man on the
couch was struggling terribly against an hysteria of emotion. It brought beads of sweat out upon the doctor's tall
forehead; for his perfect repose suggested an agony more
awful than yells and groans and struggles. The silence
was like acid; it burned without a flame. And Byrne
knew, that moment, the quality of the thing which had
wasted the rancher. It was this acid of grief or yearning
which had eaten deep into him and was now close to his
heart. The girl had said that for six months he had been
failing. Six months! Six eternities of burning at the stake!

He lay silent, waiting; and his resignation meant that
he knew death would come before that for which he
waited. Silence, that was the keynote of the room. The
girl was silent, her eyes dark with grief; yet they were
not fixed upon her father. It came thrilling home to
Byrne that her sorrow was not entirely for her dying
parent, for she looked beyond him rather than at him.
Was she, too, waiting? Was that what gave her the
touch of sad gravity, the mystery like the mystery of
distance?

And Buck Daniels. He, also, said nothing. He rolled
cigarettes one after another with amazing dexterity and
smoked them with half a dozen Titanic breaths. His was
a single-track mind. He loved the girl, and he bore the
sign of his love on his face. He wanted her desperately;
it was a hunger like that of Tantalus, too keen to be ever
satisfied. Yet, still more than he looked at the girl, he,
also, stared into the distance. He, also, was waiting!

It was the deep suspense of Cumberland which made
him so silently alert. He was as intensely alive as the
receiver of a wireless apparatus; he gathered information
from the empty air.

So that Byrne was hardly surprised when, in the midst of that grim silence, the old man raised a rigid forefinger of warning. Kate and Daniels stiffened in their chairs and Byrne felt his flesh creep. Of course it was nothing. The wind, which had shaken the house with several strong gusts before dinner, had now grown stronger and blew with steadily increasing violence; perhaps the sad old man had been attracted by the mournful chorus and imagined some sound he knew within it.

But now once more the finger was raised, the arm extended, shaking violently, and Joe Cumberland turned upon them a glance which flashed with a delirious and unhealthy joy.

"Listen!" he cried. "Again!"

"What?" asked Kate.

"I hear them, I tell you."

Her lips blanched, and parted to speak, but she checked the impulse and looked swiftly about the room with what seemed to Byrne an appeal for help. As for Buck Daniels, he changed from a dark bronze to an unhealthy yellow; fear, plain and grimly unmistakable, was in his face. Then he strode to the window and threw it open with a crash. The wind leaped in and tossed the flame in the throat of the chimney, so that great shadows waved suddenly through the room, and made the chairs seem afloat. Even the people were suddenly unreal. And the rush of the storm gave Byrne an eerie sensation of being blown through infinite space. For a moment there was only the sound of the gale and the flapping of a loose picture against the wall, and the rattling of a newspaper. Then he heard it.

First it was a single note which he could not place. It was music, and yet it was discordant, and it had the effect of a blast of icy wind.

Once he had been in Egypt and had stood in a corridor of Cheops' pyramid. The torch had been blown out in the hand of his guide. From somewhere in the black depths before them came a laugh, made unhuman by echoes. And Byrne had visioned the mummied dead pushing back the granite lids of their sarcophagi and sitting upright.

But that was nothing compared with this. Not half so wild or strange.

He listened again, breathless, with the sharp prickling running up and down his spine. It was the honking of the wild geese, flying north. And out of the sound he builded a picture of the gray triangle cleaving through the cold upper sky, sent on a mission no man could understand.

"Was I right? Was I right?" shrilled the invalid, and when Byrne turned toward him, he saw the old man sitting erect, with an expression of wild triumph. There came an indescribable cry from the girl, and a deep throated curse from Buck Daniels as he slammed down the window.

With the chill blast shut off and the flame burning steadily once more in the lamp, a great silence besieged the room, with a note of expectancy in it. Byrne was conscious of being warm, too warm. It was close in the room, and he was weighted down. It was as if another presence had stepped into the room and stood invisible. He felt it with unspeakable keenness, as when one knows certainly the thoughts which pass in the mind of another. And, more than that, he knew that the others in the room felt what he felt. In the waiting silence he saw that the old man lay on his couch with eyes of fire and gaping lips, as if he drank the wine of his joyous expectancy. And big Buck Daniels stood with his hand on the sash of the window, frozen there, his eyes bulging, his heart thundering in his throat. And Kate Cumberland sat with her eyes closed, as she had closed them when the wind first rushed upon her, and she still smiled as she had smiled then. And to Byrne, more terrible than the joy of Joseph Cumberland or the dread of Buck Daniels was the smile and the closed eyes of the girl.

But the silence held and the fifth presence was in the room, and not one of them dared speak.

6 · The Mission Starts

THEN, with a shifting of the wind, a song was blown to them from the bunkhouse, a cheerful, ringing chorus; the sound was like daylight—it drove the terror from the room. Joe Cumberland asked them to leave him. That night, he said, he would sleep. He felt it, like a promise. The other three went out from the room.

In the hall Kate and Daniels stood close together under a faint light from the wall-lamp, and they talked as if they had forgotten the presence of Byrne.

"It had to come," she said. "I knew it would come to him sooner or later, but I didn't dream it would be as terrible as this. Buck, what are we going to do?"

"God knows," said the big cowpuncher. "Just wait, I s'pose, same as we've been doing."

He had aged wonderfully in that moment of darkness.

"He'll be happy now for a few days," went on the girl, "but afterward—when he realizes that it means nothing—what then, Buck?"

The man took her hands and began to pat them softly as a father might soothe a child.

"I seen you when the wind come in," he said gently. "Are you going to stand it, Kate? Is it going to be hell for you, too, every time you hear 'em?"

She answered: "If it were only I! Yes, I could stand it. Lately I've begun to think that I can stand anything. But when I see Dad it breaks my heart—and you—oh, Buck, it hurts, it hurts!" She drew his hands impulsively against her breast. "If it were only something we could fight outright!"

Buck Daniels sighed.

"Fight?" he echoed hopelessly. "Fight? Against him? Kate, you're all tired out. Go to bed, honey, and try to stop thinkin'—and—God help us all!"

33

She turned away from him and passed the doctor—blindly.

Buck Daniels had set his foot on the stairs when Byrne hurried after him and touched his arm; they went up together.

"Mr. Daniels," said the doctor, "it is necessary that I speak with you, alone. Will you come into my room for a few moments?"

"Doc," said the cattleman, "I'm short on my feed and I don't feel a pile like talkin'. Can't you wait till the morning?"

"There has been a great deal too much waiting, Mr. Daniels,' said the doctor. "What I have to say to you must be said now. Will you come in?"

"I will," nodded Buck Daniels. "But cut it short."

Once in his room the doctor lighted the lamp and then locked the door.

"What's all the mystery and hush stuff?" growled Daniels, and with a gesture he refused the proffered chair. "Cut loose, doc, and make it short."

The little man sat down, removed his glasses, held them up to the light, found a speck upon them, polished it carefully away, replaced the spectacles upon his nose, and peered thoughtfully at Buck Daniels.

Buck Daniels rolled his eyes toward the door and then even toward the window, and then, as one who accepts the inevitable, he sank into a chair and plunged his hands into his pockets, prepared to endure.

"I am called," went on the doctor dryly, "to examine a case in which the patient is dangerously ill—in fact, hopelessly ill, and I have found that the cause of his illness is a state of nervous expectancy on the part of the sufferer. It being obviously necessary to know the nature of the disease and its cause before that cause may be removed, I have asked you to sit here this evening to give me whatever explanation you may have for it."

Buck Daniels stirred uneasily. At length he broke out: "Doc, I size you up as a gent with brains. I got one piece of advice for you: get the hell away from the Cumberland Ranch and never come back again!"

The doctor flushed and his lean jaw thrust out.

"Although," he said, "I cannot pretend to be classed

among those to whom physical fear is an unknown, yet I wish to assure you, sir, that with me physical trepidation is not an overruling motive."

"Oh, hell!" groaned Buck Daniels. Then he explained more gently: "I don't say you're yellow. All I say is this mess ain't one that you can straighten out—nor no other man can. Give it up, wash your hands, and git back to Elkhead. I dunno what Kate was thinkin' of to bring you out here!"

"The excellence of your intention," said the doctor, "I shall freely admit, though the assumption that difficulty in the essential problem would deter me from the analysis is an hypothesis which I cannot leave uncontested. In the vulgar, I may give you to understand that I am in this to stay!"

Buck Daniels started to speak, but thinking better of it he shrugged his shoulders and sat back, resigned.

"Well," he said, "Kate brought you out here. Maybe she has a reason for it. What d'you want to know?"

"What connection," said the doctor, "have wild geese with a man, a horse, and a dog?"

"What in hell d'you know about a horse and a man and a dog—and wild geese?" inquired Buck in a strained voice.

"Rumor," said the doctor, "has been in this instance, unfortunately, my only teacher. But, sir, I have ascertained that Mr. Cumberland, his daughter, and you, sir, are all waiting for a certain thing to come to this ranch, and that thing I naturally assume to be a man."

"Doc," said the cowpuncher sarcastically, "there ain't no doubt you got a wonderful brain!"

"Mockery," pronounced the man of learning, "is a use of the mental powers which is both unworthy and barren and does not in this case advance the argument, which is: Who and what is this man for whom you wait?"

"He came," said Buck Daniels, "out of nowhere. That's all we know about who he is. What is he? I'll tell you easy. He's a gent that looks like a man, and walks like a man, and talks like a man—but he *ain't* a man."

"Ah," nodded the philosopher, "a crime of extraordinary magnitude has, perhaps, cut off this unfortunate fellow from communication with others of his kind. Is this the case?"

"It ain't," replied Buck. "Doc, tell me this: Can a wolf commit a crime?"

"Admitting this definition: that crime is the breaking of law, and that law is a force created by reason to control the rational, it may be granted that the acts of the lower animals lie outside of categories framed according to ethical precepts. To directly answer your not incurious question: I believe that a wolf cannot commit a crime."

Buck Daniels sighed.

"D'you know, doc," he said gravely, "that you remind me of a side-hill goat?"

"Ah," murmured the man of learning, "is it possible? And what, Mr. Daniels, is the nature of a side-hill goat?"

"It's a goat that's got the legs of one side shorter than the legs on the other side, and the only way he can get to the top of a hill is to keep trottin' around and around the hill like a five per cent grade. He goes a mile to get ten feet higher."

"This fact," said Byrne, and he rubbed his chin thoughtfully, "is not without interest, though I fail to perceive the relation between me and such a creature, unless, perhaps, there are biological similarities of which I have at present no cognition."

"I didn't think you'd follow me," replied Buck with an equal gravity. "But you can lay to this, Doc: this gent we're waitin' for ain't committed any more crimes than a wolf has."

"Ah, I see," murmured the doctor, "a man so near the brute that his enormities pass beyond——"

"Get this straight," said Buck, interrupting with a sternly pointed finger: "There ain't a kinder or a gentler man in the mountain-desert than him. He's got a voice softer than Kate Cumberland's, which is some soft voice, and as for his heart—Doc, I've seen him get off his horse to put a wounded rabbit out of its pain!"

A ring of awe came in the throat of Daniels as he repeated the incredible fact.

He went on: "If I was in trouble, I'd rather have him beside me than ten other men; if I was sick I'd rather have him than the ten best doctors in the world; if I wanted a pal that would die for them that done him good and go to hell to get them that done him bad, I'd choose him first, and there ain't none that come second."

The panegyric was not a burst of imagination. Buck Daniels was speaking seriously, hunting for words, and if he used superlatives it was because he needed them.

"Extraordinary!" murmured the doctor, and he repeated the word in a louder tone. It was a rare word for him; in all his scholastic career and in all of his scientific investigations he had found occasion to use so strong a term not more than half a dozen times at the most. He went on, cautiously, and his weak eyes blinked at Daniels: "And there is a relation between this man and a horse and dog?"

Buck Daniels shuddered and his color changed.

"Listen!" he said, "I've talked enough. You ain't going to get another word out of me except this: Doc, have a good sleep, get on your hoss tomorrow mornin', and beat it. Don't even wait for breakfast. Because, if you *do* wait, you may get a hand in this little hell of ours. You may be waiting, too!" A sudden thought brought him to his feet. He stood over the doctor. "How many times," he thundered, "have you seen Kate Cumberland?"

"Today, for the first time."

"Well," said Daniels, growling with relief, "you've seen her enough. I *know*." And he turned toward the door. "Unlock," he commanded. "I'm tired out—and sick—of talking about *him*."

But the doctor did not move.

"Nevertheless," he stated, "you will remain. There is something further which you know and which you will communicate to me."

Buck Daniels turned at the door; his face was not pleasant.

"While observing you as you talked with the girl," Byrne said, "it occurred to me that you were holding information from her. The exact nature of that information I cannot state, but it is reasonable to deduce that you could, at the present moment, name the place where the man for whom Mr. Cumberland and his daughter wait is now located."

Buck Daniels made no reply, but he returned to his chair and slumped heavily into it, staring at the little doctor. And Byrne realized with a thrill of pleasure that he was not afraid of death.

"I may further deduce," said the doctor, "that you will go in person to the place where you know this man may be found and induce him to come to this ranch."

The silent anger of Daniels died away. He smiled, and at length he laughed without mirth.

"Doc," he said, "if you knew where there was a gun, would that make you want to put it up agin your head and pull the trigger?"

But the doctor proceeded inexorably with his deductions: "Because you are aware, Mr. Daniels, that the presence of this man may save the life of Mr. Cumberland, a thought, to be sure, which might not be accepted by the medical fraternity, but which may without undue exaggeration devolve from the psychological situation in this house."

"Doc," said Daniels huskily, "you talk straight, and you act straight, and I think you *are* straight, so I'll take off the bridle and talk free. I know where Whistling Dan is—just about. But if I was to go to him and bring him here I'd bust the heart of Kate Cumberland. D'you understand?" His voice lowered with an intense emotion. "I've thought it out sideways and backwards. It's Kate or old Joe. Which is the most important?"

The doctor straightened in the chair, polished his glasses, and peered once more at the cowpuncher.

"You are quite sure, also, that the return of this man, this strange wanderer, might help Mr. Cumberland back to health?"

"I am, all right. He's sure wrapped up in Whistlin' Dan."

"What is the nature of their relations; what makes him so oddly dependent upon the other?"

"I dunno, doc. It's got us all fooled. When Dan is here it seems like old Cumberland jest nacherally lives on the things Dan does and hears and sees. We've seen Cumberland prick up his ears the minute Dan comes into the room, and show life. Sometimes Dan sits with him and tells him what he's been doin'—maybe it ain't any more than how the sky looks that day, or about the feel of the wind—but Joe sits with his eyes dreamin', like a little kid hearin' fairy stories. Kate says it's been that way since her dad first brought Dan in off'n the range. He's been sort of necessary to old Joe—almost like air to breathe. I tell you, it's jest a picture to see them two together."

"Very odd, very odd," brooded the doctor, frowning, "but this seems to be an odd place and an odd set of people. You've no real idea why Dan left the ranch?"

"Ask the wild geese," said Buck bitterly. He added: "Maybe you'd better ask Dan's black hoss or his dog, Bart. They'd know better'n anything else."

"But what has the man been doing since he left? Have you any idea?"

"Get a little chatter, now and then, of a gent that's rid into a town on a black hoss, prettier'n anything that was ever seen before.

"It's all pretty much the same, what news we get. Mostly I guess he jest wanders around doin' no harm to nobody. But once in a while somebody sicks a dog on Bart, and Bart jest nacherally chaws that dog in two. Then the owner of the dog may start a fight, and Dan drops him and rides on."

"With a trail of dead men behind him?" cried the doctor, hunching his shoulders as if to shake off a chill.

"Dead? Nope. You don't have to shoot to kill when you can handle a gun the way Dan does. Nope, he jest wings 'em. Plants a chunk of lead in a shoulder, or an arm, or a leg. That's all. They ain't no love of blood in Dan—except——"

"Well?"

"Doc," said Buck with a shudder, "I ain't goin' to talk about the exceptions. Mostly the news we gets of Dan is about troubles he's had. But sometimes we hear of gents he's helped out when they was sick, and things like that. They ain't nobody like Dan when a gent is down sick, I'll tell a man!"

The doctor sighed.

He said: "And do I understand you to say that the

girl and this man—Whistling Dan, as you call him—are intimately and sentimentally related?"

"She loves him," said Daniels slowly. "She loves the ground he walks on and the places where he's been."

"But, sir, it would seem probable from your own reasoning that the return of the man, in this case, will not be unwelcome to her."

"Reason?" broke out Daniels bitterly. "What the hell has reason got to do with Whistling Dan? Man, man! if Barry was to come back d'you suppose he'd remember that he'd once told Kate he loved her? Doc, I know him as near as any man can know him. I tell you, he thinks no more of her than—than the wild geese think of her. If old Joe dies because Dan is away—well, Cumberland is an old man anyway. But how could I stand to see Barry pass Kate by with an empty eye, the way he'd do if he come back? I'd want to kill him, and I'd get bumped off tryin' it, like as not. And what would it do to Kate? It'd kill her, Doc, as sure as you're born."

"Your assumption being," murmured the doctor, "that if she never sees the man again she will eventually forget him."

"D'you forget a knife that's sticking into you? No, she won't forget him. But maybe after a while she'll be able to stand thinkin' about him. She'll get used to the hurt. She'll be able to talk and laugh the way she used to. Oh, doc, if you could of seen her as I've seen her in the old days——"

"When the man was with her?" cut in the doctor.

Buck Daniels caught his breath.

"Damn your eternal soul, doc!" he said softly.

And for a time neither of them spoke. Whatever went on in the mind of Daniels, it was something that contorted his face. As for Byrne, he was trying to match fact and possibility and he was finding a large gap between the two; for he tried to visualize the man whose presence had been food to old Joe Cumberland, and whose absence had taken the oil from the lamp so that the flame now flickered dimly, nearly out. But he could build no such picture. He could merely draw together a vague abstraction of a man to whom the storm and the wild geese who ride the storm had meaning and relationship. The logic which he loved was breaking to pieces in the hands of Randall Byrne.

Silence, after all, is only a name, never a fact. There are noises in the most absolute quiet. If there is not even the sound of the cricket or the wind, if there are not even ghost whispers in the house, there is the sigh of one's own breathing, and in those moments of deadly waiting the beat of the heart may be as loud and as awful as the rattle of the death-march. Now, between the doctor and the cowpuncher, such a silence began. Buck Daniels wanted nothing more in the world than to be out of that room, but the eye of the doctor held him, unwillingly. And there began once more that eternal waiting, waiting, waiting, which was the horror of the place, until the faint creakings through the windshaken house took on the meaning of footsteps stalking down the hall and pausing at the door, and there was the hushing breath of one who listened and smiled to himself! Now the doctor became aware that the eye of Buck Daniels was widening, brightening; it was as if the mind of the big man were giving way in the strain. His face blanched. Even the lips had no color, and they moved, gibberingly.

"Listen!" he said.

"It is the wind," answered the doctor, but his voice was hardly audible.

"Listen!" commanded Daniels again.

The doctor could hear it then. It was a pulse of sound obscure as the thudding of his heart. But it was a human sound and it made his throat close up tightly, as if a hand were settling around his windpipe. Buck Daniels rose from his chair; that half-mad, half-listening look was still in his eyes—behind his eyes. Staring at him the doctor understood, intimately, how men can throw their lives away gloriously in battle, fighting for an idea; or how they can commit secret and foul murder. Yet he was more afraid of that pulse of sound than of the face of Buck Daniels. He, also, was rising from his chair, and when Daniels stalked to the side door of the room and leaned there, the doctor followed.

Then they could hear it clearly. There was a note of music in the voice; it was a woman weeping in that room where the chain lay on the floor, coiled loosely like a snake. Buck Daniels straightened and moved away from the door. He began to laugh, guarding it so that not a whisper could break outside the room, and his silent laughter was the most horrible thing the doctor had ever seen. It was only for a moment. The hysteria passed and left the big man shaking like a dead leaf.

"Doc," he said, "I can't stand it no longer. I'm going out and try to get him back here. And God forgive me for it."

He left the room, slamming the door behind him, and then he stamped down the hall as if he were trying to make a companion out of his noise. Doctor Randall Byrne sat down to put his thoughts in order. He began at the following point: "The physical fact is not; only the immaterial is." But before he had carried very far his deductions from this premise, he caught the neighing of a horse near the house; so he went to the window and threw it open. At the same time he heard the rattle of galloping hoofs, and then he saw a horseman riding furiously into the heart of the wind. Almost at once the rider was lost from sight.

7 · Jerry Strann

THE wrath of the Lord seems less terrible when it is localized, and the world at large gave thanks daily that the range of Jerry Strann was limited to the Three B's. As everyone in the mountain-desert knows, the Three B's are Bender, Buckskin, and Brownsville; they make the points of a loose triangle that is cut with canyons and tumbled with mountains, and that triangle was the chosen stamping ground of Jerry Strann. Jerry was not born in the region of the Three B's and why it should have been chosen specially by him was a matter which the inhabitants could not puzzle out; but they felt that for their sins the Lord had probably put his wrath among them in the form of Jerry Strann.

He was only twenty-four, this Jerry, but he was already grown into a proverb. Men of the Three B's reckoned their conversational dates by the visits of the youth; if a storm hung over the mountains someone might remark: "It looks like Jerry Strann is coming," and such a remark was always received in gloomy silence; mothers had been known to hush their children by chanting: "Jerry Strann will get you if you don't watch out." Yet he was not an ogre with a red knife between his teeth. He stood at exactly the perfect romantic height; he was just six feet tall; he was as graceful as a young cottonwood in a windstorm and he was as strong and tough as the roots of the mesquite. He was one of those rare men who are beautiful without being unmanly. His face was modelled with the care a Praxiteles would lavish on a Phœbus. His brown hair was thick and dark and every touch of wind stirred it, and his hazel eyes were brilliant with an enduring light—the inextinguishable joy of life.

Consider that there was no malice in Jerry Strann. But he loved strife as the young Apollo loved strife—or a pure-blooded bull terrier. He fought with distinction and grace and abandon and was perfectly willing to use fists or knives or guns at the pleasure of the other contracting party. In another age, with armor and a golden chain and spurs, Jerry Strann would have been—but why think of that? Swords are not forty-fives, and the Twentieth Century is not the Thirteenth. He was, in fact, born just six hundred years too late. From his childhood he had thirsted for battle as other children thirst for milk: and now he rode anything on hoofs and threw a knife like a Mexican—with either hand—and at short range he did snap shooting with two revolvers that made rifle experts sick at heart.

However, the men of the Three B's, as everyone understands, are not gentle or long-enduring, and you will wonder why this young destroyer was allowed to range at large so long. There was a vital reason. Up in the mountains lived Mac Strann, the hermit-trapper, who hated everything in the wide world except his young brother, the beautiful, wild, and sunny Jerry Strann. And Mac Strann loved his brother as much as he hated everything else; it is impossible to state it more strongly. It was not long before the men of the Three B's discovered how Mac Strann felt about his brother. After Jerry's famous Hallowe'en party in Buckskin, for instance, Williamson, McKenna, and Rath started out to rid the country of the disturber. They went out to hunt him as men go out to hunt a wild mustang. And they caught him and bent him down—those three stark men—and he lay in bed for a month; but before the month was over Mac Strann came down from his mountain and went to Buckskin and gathered Williamson and McKenna and Rath in one public place. And when the morning came Williamson and McKenna and Rath had left this vale of tears and Mac Strann was back on his mountain. He was not even arrested. For there was a devilish cunning about the fellow and he made his victims, without exception, attack him first; then he destroyed them, suddenly and surely, and retreated to his lair. Things like this happened once or twice and then the men of the Three B's understood that it was not wise to lay plots for Jerry Strann. They accepted him, as I have said before, as men accept the wrath of God.

Let it not be thought that Jerry Strann was a solitary like his brother. When he went out for a frolic the young men of the community gathered around him, for Jerry paid all scores and the red-eye flowed in his path like wine before the coming of Bacchus, where Jerry went there was never a dull moment, and young men love action. So it happened that when he rode into Brownsville this day he was the leader of a cavalcade. Rumor rode before them, and doors were locked and windows were darkened, and men sat in the darkness within with their guns across their knees. For Brownsville lay at the extreme northern tip of the triangle and it was rarely visited by Jerry; and it is well established that men fear the unfamiliar more than the known.

As has been said, Jerry headed the train of revellers, partially because it was most unwise to cut in ahead of

Jerry and partially because there was not a piece of horseflesh in the Three B's which could outfoot his chestnut. It was a gelding out of the loins of the north wind and sired by the devil himself, and its spirit was one with the spirit of Jerry Strann; perhaps because they both served one master. The cavalcade came with a crash of racing hoofs in a cloud of dust. But in the middle of the street Jerry raised his right arm stiffly overhead with a whoop and brought his chestnut to a sliding stop; the cloud of dust rolled lazily on ahead. The young men gathered quickly around the leader, and there was silence as they waited for him to speak—a silence broken only by the wheezing of the horses, and the stench of sweating horseflesh was in every man's nostrils.

"Who owns that hoss?" asked Jerry Strann, and pointed.

He had stopped just opposite O'Brien's hotel, store, blacksmith shop, and saloon, and by the hitching rack was a black stallion. Now, there are some men who carry tidings of their inward strength stamped on their foreheads and written in their eyes. In times of crises crowds will turn to such men and follow them as soldiers follow a captain; for it is patent at a glance that this is a man of men. It is likewise true that there are horses which stand out among their fellows, and this was such a horse. He was such a creature that, if he had been led to a barrier, the entire crowd at the race track would rise as one man and say: "What is that horse?" There were points in which some critics would find fault; most of the men of the mountain-desert, for instance, would have said that the animal was too lightly and delicately limbed for long endurance; but as the man of men bears the stamp of his greatness in his forehead and his eyes, so it was with the black stallion. When the thunder of the cavalcade had rushed upon him down the street he had turned with catlike grace and raised his head to see; and his forehead and his eyes arrested Jerry Strann like a levelled rifle. Looking at that proud head one forgot the body of the horse, the symmetry of curves exquisite beyond the sculptor's dream, the arching neck and the steel muscles; one was only conscious of the great spirit. In human beings we refer to it as "person-ality."

After a little pause, seeing that no one offered a sug-gestion as to the identity of the owner, Strann said, softly: "That hoss is mine."

It caused a stir in the crowd of his followers. In the mountain-desert one may deal lightly with a man's wife and lift a random cow or two and settle the score, at need, with a snug "forty-five" chunk of lead. But with horses it is different. A horse in the mountain-desert lies outside of all laws—and above all laws. It is greater than honor and dearer than love, and when a man's horse is taken from him the men of the desert gather together and hunt the thief whether it be a day or whether it be a month, and when they have reached him they shoot him like a dog and leave his flesh to the buzzards and his bones to the merciless stars. For all of this there is a reason. But Jerry Strann swung from his mount, tossed the reins over the head of the chestnut, and walked toward the black with hungry eyes. He was careless, also, and venturing too close—the black whirled with his sudden, catlike agility, and two black hoofs lashed within a hair's breadth of the man's shoul-der. There was a shout from the crowd, but Jerry Strann stepped back and smiled so that his teeth showed.

"Boys," he said, but he was really speaking to him-self, "there's nothing in the world I want as bad as I want that hoss. Nothing! I'm going to buy him; where's the owner?"

"Don't look like a hoss a man would want to sell, Jerry," came a suggestion from the cavalcade, who had dismounted and now pressed behind their leader.

Jerry favored the speaker with another of his enig-matic smiles: "Oh," he chuckled, "he'll sell, all right! Maybe he's inside. You gents stick out here and watch for him; I'll step inside."

And he strode through the swinging doors of the sa-loon.

It was a dull time of day for O'Brien, so he sat with his feet on the edge of the bar and sipped a tall glass of beer; he looked up at the welcome click of the doors, however, and then was instantly on his feet. The good red went out of his face and the freckles over his nose stood out like ink marks.

"There's a black hoss outside," said Jerry, "that I'm going to buy. Where's the owner?"

"Have a drink," said the bartender, and he forced an amiable smile.

"I got business on my hands, not drinking," said Jerry Strann.

"Lost your chestnut?" queried O'Brien in concern.

"The chestnut was all right until I seen the black. And now he ain't a hoss at all. Where's the gent I want?"

The bartender had fenced for time as long as possible.

"Over there," he said, and pointed.

It was a slender fellow sitting at a table in a corner of the long room, his sombrero pushed back on his head. He was playing solitaire and his back was toward Jerry Strann, who now made a brief survey, hitched his cartridge belt, and approached the stranger with a grin. The man did not turn; he continued to lay down his cards with monotonous regularity, and while he was doing it he said in the gentlest voice that had ever reached the ear of Jerry Strann: "Better stay where you are, stranger. My dog don't like you."

And Jerry Strann perceived, under the shadow of the table, a blacker shadow, huge and formless in the gloom, and two spots of incandescent green twinkling toward him. He stopped; he even made a step back; and then he heard a stifled chuckle from the bartender.

If it had not been for that untimely mirth of O'Brien's probably nothing of what followed would have passed into the history of the Three B's.

8 · The Gift-Horse

"YOUR dog is your own dog," remarked Jerry Strann, still to the back of the card-playing stranger, "but this ain't your backyard. Keep your eye on him, or I'll fix him so he won't need watching!"

So saying he made another step forward, and it brought a snarl from the dog; not one of those high-whining noises, but a deep guttural that sounded like indrawn breath. The gun of Jerry Strann leaped into his hand.

"Bart," said the gentle-voiced stranger, "lie down and don't talk." And he turned in his chair, pulled his hat straight, and looked mildly upon the gunman. An artist would have made much of that picture, for there was in this man, as in Strann, a singular portion of beauty. It was not, however, free from objection, for he had not the open manliness of the larger of the two. Indeed, a feminine grace and softness marked him; his wrists were as round as a girl's, and his hands as slender and as delicately finished. Whether it be the white-hot sun of summer or the hurricane snows of winter, the climate of the mountain-desert roughens the skin, and it cuts away spare flesh, hewing out the face in angles; but with this man there were no rough edges, but all was smoothed over and rounded with painful care; as if nature had concentrated in that birth to show what she could do. Such fine workmanship, perhaps, would be appreciated more by women than by men; for men like a certain weight and bulk of bone and muscle—whereas this fellow seemed as light of body as he was of hand. He sat now watching Strann with the utmost gravity. He had very large brown eyes of a puzzling quality; perhaps that was because there seemed to be no thought behind them and one caught the mystery and the wistfulness of some animals from a glance at him.

48

The effect of that glance on Strann was to make him grin again, and he at once banished the frown from his forehead and put away his gun; the big dog had slunk deeper into the shadow and closer to his master.

"I'm Strann. Maybe you've heard of me."

"My name is Barry," said the other. "I'm sorry that I haven't heard of you before."

And the sound of his voice made Jerry Strann grin again; it was such a low, soft voice with the velvet of a young girl's tone in it; moreover, the brown eyes seemed to apologize for the ignorance concerning Strann's name.

"You got a hoss out in front."

A nod of agreement.

"What's your price?"

"None."

"No price? Look here," argued Strann, "everythings got a price, and I got to have that hoss, understand? *Got* to! I ain't bargaining. I won't try to beat you down. You just set a figger and I'll cover it. I guess that's square!"

"He ain't a gentle hoss," said Barry. "Maybe you wouldn't like him."

"Oh, that's all right about being gentle," chuckled Strann. Then he checked his mirth and stared piercingly at the other to make out if there were a secret mockery. It could not, however, be possible. The eyes were as gravely apologetic as ever. He continued: "I seen the hell-fire in him. That's what stopped me like a bullet. I like 'em that way. Much rather have 'em with a fight. Well, let's have your price. Hey, O'Brien, trot out your redeye; I'm going to do some business here!"

O'Brien came hastily, with drinks, and while they waited Strann queried politely: "Belong around these parts?"

"No," answered the other softly.

"No? Where you come from?"

"Over there," said Barry, and waved a graceful hand toward half the points of the compass.

"H-m-m!" muttered Strann, and once more he bent a keen gaze upon his companion. The drinks were now placed before them. "Here," he concluded, "is to the black devil outside!" And he swallowed the liquor at a gulp, but as he replaced the empty glass on the table he observed, with breathless amazement, that the whiskey glass of the stranger was still full; he had drunk his chaser!

"Now, by God!" said Strann in a ringing voice, and struck a heavy hand upon the top of the table. He regained his control, however, instantly. "Now about that price!"

"I don't know what horses are worth," replied Barry.

"To start, then—five hundred bucks in cold cash—gold!—for your—what's his name?"

"Satan."

"Eh?"

"Satan."

"H-m-m!" murmured Strann again. "Five hundred for Satan, then. How about it?"

"If you can ride him," began the stranger.

"Oh, hell," smiled Strann with a large and careless gesture, "I'll *ride* him, all right."

"Then I would let you take him for nothing," concluded Barry.

"You'd—what?" said Strann. Then he rose slowly from his chair and shouted; instantly the swinging doors broke open and a throng of faces appeared at the gap. "Boys, this gent here is going to give me the black—ha, ha, ha! —if I can ride him!" He turned back on Barry. "They've heard it," he concluded, "and this bargain is going to stick just this way. If your hoss can throw me the deal's off. Eh?"

"Oh, yes," nodded the brown-eyed man.

"What's the idea?" asked one of Jerry's followers as the latter stepped through the doors of the saloon onto the street.

"I dunno," said Jerry. "That gent looks kind of simple; but it ain't my fault if he made a rotten bargain. Here, you!"

And he seized the bridle reins of the black stallion. Speed, lightning speed, was what saved him, for the instant his fingers touched the leather Satan twisted his head and snapped like an angry dog. The teeth clicked beside Strann's shoulder as he leaped back. He laughed savagely.

"That'll be took out of him," he announced, "and damned quick!"

Here the voice of Barry was heard, saying: "I'll help you mount, Mr. Strann." And he edged his way through the little crowd until he stood at the head of the stallion.

"Look out!" warned Strann in real alarm, "or he'll take your head off!"

But Barry was already beside his horse, and, with his back toward those vicious teeth, he drew the reins over its head. As for the stallion, it pricked one ear forward and then the other, and muzzled the man's shoulder confidingly. There was a liberal chorus of astonished oaths from the gathering.

"I'll hold his head while you get on," suggested Barry, turning his mild eyes upon Strann again.

"Well," muttered the big man, "may I be eternally damned!" He added: "All right. Hold his head, and I'll ride him without pulling leather. Is that square?"

Barry nodded absently. His slender fingers were patting the velvet nose of the stallion and he was talking to it in an affectionate undertone—meaningless words, perhaps, such as a mother uses to soothe a child. When Strann set his foot in the stirrup and gathered up the reins the black horse cringed and shuddered; it was not a pleasant thing to see; it was like a dog crouching under the suspended whip. It was worse than that; it was almost the horror of a man who shivers at the touch of an unclean animal. There was not a sound from the crowd; and every grin was wiped out. Jerry Strann swung into the saddle lightly.

There he sat, testing the stirrups. They were too short by inches but he refused to have them lengthened. He poised his quirt and tugged his hat lower over his eyes.

"Turn him loose!" he shouted. "Hei!"

And his shrill yell went down the street and the echoes sent it barking back from wall to wall; Barry stepped back from the head of the black. But for an instant the horse did not stir. He was trembling violently, but his blazing eyes were fixed upon the face of his owner. Barry raised his hand.

And then it happened. It was like the release of a

coiled watch spring; the black whirled as a top spins
and Strann sagged far to the left; before he could re-
cover the stallion was away in a flash, like a racer leaving the barrier and reaching full speed in almost a stride.
Not far—hardly the breadth of the street—before he
pitched up in a long leap as if to clear a barrier, landed
stiff-legged with a sickening jar, whirled again like a spinning top, and darted straight back. And Jerry Strann
pulled leather—with might and main—but the short stirrups were against him, and above all the suddenness of
the start had taken him off guard for all his readiness.
When the stallion dropped stiff-legged Jerry was thrown
forward and an unlucky left foot jarred loose from the
stirrup; and when the horse whirled Strann was flung
from the saddle. It was a clean fall. He twisted over in
the air as he fell and landed in deep dust. The black stallion had reached his master and now he turned, in that
same catlike manner, and watched with pricking ears as
Strann dragged himself up from the dust.

There was no shout of laughter—no cheer for that
fall, and without a smile they watched Strann returning.
Big O'Brien had seen from his open door and now he
laid a hand on the shoulder of one of the men and
whispered at his ear: "There's going to be trouble; bad
trouble, Billy. Go for Fatty Matthews—he's a deputy
marshal now—and get him here as quick as you can.
Run!"

The other spared time for a last glance at Strann and
then hurried down the street.

Now, a man who can lose and smile is generally considered the most graceful of failures, but the smile of
Jerry Strann as he walked slowly back worried his followers.

"We all hit dust sometime," he philosophized. "But
one try don't prove nothin'. I ain't near through with
that hoss!"

Barry turned to Strann. If there had been mockery in
his eyes or a smile on his lips as he faced Jerry there
would have been gunplay on the spot; but, instead, the
brown eyes were as dumbly apologetic as ever.

"We didn't talk about two tries," he observed.

"We talk about it now," said Strann.

There was one man in the crowd a little too old to be dangerous and therefore there was one man who was in a position to speak openly to Strann. It was big O'Brien.

"Jerry, you named your game and made your play and lost. I guess you ain't going to turn up a hard loser. Nobody plays twice for the same pot."

The hazel eye of Strann was gray with anguish of the spirit as he looked from O'Brien to the crowd and from the crowd to Satan, and from Satan to his meek-eyed owner. Nowhere was there a defiant eye or a glint of scorn on which he could wreak his wrath. He stood poised in his anger for the space of a breath; then, in the sharp struggle, his better nature conquered.

"Come on in, all of you," he called. "We'll liquor, and forget this."

9 · Battle Light

O'BRIEN pressed close to Barry.

"Partner," he said rapidly, "you're clear now—you're clear of more hell than you ever dream. Now climb that hoss of yours and feed him leather till you get clear of Brownsville—and if I was you I'd never come within a day's ride of the Three B's again."

The mild, brown eyes widened.

"I don't like crowds," murmured Barry.

"You're wise, kid," grinned the bartender—"a hell of a lot wiser than you know right now. On your way!"

And he turned to follow the crowd into the saloon. But Jerry Strann stood at the swinging doors, watching, and he saw Barry linger behind.

"Are you coming?" he called.

"I got an engagement," answered the meek voice.

"You got another engagement here," mocked Strann. "Understand?"

The other hesitated for an instant, and then sighed deeply. "I suppose I'll stay," he murmured, and walked into the bar. Jerry Strann was smiling in the way that showed his teeth. As Barry passed he said softly: "I see we ain't going to have no trouble, you and me!" and he moved to clap his strong hand on the shoulder of the smaller man. Oddly enough, the hand missed, for Barry swerved from beneath it as a wolf swerves from the shadow of a falling branch. No perceptible effort—no sudden start of tensed muscles, but a movement so smooth that it was almost unnoticeable. But the hand of Strann fell through thin air.

"You're quick," he said. "If you was as quick with your hands as you are with your feet——"

Barry paused and the melancholy brown eyes dwelt on the face of Strann.

"Oh, hell!" snorted the other, and turned on his heel to the bar. "Drink up!" he commanded.

A shout and a snarl from the further end of the room.

"A wolf, by God!" yelled one of the men.

The owner of the animal made his way with unobtrusive swiftness the length of the room and stood between the dog and a man who fingered the butt of his gun nervously.

"He won't hurt you none," murmured that softly assuring voice.

"The hell he won't!" responded the other. "He took a pass at my leg just now and dam' near took it off. Got teeth like the blades of a pocketknife!"

"You're on a cold trail, Sam," broke in one of the others. "That ain't any wolf. Look at him now!"

The big, shaggy animal had slunk to the feet of his master and with head abased stared furtively up into Barry's face. A gesture served as sufficient command, and he slipped shadow-like into the corner and crouched with his head on his paws, the incandescent green of his eyes glimmering; Barry sat down in a chair nearby.

O'Brien was happily spinning bottles and glasses the length of the bar; there was the chiming of glass and the rumble of contented voices.

"Redeye all 'round," said the loud voice of Jerry Strann, "but there's one out. Who's out? Oh, it's *him*. Hey O'Brien, lemonade for the lady."

It brought a laugh, a deep, good-natured laugh, and

then a chorus of mockery; but Barry stepped uncon-fused to the bar, accepted the glass of lemonade, and when the others downed their firewater, he sipped his drink thoughtfully. Outside, the wind had risen, and it shook the hotel and carried a score of faint voices as it whirred around corners and through cracks. Perhaps it was one of those voices which made the big dog lift its head from its paws and whine softly! Surely it was something he heard which caused Barry to straighten at the bar and cant his head slightly to one side—but, as certainly, no one else in the barroom heard it. Barry set down his glass.

"Mr. Strann?" he called.

And the gentle voice carried faintly down through the uproar of the bar.

"Sister wants to speak to you," suggested O'Brien to Strann.

"Well?" roared the latter, "what d'you want?"

The others were silent to listen; and they smiled in anticipation.

"If you don't mind, much," said the musical voice, "I think I'll be moving along."

There is an obscure little devil living in all of us. It makes the child break his own toys; it makes the hus-band strike the helpless wife; it makes the man beat the cringing, whining dog. The greatest of American writers has called it the Imp of the Perverse. And that devil came in Jerry Strann and made his heart small and cold. If he had been by nature the bully and the ruffian there would have been no point in all that followed, but the heart of Jerry Strann was ordinarily as warm as the yellow sunshine itself; and it was a common saying in the Three B's that Jerry Strann would take from a child what he would not endure from a mountain lion. Women loved Jerry Strann, and children would crowd about his knees, but this day the small demon was in him.

"You want to be moving along," mimicked the devil in Jerry Strann. "Well, you wait a while. I ain't through with you yet. Maybe——" he paused and searched his mind. "You've given me a fall, and maybe you can give the rest of us—a laugh!"

The chuckle of appreciation went up the bar and down it again.

"I want to ask you," went on the devil in Jerry Strann, "where you got your hoss?"

"He was running wild," came the gentle answer. "So I took a walk, one day, and brought him in."

A pause.

"Maybe," grinned the big man, "you creased him?"

For it is one of the most difficult things in the world to capture a wild horse, and some hunters, in their desperation at seeing the wonderful animals escape, have tried to "crease" them. That is, they strive to shoot so that the bullet will barely graze the top of the animal's vertebrae, just behind the ears, stunning the horse and making it helpless for the capture. But necessarily such shots are made from a distance, and little short of a miracle is needed to make the bullet strike true—for a fraction of an inch too low means death. So another laugh of appreciation ran around the barroom at the mention of creasing.

"No," answered Barry, "I went out with a halter and after a while Satan got used to me and followed me home."

They waited only long enough to draw deep breath; then came a long yell of delight. But the obscure devil was growing stronger and stronger in Strann. He beat on the bar until he got silence. Then he leaned over to meet the eyes of Barry.

"That," he remarked through his teeth, "is a damned —lie!"

There is only one way of answering that word in the mountain-desert, and Barry did not take it. The melancholy brown eyes widened; he sighed, and raising his glass of lemonade sipped it slowly. Came a sick silence in the barroom. Men turned their eyes toward each other and then flashed them away again. It is not good that one who has the eyes and the tongue of a man should take water from another—even from a Jerry Strann. And even Jerry Strann withdrew his eyes slowly from his prey, and shuddered; the sight of the most grisly death is not so horrible as cowardice.

And the devil which was still strong in Strann made

him look about for a new target; Barry was removed from all danger by an incredible barrier. He found that new target at once, for his glance reached to the corner of the room and found there the greenish, glimmering eyes of the dog. He smote upon the bar.

"Is this a damned kennel?" he shouted. "Do I got to drink in a barnyard? What's the dog doin' here?"

And he caught up the heavy little whiskey glass and hurled it at the crouching dog. It thudded heavily, but it brought no yelp of pain; instead, a black thunderbolt leaped from the corner and lunged down the room. It was the silence of the attack that made it terrible, and Strann cursed and pulled his gun. He could never have used it. He was a whole half second too late, but before the dog sprang a voice cut in: "Bart!"

It checked the animal in its very leap; it landed on the floor and slid on stiffly extended legs to the feet of Strann.

"Bart!" rang the voice again.

And the beast, flattening to the floor, crawled backward, inch by inch; it was slavering, and there was a ravening madness in its eyes.

"Look at it!" cried Strann. "By God, it's mad!"

And he raised his gun to draw the bead.

"Wait!" called the same voice which had checked the spring of the dog. Surely it could not have come from the lips of Barry. It held a resonance of chiming metal; it was not loud, but it carried like a brazen bell. "Don't do it, Strann!"

And it came to every man in the barroom that it was unhealthy to stand between the two men at that instant; a sudden path opened from Barry to Strann.

"Bart!" came the command again. "Heel!"

The dog obeyed with a slinking swiftness; Jerry Strann put up his gun and smiled.

"I don't take a start on no man," he announced quite pleasantly. "I don't need it. But—you yaller hearted houn'—get out from between. When I make my draw I'm goin' to kill that damn wolf."

Now, the fighting face of Jerry Strann was well known in the Three B's, and it was something for men to remember until they died in a peaceful bed. Yet there was not a glance from the bystanders, for Strann. They stood back against the wall, flattening themselves, and they stared, fascinated, at the slender stranger. Not that his face had grown ugly by a sudden metamorphosis. It was more beautiful than ever, for the man was smiling. It was his eyes which held them. Behind the brown a light was growing, a yellow and unearthly glimmer which one felt might be seen on the darkest night.

There was none of the coward in Jerry Strann. He looked full into that yellow, glimmering, changing light— he looked steadily—and a strange feeling swept over him. No, it was not fear. Long experience had taught him that there was not another man in the Three B's, with the exception of his own terrible brother, who could get a gun out of the leather faster than he, but now it seemed to Jerry Strann that he was facing something more than mortal speed and human strength and surety. He could not tell in what the feeling was based. But it was a giant, dim foreboding holding dominion over other men's lives, and it sent a train of chilly weakness through his blood.

"It's a habit of mine," said Jerry Strann, "to kill mad dogs when I see 'em." And he smiled again.

They stood for another long instant, facing each other. It was plain that every muscle in Strann's body was growing tense; the very smile was frozen on his lips. When he moved, at last, it was a convulsive jerk of his arm, and it was said, afterward, that his gun was all clear of the leather before the calm stranger stirred. No eye followed what happened. Can the eye follow such speed as the cracking lash of a whip?

There was only one report. The forefinger of Strann did not touch his trigger, but the gun slipped down and dangled loosely from his hand. He made a pace forward with his smile grown to an idiotic thing and a patch of red sprang out in the center of his breast. Then he lurched headlong to the floor.

10 · "Sweet Adeline"

FATTY MATTHEWS came panting through the doors. He was one of those men who have a leisurely build and a purely American desire for action; so that he was always hurrying and always puffing. If he mounted a horse, sweat started out from every pore; if he swallowed a glass of redeye he breathed hard thereafter. Yet he was capable of great and sustained exertions, as many and many a man in the Three B's could testify. He was ashamed of his fat. Imagine the soul of a Bald Eagle in the body of a Poland China sow and you begin to have some idea of Fatty Matthews. Fat filled his boots as with water and he made a "squinching" sound when he walked; fat rolled along his jowls; fat made his very forehead flabby; fat almost buried his eyes. But nothing could conceal the hawk-line of his nose or the gleam of those half-buried eyes. His hair was short-cropped, gray, and stood on end like bristles, and he was in the habit of using his panting breath in humming—for that concealed the puffing. So Fatty Matthews came through the doors and his little, concealed eyes darted from face to face. Then he kneeled beside Strann.

He was humming as he opened Jerry's shirt; he was humming as he pulled from his bag—for Fatty was almost as much doctor as he was marshal, cowpuncher, miner, and gambler—a roll of cotton and another roll of bandages. The crowd grouped around him, fascinated, and at his directions some of them brought water and others raised and turned the body while the marshal made the bandages; Jerry Strann was unconscious. Fatty Matthews began to intersperse talk in his humming.

"You was plugged from in front—my beauty—was you?" grunted Fatty, and then running the roll of bandage around the wounded man's chest he hummed a bar of:

"Sweet Adeline, my Adeline,
At night, dear heart, for you I pine."

"Was Jerry lookin' the other way when he was potted?" asked Fatty of the bystanders. "O'Brien, you seen it?"

O'Brien cleared his throat.

"I didn't see nothin'," he said mildly, and began to mop his bar, which was already polished beyond belief.

"Well," muttered Fatty Matthews, "all these birds get it. And Jerry was some overdue. Lew, you seen it?"

"Yep."

"Some drunken bum do it?"

Lew leaned to the ear of the kneeling marshal and whispered briefly. Fatty opened his eyes and cursed until his panting forced him to break off and hum.

"Beat him to the draw?" he gasped at length.

"Jerry's gun was clean out before the stranger made a move," asserted Lew.

"It ain't possible," murmured the deputy, and hummed softly:

"In all my dreams, your fair face beams."

He added sharply, as he finished the bandaging: "Where'd he head for?"

"No place," answered Lew. "He just now went out the door."

The deputy swore again, but he added, enlightened: "Going to plead self-defense, eh?"

Big O'Brien leaned over the bar.

"Listen, Fatty," he said earnestly, "there ain't no doubt of it. Jerry had his war paint on. He tried to kill this feller Barry's wolf."

"Wolf?" cut in the deputy marshal.

"Dog, I guess," qualified the bartender. "I dunno. Anyway, Jerry made all the leads; this Barry simply done the finishing. I say, don't put this Barry under arrest. You want to keep him here for Mac Strann."

"That's *my* business," growled Fatty. "Hey, half a dozen of you gents. Hook on to Jerry and take him up to a room. I'll be with you in a minute."

And while his directions were being obeyed he trotted

heavily up the length of the barroom and out the swinging doors. Outside, he found only one man, and in the act of mounting a black horse; the deputy marshal made straight for that man until a huge black dog appeared from nowhere blocking his path. It was a silent dog, but its teeth and eyes said enough to stop Fatty in full career.

"Are you Barry?" he asked.

"That's me. Come here, Bart."

The big dog backed to the other side of the horse without shifting his eyes from the marshal. The latter gingerly approached the rider, who sat perfectly at ease in the saddle; most apparently he was in no haste to leave.

"Barry," said the deputy, "don't make no play when I tell you who I am; I don't mean you no harm, but my name's Matthews, and——" he drew back the flap of his vest enough to show the glitter of his badge of office. All the time his little beady eyes watched Barry with birdlike intentness. The rider made not a move. And now Matthews noted more in detail the feminine slenderness of the man and the large, placid eyes. He stepped closer and dropped a confidential hand on the pommel of the saddle.

"Son," he muttered, "I hear you made a clean play inside. Now, I know Strann and his ways. He was in the wrong. There ain't a doubt of it, and if I held you, you'd get clear on self-defense. So I ain't going to lay a hand on you. You're free; but one thing more. You cut off there—see?—and bear away north from the Three B's. You got a hoss that *is,* and believe me, you'll need him before you're through." He lowered his voice and his eyes bulged with the terror of his tidings: "Feed him the leather, ride to beat hell; never stop while your hoss can raise a trot; and then slide off your hoss and get another. Son, in three days Mad Strann'll be on your trail!"

He stepped back and waved his arms.

"Now, *vamos!*"

The black stallion flicked back its ears and winced from the outflung hands, but the rider remained imperturbed.

"I never heard of Mac Strann," said Barry.

"You never heard of Mac Strann?" echoed the other.

"But I'd like to meet him," said Barry.

The deputy marshal blinked his eyes rapidly, as though he needed to clear his vision.

"Son," he said hoarsely. "I c'n see you're game. But don't make a fall play. If Mac Strann gets you, he'll California you like a yearling. You won't have no chance. You've done for Jerry, there ain't a doubt of that, but Jerry to Mac is like a tame cat to a mountain lion. Lad, I c'n see you're a stranger to these parts, but ask me your questions and I'll tell you the best way to go."

Barry slipped from the saddle.

He said. "I'd like to know the best place to put up my hoss."

The deputy marshal was speechless.

"But I s'pose," went on Barry, "I can stable him over there behind the hotel."

Matthews pushed off his sombrero and rubbed his short fingers through his hair. Anger and amazement still shocked him, but he controlled himself by a praiseworthy effort.

"Barry," he said, "I don't make you out. Maybe you figure to wait till Mac Strann gets to town before you leave; maybe you think your hoss can outrun anything on four feet. And maybe it can. But listen to me: Mac Strann ain't fast on a trail, but the point about him is that he never leaves it! You can go through rain and over rocks, but you can't never shake Mac Strann—not once he gets the wind of you."

"Thanks," returned the gentle-voiced stranger. "I guess maybe he'll be worth meeting."

And so saying he turned on his heel and walked calmly toward the big stables behind the hotel and at his heels followed the black dog and the black horse. As for the deputy marshal Matthews, he moistened his lips to whistle, but when he pursed them, not a sound came. He turned at length into the barroom and as he walked his eye was vacant. He was humming brokenly:

> "*Sweet Adeline, my Adeline,*
> *At night, dear heart, for you I pine.*"

Inside, he took firm hold upon the bar with both pudgy hands.

"O'Brien," he said, "redeye."

He pushed away the small glass which the bartender spun toward him and seized in its place a mighty water-tumbler.

"O'Brien," he explained, "I need strength, not encouragement." And filling the glass nearly to the brim he downed the huge potion at a single draught.

11 · The Buzzard

MOST animals have their human counterparts, and in that room where Jerry Strann had fallen a whimsical observer might have termed Jerry, with his tawny head, the lion, and O'Brien behind the bar, a shaggy bear, and the deputy marshal a wolverine, fat but dangerous, and here stood a man as ugly and hardened as a desert cayuse, and there was Dan Barry, sleek and supple as a panther; but among the rest this whimsical observer must have noticed a fellow of prodigious height and negligible breadth, a structure of sinews and bones that promised to rattle in the wind, a long, narrow head, a nose like a beak, tiny eyes set close together and shining like polished buttons, and a vast Adam's apple that rolled up and down the scraggy throat. He might have done for the spirit of Famine in an old play; but every dweller of the mountain-desert would have found an apter expression by calling him the buzzard of the scene. Through his prodigious ugliness he was known far and wide as "Haw-Haw" Langley; for on occasion Langley laughed, and his laughter was an indescribable sound that lay somewhere between the braying of a mule and the cawing of a crow. But Haw-Haw Langley was usually silent, and he would sit for hours without words, twisting his head and making little pecking motions as his eyes fastened on face after face. All the bitterness of the mountain-desert was in Haw-Haw Langley; if his body looked like a buzzard, his soul was the soul of the vulture itself, and therefore he had followed the courses of Jerry Strann up and down the range. He stuffed his gorge with the fragments of his leader's food; he fed his soul with the dangers which Jerry Strann met and conquered.

In the barroom Haw-Haw Langley had stood turning his sharp little eyes from Jerry Strann to Dan Barry, and from Dan Barry back to Strann; and when the shot was fired something like a grin twisted his thin lips; and when the spot of red glowed on the breast of the staggering man, the eyes of Haw-Haw blazed as if with the reflection of a devouring fire. Afterward he lingered for a few minutes making no effort to aid the fallen man, but when he had satisfied himself with the extent of the injury, and when he had noted the froth of bloody bubbles which stained the lips of Strann, Haw-Haw Langley turned and stalked from the room. His eyes were points of light and his soul was crammed to repletion with ill-tidings.

At the hitching rack he stepped into the saddle of a diminutive horse, whirled it into the street with a staggering jerk of the reins, and buried the spurs deep in the cow pony's flanks. The poor brute snorted and flirted its heels in the air, but Langley wrapped his long legs around the barrel of his mount and goaded it again.

His smile, which began with the crack of Barry's gun in O'Brien's place, did not die out until he was many a mile away, headed far up through the mountains; but as he put peak after peak behind him and as the white light of the day diminished and puffs of blue shadow drowned the valleys, the grin disappeared from Haw-Haw's face. He became keenly intent on his course until, having reached the very summit of a tall hill, he came to a halt and peered down before him.

It was nearly dusk by this time and the eyes of an ordinary man could not distinguish a tree from a rock at any great distance; but it seemed that Haw-Haw was gifted with eyes extraordinary—the buzzard at the top of its sky-towering circles does not see the brown carcass far below with more certainty than Haw-Haw sensed his direction. He waited only a few seconds before he rolled the rowel once more along the scored flanks of his mustang and then plunged down the slope at a reckless gallop.

His destination was a hut, or rather a lean-to, that pressed against the side of the mountain, a crazy structure with a single length of stove pipe leaning away from the roof. And at the door of this house Haw-Haw Langley drew rein and stepped to the ground. The interior of the hut was dark, but Haw-Haw stole with the caution of a wild Indian to the entrance and reconnoitered the interior, probing every shadowy corner with his glittering eyes. For several long moments he continued this examination, and even when he was satisfied that there was no one in the place he did not enter, but moved back several paces from the door and swept the sides of the mountains with an uneasy eye. He made out, a short distance from the door, a picketed horse which now reared up its head from the miserable scattering of grass on which it fed and stared at the stranger. The animal must have bulked at least twice as large as the mount which had brought Langley to the mountainside. And it was muscled even out of porportion to its bulk. The head was so tremendously broad that it gave an almost square appearance, the neck, short and thick, the forelegs disproportionately small but very sturdy; and the whole animal was built on a slope toward the hind quarters which seemed to equal in massiveness all the rest of the body. One would have said that the horse was a freak meant by nature for the climbing of hills. And to glance at it no man could suppose that those ponderous limbs might be moved to a gallop. However, Haw-Haw Langley well knew the powers of the ugly beast, and even made a detour and walked about the horse to view it more closely.

Now he again surveyed the darkening landscape and then turned once more to the house. This time he entered with the boldness of a possessor approaching his hearth. He lighted a match and with this ignited a lantern hanging from the wall to the right of the door. The furnishings of the dwelling were primitive beyond compare. There was no sign of a chair; a huddle of blankets on the bare boards of the floor made the bed, a saddle hung by one stirrup on one side and on the other side leaned the skins of bobcats, lynx, and coyotes on their stretching and drying boards. Haw-Haw took down the lantern and examined the pelts. The animals had been skinned with the utmost dexterity. As far as he could see the hides had not been marred in a single place by slips of the knife, nor were there any blood stains to attest hurried work, or careless shooting in the first place. The inner surfaces shone with the pure white of old parchment. But Haw-Haw gave his chief attention to the legs and heads of the skins, for these were the places where carelessness or stupidity with the knife were sure to show; but the work was perfect in every respect. Until even the critical Haw-Haw Langley was forced to step back and shake his head in admiration. He continued his survey of the room.

In one corner stood a rifle and a shotgun; in another was a pile of provisions—bacon, flour, salt, meal, and little else. Spices and condiments were apparently unknown to this hermit; nor was there even the inevitable coffee, nor any of the molasses or other sweets which the tongue of the desert-mountaineer cannot resist. Flour, meat, and water, it seemed, made up the entire fare of the trapper. For cookery there was an unboarded space in the very center of the floor with a number of rocks, grouped around in the hole and blackened with soot. The smoke must rise, therefore, and escape through the small hole in the center of the roof. The length of stovepipe which showed on the roof must have been simply the inhabitant's idea of giving the last delicate touch of civilization; it was like a tassel to the cap of the Turk.

As Haw-Haw's observations reached this point his sharp ear caught the faint whinny of the big horse outside. He started like one caught in a guilty act, and sprang to the lantern. However, with his hands upon it he thought better of it, and he placed the light against the wall; then he turned to the entrance and looked anxiously up the hillside.

What he saw was a form grotesque beyond belief. It seemed to be some gigantic wild beast—mountain lion or great bear, though of a size beyond credence—which slowly sprawled down the slope walking erect upon its hind feet with its forelegs stretched out horizontal, as if it were warning all who might behold it away. Haw-

Haw grew pale and involuntarily reached for his gun as he first beheld this apparition, but instantly he saw the truth. It was a man who carried a burden down the mountainside. The burden was the carcass of a bear; the man had drawn the forelegs over his shoulders—his jutting elbows making what had seemed the outstretched arms—and above the head of the burden-bearer rose the great head of the bear. As the man came closer the animal's head flopped to one side and a red tongue lolled from its mouth. Haw-Haw Langley moved back step by step through the cabin until his shoulders struck the opposite wall, and at the same time Mac Strann entered the room. He had no ear for his visitor's hail, but cast his burden to the floor. It dropped with a shock that shook the house from the rattling stovepipe to the crackling boards. For a moment Mac Strann regarded his prey. Then he stooped and drew open the great jaws. The mouth within was not so red as the bloody hands of Mac Strann; and the big white fangs, for some reason, did not seem terrible in comparison with the hunter. Having completed his survey he turned slowly upon Haw-Haw Langley and lowered his eyebrows to stare.

So doing, the light for the first time struck full upon his face. Haw-Haw Langley bit his thin lips and his eyes widened almost to the normal.

For the ugliness of Mac Strann was that most terrible species of ugliness—not disfigured features but a discord which pervaded the man and came from within him—like a sound. Feature by feature his face was not ugly. The mouth was very large, to be sure, and the jaw too heavily square, and the nose needed somewhat greater length and less width for real comeliness. The eyes were truly fine, being very large and black, though when Mac Strann lowered his bush of brows his eyes were practically reduced to gleams of light in the consequent shadow. There was a sharp angle in his forehead, the lines of it meeting in the center and shelving up and down. One felt, unpleasantly, that there were heavy muscles overlaying that forehead. One felt that to the touch it would be a pad of flesh, and it gave to Mac Strann, more than any other feature, a peculiar impression of resistless physical power.

In the catalogue of his features, indeed, there was nothing severely objectionable; but out of it came a feeling of *too much strength!* A glance at his body reinsured the first thought. It was not normal. His shirt bulged tightly at the shoulders with muscles. He was not tall—inches shorter than his brother Jerry, for instance—but the bulk of his body was incredible. His torso was a veritable barrel that bulged out both in the chest and the back. And even the tremendous thighs of Mac Strann were perceptibly bowed out by the weight which they had to carry. And there was about his management of his arms a peculiar awkwardness which only the very strongest of men exhibit—as if they were burdened by the weight of their mere dangling hands.

This giant, having placed his eyes in shadow, peered for a long moment at Haw-Haw Langley, but very soon his glance began to waver. It flashed toward the wall—it came back and rested upon Langley again. He was like a dog, restless under a steady stare. And as Haw-Haw Langley noted this a glitter of joy came in his beady eyes.

"You're Jerry's man," said Mac Strann at length.

There was about his voice the same fleshy quality that was in his face; it came literally from his stomach, and it made a peculiar rustling sound such as comes after one has eaten sticky sweet things. People could listen to the voice of Mac Strann and forget that he was speaking words. The articulation ran together in a sort of glutinous mass.

"I'm a friend of Jerry's," said the other. "I'm Langley."

The big man stretched out his hand. The hair grew black, down to the knuckles; the blood of the bear still streaked it; it was large enough to be an organism with independent life. But when Langley, with some misgiving, trusted his own bony fingers within that grasp, it was only as if something fleshy, soft, and bloodless had closed over them. When his hand was released he rubbed it covertly against his trouser leg—to remove dirt—restore the circulation. He did not know why.

"Who's bothering Jerry?" asked Mac Strann. "And where is he?"

He went to the wall without waiting for an answer and took down the saddle. Now the cowpuncher's saddle is a heavy mass of leather and steel, and the saddle of Mac Strann was far larger than the ordinary. Yet he took down the saddle as one might remove a card from a rack. Haw-Haw Langley moved toward the door, to give himself a free space for exit.

"Jerry's hurt," he said, and he watched.

There was a ripple of pain on the face of Mac Strann.

"Hoss kicked him—fall on him?" he asked.

"It weren't a hoss."

"Huh? A cow?"

"It weren't no cow. It weren't no animal."

Mac Strann faced full upon Langley. When he spoke it seemed as if it were difficult for him to manage his lips. They lifted an appreciable space before there was any sound.

"What was it?"

"A man."

Langley edged back toward the door.

"What with?"

"A gun."

And Langley saw the danger that was coming even before Mac Strann moved. He gave a shrill yelp of terror and whirled and sprang for the open. But Mac Strann sprang after him and reached. His whole body seemed to stretch like an elastic thing, and his arm grew longer. The hand fastened on the back of Langley, plucked him up, jammed him against the wall. Haw-Haw crumpled to the floor.

He gasped: "It weren't me, Mac. For Gawd's sake, it weren't me!"

His face was a study. There was abject terror in it, and yet there was also a sort of grisly joy, and his eyes feasted on the silent agony of Mac Strann.

"Where?" asked Mac Strann.

"Mac," pleaded the vulture who cringed on the floor, "gimme your word you ain't goin' to hold it agin me."

"Tell me," said the other, and he framed the face of the vulture between his large hands. If he pressed the heels of those hands together bones would snap, and Haw-Haw Langley knew it. And yet nothing but a wild delight could have set that glitter in his eyes, just as nothing but a palsy of terror could have set his limbs twitching so.

"Who shot him from behind?" demanded the giant.

"It wasn't from behind," croaked the bearer of ill-tidings. "It was from the front."

"While he wasn't looking?"

"No. He was beat to the draw."

"You're *lyin'* to me," said Mac Strann slowly.

"So help me God!" cried Langley.

"Who done it?"

"A little feller. He ain't half as big as me. He's got a voice like Kitty Jackson, the schoolmarm; and he's got eyes like a starved pup. It was him that done it."

The eyes of Mac Strann grew vaguely meditative.

"Nope," he mused, in answer to his own thoughts, "I won't use no rope. I'll use my hands. Where'd the bullet land?"

A fresh agony of trembling shook Langley, and a fresh sparkle came in his glance.

"Betwixt his ribs, Mac. And right on through. And it come out his back!"

But there was not an answering tremor in Mac Strann. He let his hands fall away from the face of the vulture, and he caught up the saddle. Langley straightened himself. He peered anxiously at Strann, as if he feared to miss something.

"I dunno whether he's livin' right now, or not," suggested Haw-Haw.

But Mac Strann was already striding through the door.

Sweat was pouring from the lather-flecked bodies of their horses when they drew rein, at last, at the goal of their long fierce ride, and Haw-Haw slunk behind the broad form of Mac Strann when the latter strode into the hotel. Then the two started for the room in which, they were told, lay Jerry Strann.

"There it is," whispered Haw-Haw, as they reached the head of the stairs. "The door's open. If he was dead the door would be closed, most like."

They stood in the hall and looked in upon a strange picture, for flat in the bed lay Jerry Strann, his face very white and oddly thin, and over him leaned the man who had shot him down.

They heard Dan Barry's soft, gentle voice query: "How you feelin' now, partner?"

He leaned close beside the other, his fingers upon the wrist of Jerry.

"A pile better," muttered Jerry Strann. "Seems like I got more'n a fightin' chance to pull through now."

"Jest you keep lyin' here quiet," advised Dan Barry, "and don't stir around none. Don't start no worryin'. You're goin' to live's long as you don't lose no more blood. Keep your thoughts quiet. They ain't no cause for you to do nothin' but jest keep your eyes closed, and breathe, and think of yaller sunshine, and green grass in the spring, and the wind lazyin' the clouds along across the sky. That's all you got to think about. Jest keep quiet, partner."

"It's easy to do it now you're with me. Seems like they's a pile of strength runnin' into me from the tips of your fingers, my frien'. And—I was *some* fool to start that fight with you, Barry."

"Jest forget all that," murmured the other. "And keep your voice down. I've forgot it; you forget it. It ain't never happened."

"What's it mean?" frowned Mac Strann, whispering to Haw-Haw.

The eyes of the latter glittered like beads.

"That's him that shot Jerry," said Haw-Haw. "Him!"

"Hell!" snarled Mac Strann, and went through the door.

At the first sound of his heavy footfall, the head of Barry raised and turned in a light, swift movement. The next instant he was on his feet. A moment before his face had been as gentle as that of a mother leaning over a sick child; but one glimpse of the threat in the contorted brows of Mac Strann set a gleam in his own eyes, an answer as distinct as the click of metal against metal. Not a word had been said, but Jerry, who had lain with eyes closed, seemed to sense a change in the atmosphere of peace which had enwrapped him the moment before. His eyes flashed open; and he saw his burly brother.

But Mac Strann had no eye for any saving Dan Barry.

"Are you the creepin', sneakin' snake that done—this?"

"You got me figured right," answered Dan coldly.

"Then, by God——" began the roaring voice of Mac, but Jerry Strann stirred wildly on the bed.

"Mac!" he called, "Mac!" His voice went suddenly horribly thick, a bubbling, liquid sound. "For God's sake, Mac!"

He had reared himself up on one elbow, his arm stretched out to his brother. And a foam of crimson stood on his lips.

"Mac, don't pull no gun! It was me that was in wrong!"

And then he fell back in the bed, and into the arms of Mac, who was beside him, moaning: "Buck up, Jerry. Talk to me, boy!"

"Mac, you've finished the job," came the husky whisper.

Mac Strann raised his head, and his terrible eyes fixed upon Dan Barry. And there was no pity in the face of the other. The first threat had wiped every vestige of human tenderness out of his eyes, and now, with something like a sneer on his lips, and with a glimmer of yellow light in his eyes, he was backing toward the door, and noiselessly as a shadow he slipped out and was gone.

12 · Finesse

"A MAN talks because he's drunk or lonesome; a girl talks because that's her way of takin' exercise."

This was a maxim of Buck Daniels, and Buck Daniels knew a great deal about women, as many a schoolmarm and many a rancher's daughter of the mountain-desert could testify.

Also Buck Daniels said of women: "It ain't what you say to 'em so much as the tune you put it to."

Now he sat this day in O'Brien's hotel dining room.

It was the lazy and idle hour between three and four
in the afternoon, and since the men of the mountain-
desert eat promptly at six, twelve, and six, there was
not a soul in the room when he entered. Nor was there
a hint of eating utensils on the tables. Nevertheless Buck
Daniels was not dismayed. He selected a corner-table
by instinct and smote upon the surface with the flat of
his hand. It made a report like the spat of a forty-five;
heavy footsteps approached, a door flung open, and a
cross-eyed slattern stood in the opening. At the sight of
Buck Daniels sitting with his hands on his hips and his
sombrero pushed back to a good-natured distance on
his head the lady puffed with rage.

"What in hell d'you think this is?" bellowed this gentle creature, and the tone echoed heavily back from all
four walls. "You're three hours late and you get no chuck
here. On your way, stranger!"

Buck Daniels elevated himself slowly from the chair
and stood at his full height. With a motion fully as
deliberate he removed his sombrero and bowed to such
a depth that the brim of the hat brushed the floor.

"Lady," he said humbly, "I was thinkin' that some gent
run this here eatin' place. Which if you'll excuse me
half a minute I'll ramble outside and sluice off some of
the dust. If I'd known you was here I wouldn't of
thought of comin' in here like this."

The lady with the defective eyes glared fiercely at
him. Her judgment wavered two ways. Her first inclina-
tion was to hold that the fellow was jibing at her covertly, and she followed her original impulse far enough
to clasp a neighboring sugar bowl in a large, capable
hand. A second and more merciful thought entered her
brain and stole slowly through it, like a faint echo in a
great cave.

"You don't have to make yourself pretty to talk to
me," she said thoughtfully. "But if you're here for chow
you're too late."

"Ma'am," said Buck Daniels instantly, "when I come
in here I was hungry enough to eat nails; but I'll forget about chuck if you'll sit down an' chin with me a
while."

The large hand of the cross-eyed lady stole out once more and rested upon the sugar bowl.

"D'you mind sayin' that over again?" she queried.

"Lonesomeness is worse'n hunger," said Buck Daniels, and he met her gaze steadily with his black eyes.

The hand released the sugar bowl once more; something resembling color stole into the brown cheeks of the maiden.

She said, relentingly: "Maybe you been off by yourse'f mining, stranger?"

Buck Daniels drew a long breath.

"Mines?" he said, and then laughed bitterly. "If that was all I been doin'——" he began darkly—and then stopped.

The waitress started.

"Maybe this here is my last chance to get chuck for days an' days. Well, let it go. If I stayed here with you I'd be talkin' too much!"

He turned slowly toward the door. His step was very slow indeed.

"Wait a minute," called the maiden. "There ain't any call for that play. If you're in wrong somewhere—well, stranger, just take that chair and I'll have some ham-and-in front of you inside of a minute."

She had slammed through the door before Buck turned, and he sat down, smiling pleasantly to himself. Half of a mirror decorated the wall beside his table, and into this Buck peered. His black locks were sadly disarrayed, and he combed them into some semblance of order with his fingers. He had hardly finished this task when the door was kicked open with such force that it whacked against the wall, and the waitress appeared with an armful of steaming food. Before Buck's widening eyes she swiftly set forth an array of bread, butter in chunks, crisp French-fried potatoes, a large slab of ham on one plate and several fried eggs on another, and above all there was a mighty pewter cup of coffee blacker than the heart of night. Yearning seized upon Buck Daniels, but policy was stronger than hunger in his subtle mind. He rose again; he drew forth the chair opposite his own.

"Ma'am," said Buck Daniels, "ain't you going to favor me by settin' down?"

The lady blinked her unfocused eyes.

"Ain't I what?" she was finally able to ask.

"I know," said Buck Daniels swiftly, "that you're terrible busy; which you ain't got time to waste on a stranger like me."

She turned upon Buck those uncertain and wistful eyes. It was a generous face. Mouth, cheekbones, and jaw were of vast proportions, while the forehead, eyes, and nose were as remarkably diminutive. Her glance lowered to the floor; she shrugged her wide shoulders and began to wipe the vestiges of dishwater from her freckled hands.

"You men are terrible foolish," she said. "There ain't no tellin' what you mean by what you say."

And she sank slowly into the chair. It gave voice in sharp protest at her weight. Buck Daniels retreated to the opposite side of the table and took his place.

"Ma'am," he began, "don't I look honest?" So saying, he slid half a dozen eggs and a section of ham from the platter to his plate.

"I dunno," said the maiden, with one eye upon him and the other plunging into the future. "There ain't no trusting men. Take 'em by the lot and they're awful forgetful."

"If you knowed me better," said Buck sadly, disposing of a slab of bread spread thick with the pale butter and following this with a pile of fried potatoes astutely balanced on his knife. "If you knowed me better, ma'am, you wouldn't have no suspicions."

"What might it be that you been doin'?" asked the girl.

Buck Daniels paused in his attack on the food and stared at her.

He quoted deftly from a magazine which had once fallen in his way: "Some day maybe I can tell you. There's something about your eyes that tells me you'd understand."

At the mention of her eyes the waitress blinked and stiffened in her chair, while a huge, red fist balled itself in readiness for action. But the expression of Buck Daniels was as blandly open as the smile of infancy. The lady relaxed and an unmistakable blush tinged even her nose with color.

"It ain't after my nature to be askin' questions," she announced. "You don't have to tell me no more'n you want to."

"Thanks," said Buck instantly. "I knew you was that kind. It ain't hard," he went on smoothly, "to tell a lady when you see one. I can tell you this much to start with. I'm lookin' for a quiet town where I can settle down permanent. And as far as I can see, Brownsville looks sort of quiet to me."

So saying, he disposed of the rest of his food by an act akin to legerdemain, and then fastened a keen eye upon the lady. She was in the midst of a struggle of some sort. But she could not keep the truth from her tongue.

"Take it by and large," she said at length, "Brownsville is as peaceable as most; but just now, stranger, it's all set for a big bust." She turned heavily in her chair and glanced about the room. Then she faced Daniels once more and cupped her hands about her mouth. "Stranger," she said in a stage whisper, "Mac Strann is in town!"

The eyes of Buck Daniels wandered.

"Don't you know him?" she asked.

"Nope."

"Never heard of him?"

"Nope."

"Well," sighed the waitress, "you've had *some* luck in your life. Take a cross between a bulldog and a mustang and a mountain lion—that's Mac Strann. He's in town, and he's here for killin'."

"You don't say, ma'am. And why don't they lock him up?"

"Because he ain't done nothin' yet to be locked up about. That's the way with him. And when he does a thing he always makes the man he's after pull his gun first. Smart? I'll say he's just like an Indian, that Mac Strann!"

"But who's he after?"

"The feller that plugged his brother, Jerry."

"Kind of looks like he had reason for a killing, then."

"Nope. Jerry had it comin' to him. He was always rais-ing trouble, Jerry was. And this time, he pulled his gun first. Everybody seen him."

"He run into a gunman?"

"Gunman?" she laughed heartily. "Partner, if it wasn't for something funny about his eyes, I wouldn't be no more afraid of that gunman than I am of a tabby-cat. And me a weak woman. The quietest lookin' sort that ever come to Brownsville. But there's something queer about him. He knows that Mac Strann is here in town. He knows that Mac Strann is waiting for Jerry to die. He knows that when Jerry dies Mac will be out for a killin'. And this here stranger is just sittin' around and waitin' to be killed! Can you beat that?"

But Buck Daniels had grown strangely excited.

"What did you say there was about his eyes?" he asked sharply.

She grew suddenly suspicious.

"D' you know him?"

"No. But you was talkin' about his eyes?"

"I dunno what it is. I ain't the only one that's seen it. There ain't no word you can put to it. It's just there. That's all."

The voice of Buck Daniels fell to a whisper.

"It's sort of fire," he suggested. "Ain't it a kind of light *behind* his eyes?"

But the waitress stared at him in amazement.

"Fire?" she gasped. "A light *behind* his eyes? M'frien', are you tryin' to string me?"

"What's his name?"

"I dunno."

"Ma'am," said Daniels, rising hastily. "Here's a dol-lar if you'll take me to him."

"You don't need no guide," she replied. "Listen to that, will you?"

And as he hearkened obediently Buck Daniels heard a strain of whistling, needle-sharp with distance.

"That's him," nodded the woman. "He's always goin' about whistling to himself. Kind of a nut, he is."

"It's him!" cried Buck Daniels. "It's him!"

And with this ungrammatical burst of joy he bolted from the room.

13 · The Three

THE whistling came from behind the hotel, and although it ended as soon as he reached the veranda of the building, Buck Daniels hurried to the rear of the place. There were the long, low sheds of the barn, and behind these, he knew, must be the corrals. He raced around the corner of the shed and there came to a halt, for he saw a thing that turned his blood to ice.

One of those rare rains of the mountain-desert had recently fallen and the corrals behind the barn were carpeted with a short, thick grass. In the small corral nearest him he beheld, rolling on that carpet of grass, a great wolf—or a dog as large and as rough-coated as a wolf, and a man; and they were engaged in a desperate and silent struggle for mastery. Their movements were so lightning fast that Buck Daniels could not make out distinct forms from the tangle. But he saw the great white teeth of the wolf flash in the sun one instant, and the next the man had whirled on top. It was Dan and Bart at play.

No outcry from Dan; no growl from the wolf. Buck felt the old chill which never left him when he saw the fierce game of the wolf and the wolfman. All this passed in the twinkling of an eye, and then Dan, by a prodigious effort, had thrown the great beast away from him, so that Bart fell upon his back. Dan leaped with outstretched arms upon the fallen animal, and buried his clutching hands in the throat of the beast.

Yet still there was a thrill to add to these, for now a black horse appeared in the picture, a miracle of slender, shimmering grace—and he rushed with flattened ears upon the two twisting, writhing, prostrate figures. His teeth were bared—he was more like a prodigious dog than a horse. And those teeth closed on the back of the man's neck—or did they merely pinch his shirt?—and then Dan was dragged bodily away from the wolf and thrown through the air by a flirt of the stallion's head.

Horrible! Buck Daniels shuddered and then he grinned shamefacedly in apology to himself.

"The three of 'em!" he grunted, and stepped closer to the fence to watch.

The instant the man was torn away by the intercession of the horse, the wolf regained its feet and rushed upon him; but Dan had landed from his fall upon his feet, with cat-like agility, and now he dodged the rush of the wolf and the arrowy spring of the creature, and sprang in his turn toward the stallion.

The black met this attack by rearing, his ears flattened, his teeth bared, his eyes terrible to behold. As the man raced close the stallion struck with lightning hoofs, but the blow failed of its mark—by the breadth of a hair. And the assailant, swerving like a will-o'-the-wisp, darted to the side of the animal and leaped upon its back. At the same instant the wolf left the ground with terribly gaping mouth in a spring for the rider; but Dan flattened himself along the shining back of his mount and the wolf catapulted harmlessly past.

After this failure the wolfdog seemed to desire no further active part in the struggle, but took up a position to one side, and there, with lolling tongue and red-stained eyes, watched the battle continue. The stallion, to be sure, kept up the conflict with a wholehearted energy. Never had Buck Daniels in a long and varied career seen such wild pitching. The black leaped here and there, doubling about with the sinuous speed of a snake, springing high in the air one instant, and landing the next to stiff legs; dropping to the ground the next second, and rolling to catch the rider; up again like a leaf jerked up by a gale of wind, and so the fierce struggle continued, with the wild rider slapping the neck of the horse as if he would encourage it to more terrible efforts, and drumming its round barrel with vindictive heels. His hair blew back; his face flushed; and in his eyes there was the joy of the sailor, long land-bound, who climbs at last the tallest mast and feels it pitch beneath him and catches the sharp tang of the traveled wind.

The struggle ceased as if in obedience to an inaudible command. From the full frenzy of motion horse and man were suddenly moveless. Then Dan slipped from his seat and stood before his mount. At once the ears of the stallion, which had been flat back, pricked sharply forward; the eyes of the animal grew luminous and soft as the eyes of a woman, and he dropped the black velvet of his muzzle beneath the master's chin. As for Dan Barry, he rewarded this outburst of affection with no touch of his hand; but his lips moved, and he seemed to be whispering a secret to his horse. The wolf in the meantime had viewed this scene with growing unrest, and now it trotted up and placed itself at the side of the man. Receiving no attention in this position, it caught the arm of the man between its great fangs and drew his hands down. The stallion, angered by this interruption, raised a delicate forefoot to strike, and was received with a terrific snarl—the first sound of the entire scene.

"Bart," said the man, and his voice was not raised or harsh, but came as softly as running water, "if you ain't going to be a gentleman, I got to teach you manners. Get up on Satan's back and lie down till I tell you to get off."

The wolf received this command with a snarl even more bloodcurdling than before, but he obeyed, slinking sidewise a reluctant pace or two, and then springing to the back of the stallion with a single bound. There he crouched, still snarling softly until his master raised a significant forefinger. At that he lowered his head and maintained a fiercely observant silence.

"Dan!" called Buck Daniels.

The other whirled.

"Speakin' of pets," observed Buck Daniels, "I heard tell once about a gent that had a tame lion. Which you got the outbeatingest pair I ever see, Dan. Gentle, ain't they, like a stampede of cows!"

But Barry left this remark unanswered. He ran to the tall fence, placed his hand on the top rail, and vaulted lightly over it. Then he clasped the hand of the larger man, and his face lighted.

"Buck," he said, "I been sort of lonesome. It feels pretty good to see you agin."

"Oh man," answered Buck Daniels, "speakin' of bein'

lonesome——" He checked himself. "How about steppin'
inside and havin' a talk?"

The other started forward agreeably, but stopped almost at once.

"Heel!" he called, without turning his head.

Black Bart left the back of the stallion in a long bound
that carried him half way to the fence. His next leap
brought him over the rail and beside his master. Buck
Daniels moved back a step involuntarily.

"Bart," he said, "d'you know me?"

He stretched out his hand; and was received with a
sudden baring of the fangs.

"Nice dog!" said Buck sarcastically. "Regular house-
pet, ain't he?"

The other apparently missed the entire point of this
remark. He said in his gentle, serious way: "He used to
be real wild, Buck. But now he don't mind people. He
let the cook feed him a chunk o' meat the other day;
and you remember he don't usually touch stuff that other
men have handled."

"Yep," grunted Buck, "it's sure disgustin' to have a
dog as tame as that. I'd bet he ain't killed another dog
for a whole day, maybe!"

And still Barry saw no irony in this.

He answered, as gravely as before: "No, it was the
day before yesterday. Somebody come to town and got
drunk. He had two dogs, and sicked 'em on Bart."

Buck Daniels controlled an incipient shudder.

"Both dead?"

"I was inside the house," said Daniels sadly, "and it
took me a couple of seconds to get outside. Of course by
that time Bart had cut their throats."

"Of course. Didn't the drunk guy try to pot Bart?"

"Yes, he got out his gun; but Mr. O'Brien, the bartender, persuaded him out of it. I was glad there wasn't
no trouble."

"My God!" exclaimed Buck Daniels. And then: "Well,
let's go inside. We'll take your man-eater along, if you
want to."

A shadow came in the eyes of Barry.

"Can't we talk jest as well out here?"

"What's the matter with findin' some chairs?"

"Because I don't like to get inside walls. You know how four walls seem like so many pairs of eyes standin' around you?"

"No," said Buck bluntly, "I don't know nothin' of the kind. What d'you mean?"

"I dunno," answered Barry, depressed. "It jest seems that way. Ain't you noticed how sort of close it is in a house? Hard to breathe? Like you had on a shirt too small for you."

"We'll stay out here, then?"

The other nodded, smiled, and made a gesture to the dog behind him. Black Bart crouched on the ground, and Dan Barry sat down cross-legged, his shoulders leaning against the shaggy pelt of Bart. Daniels followed the example with less grace. He was thinking very hard and fast, and he rolled a Durham cigarette to fill the interlude.

"I s'pose you're bustin' to find out the news about the folks," he said dryly, at last.

The other sat with his hands loosely clasped in his lap. His wide eyes looked far away, and there was about his lips that looseness, that lack of compression, which one sees so often in children. He might have sat, in that posture, for the statue of thoughtlessness.

"What folks?" he asked at last.

Buck Daniels had lighted a match, but now he sat staring blankly until the match burned down to his fingers. With an oath he tossed the remnant away and lighted another. He had drawn down several long breaths of smoke to the bottom of his lungs before he could speak again.

"Some people you used to know; I suppose you've forgotten all about 'em, eh?" His eyes narrowed; there was a spark of something akin to dread in them. "Kate Cumberland?" he queried.

A light came in the face of Dan Barry.

"Kate Cumberland?" he repeated. "How is she, Buck? Lately, I been thinkin' about her every day."

A trembling shook the body and the voice of Daniels; his errand, after all, might meet some success.

"Kate?" he repeated. "Oh, ay, she's well enough. But Joe Cumberland ain't."

"No?"

"He's dyin', Dan."

And Dan replied calmly. "He's kind of old, I s'pose."

"Old?" said Buck, with a sort of horror. "Yes, he's old, right enough. D'you know why he's dying? It's because you went away the way you done, Dan. That's what's killin' him."

Something of thought came in the face of Barry.

"Maybe I understand," he said slowly. "If I was to lose Satan, or Bart——" here the great dog whined at the mention of his name, and Barry dropped a slender hand across the scarred forehead of his servant. "If I was to lose 'em, I'd sort of mourn for 'em, maybe."

Buck Daniels set his teeth.

"I don't suppose it seems possible," he said, "that a man could miss another man the way you could miss your —dog, eh? But it is! Joe Cumberland is dying for you, Dan, as sure as if you'd put a bullet in his bowels."

The other hesitated and then frowned and made a gesture of vague dismissal.

"Don't you figure on doin' nothing about it?" asked Buck softly.

"What could I do?"

"My God A'mighty, ain't you got no human feelin's?"

"I dunno what you mean," said the soft voice.

"This! Can't you git on your hoss and ride back with me to Cumberland Ranch? Stay with the old man till he gets back on his feet. Ain't that easy to do? Is your time so damned valuable you can't spare a few days for that?"

"But I *am* goin' back," answered Dan, in a rather hurt voice. "They ain't no need for cussin' me, Buck. I been thinkin' of Kate, every day, almost."

"Since when?"

"I dunno." Dan stirred uneasily. He looked up, and far above Buck, following the direction of Dan's eyes, saw a pattern of wild geese. "I been sort of driftin' north toward the Cumberland Ranch and Kate," went on Dan. He sighed: "I been thinkin' of her eyes, which is blue, Buck, and her hair, and the soft sound of her voice. They been hangin' in my ears, stayin' behind my eyes, lately, and I been driftin' up that way steady."

"Why, man," cried Buck, "then what's there to keep

you here? Jump on your hoss, and we'll head north in ten minutes."

"I will!" said Dan, full as eagerly. "We'll start full speed."

"Come on, then."

"Wait a minute!" said Dan, his voice growing suddenly cold. "I been forgettin' something."

Buck Daniels turned and found his companion strangely changed. There was a set expression of coldness about his face, and a chill glitter in his eyes.

"I got to wait here for something."

"What's that?"

"They's a man in town that may want to see me."

"Mac Strann! I've heard about him. Dan, are you goin' to let Joe Cumberland die because you want to stay here and fight it out with a dirty cutthroat?"

"I don't want to fight," protested Barry. "No, there ain't nothin' I like less than fightin'!"

Buck Daniels cursed softly and continuously to himself.

"Dan," he said, "can you sit there and lie like that to me? Ain't I seen you in action? Don't I remember the way you trailed Jim Silent? Don't I remember how we all got down and prayed you to keep away from Jim? Don't I remember how you threw everything to hell so's you could get your hands on Jim? My God A'mighty, man, didn't I see your face when you had your fingers in Silent's throat?"

An expression of unutterable revulsion rippled over the face of Dan Barry.

"Stop!" he commanded softly, and raised his slender hand. "Don't keep on talkin' about it. It makes me sick —all through. Oh, Buck, they's a tingle in the tips of my fingers still from the time I had 'em in his throat. And it makes me feel unclean—sort of uncleanness that won't wash out with no kind of soap and water. Buck, I'd most rather die myself than fight a man!"

A vast amazement overspread the countenance of Buck Daniels as he listened to this outburst; it was as if he had heard a healthy man proclaim that he had no desire for bread and meat. Something rose to his lips, but he swallowed it.

"Then it looks kind of simple to me," he said. "You

hate fightin'. This gent Mac Strann likes it; he lives on it; he don't do nothing but wait from day to day hungerin' for a scrap. What's the out? Jest this! You hop on your hoss and ride out with me. Young Jerry Strann kicks out —Mac Strann starts lookin' for you—he hears that you've beat it—he goes off and forgets about you. Ain't that simple?"

The old uneasiness returned to the farseeing eyes of Dan Barry.

"I dunno," he said, "maybe——"

Then he paused again.

"Have you got anything to say agin it?" urged Buck, arguing desperately.

"I dunno," repeated Barry, confused, "except that I keep thinking what a terrible disappointment it'll be to this Mac Strann when his brother dies and I ain't around."

Buck Daniels stared, blinked, and then burst into unmelodious laughter. Satan trotted across the corral and raised his head above the fence, whinnying softly. Barry turned his head and smiled up to the horse.

Then he said: "Seems like if Jerry Strann died I owe somebody something. Who? Mac Strann, I reckon. I sort of got to stay and give him his chance."

"I hope to God," burst out Daniels, smashing his hands together, "that Mac Strann beats you to a pulp! That's what I hope!"

The eyes of Dan Barry widened.

"Why d'you hope that?" he asked gently.

It brought Daniels again to speechlessness.

"Is it possible?" he growled to himself. "Are you a human bein' and yet you think more of your hoss and your damned wolf dog than you do of the life of a man? Dan, I'm askin' you straight, is that a square thing to do?"

The fragile hands went out to him, palms up.

"Don't you see, Buck? I don't want to be this way. I jest can't help it!"

"Then the Lord help poor old Joe Cumberland—him that took you in out of the desert—him that raised you from the time you was a kid—him that nursed you like you was his own baby—him that loved you more'n he loved Kate—him that's lyin' back there now with fire in his eyes, waitin', waitin', waitin', for you to come back. Dan, if you was to see him you'd go down on your knees and ask him to forgive you!"

"I s'pose I would," murmured Barry thoughtfully.

"Dan, you're goin' to go with me!"

"I don't somehow think it's my time for movin', Buck."

"Is that all you got to say to me?"

"I guess maybe it is, Buck."

"If I was to beg you to come for old-time's sake, and all we been through together, you and me, wouldn't it make no difference to you?"

The large, gentle eyes focused far beyond Buck Daniels, somewhere on a point in the pale, hazy blue of the spring sky.

"I'm kind of tired of talkin', Buck,' he said at length.

And Buck Daniels rose and walked slowly ayay, with his head fallen. Behind him the stallion neighed suddenly and loud, and it was so much like a blast of defiant triumph that Buck whirled and shook his clenched fist at Satan.

14 · Music for Old Nick

A THOUGHT is like a spur. It lifts the head of a man as the spur makes the horse toss his; and it quickens the pace with a subtle addition of strength. Such a thought came to Buck Daniels as he stepped again on the veranda of the hotel. It could not have been an altogether pleasant inspiration, for it drained the color from his face and made him clench his broad hands; and next he loosened his revolver in its holster. A thought of fighting—of some desperate chance he had once taken, perhaps.

But also it was a thought which needed considerable thought. He slumped into a wicker chair at one end of the porch and sat with his chin resting on his chest while he smoked cigarette after cigarette and tossed the butts idly over the rail. More than once he pressed his hand against his lips as though there were sudden pains there. The color did not come back to his face; it continued as bloodless as ever, but there was a ponderable light in his eyes, and his jaws became more and more firmly set. It was not a pleasant face to watch at that moment, for he seemed to sit with a growing resolve.

Long moments passed before he moved a muscle, but then he heard, far away, thin, and clear, whistling from behind the hotel. It was no recognizable tune. It was rather a strange improvisation with singable fragments here and there, and then wild, free runs and trills. It was as if some bird of exquisite singing powers should be taken in a rapture of song, so that it whistled snatches here and there of its usual melody, but all between were great, whole-throated rhapsodies. As the sound of this whistling came to him, Buck raised his head suddenly. And finally, still listening, he rose to his feet and turned into the dining room.

There he found the waitress he had met before, and he asked her for the name of the doctor who took care of the wounded Jerry Strann.

"There ain't no doc," said the waitress. "It's Fatty Matthews, the deputy marshal, who takes care of that Strann—bad luck to him! Fatty's in the barroom now. But what's the matter? You seem like you was hearin' something?"

"I am," replied Daniels enigmatically. "I'm hearin' something that would be music for the ears of Old Nick."

And he turned on his heel and strode for the barroom. There he found Fatty in the very act of disposing of a stiff three-fingers of redeye. Daniels stepped to the bar, poured his own drink, and then stood toying with the glass. For thought the effect of redeye may be pleasant enough, it has an essence which appalls the stoutest heart and singes the most leathery throat; it is to full-grown men what castor oil is to a child. Why men drink it is a mystery whose secret is known only to the profound soul of the mountain-desert. But while Daniels fingered his glass he kept an eye upon the other man at the bar.

It was unquestionably the one he sought. The excess flesh of the deputy marshal would have brought his nickname to the mind of an imbecile. However, Fatty was humming softly to himself, and it is not the habit of men who treat very sick patients to sing.

"I'll hit it agin," said Fatty. "I need it."

"Have a bad time of it today?" asked O'Brien sympathetically.

"Bad time today? Yep, as' every day is the same. I tell you, O'Brien, it takes a pile of nerve to stand around that room expectin' Jerry to pass out any minute, and the eyes of that devil Mac Strann followin' you every step you make. D'you know, if Jerry dies I figure Mac to go at my throat like a bulldog."

"You're wrong, Fatty," replied O'Brien. "That ain't his way about it. He takes his time killin' a man. Waits till he can get him in a public place and make him start the picture. That's Mac Strann! Remember Fitzpatrick? Mac Strann followed Fitz nigh onto two months, but Fitz knew what was up and he never would make a move. He knowed that if he made a wrong pass it would be his last. So he took everything and let it pass by. But finally it got on his nerves. One time—it was right here in my barroom, Fatty——"

"The hell you say!"

"Yep, that was before your time around these parts. But Fitz had a couple of jolts of redeye under his vest and felt pretty strong. Mac Strann happened in and first thing you know they was at it. Well, Fitz was a big man. I ain't small, but I had to look up when I talked to Fitz. Scotch-Irish, and they got fightin' bred into their bone. Mac Strann passed him a look and Fitz come back with a word. Soon as he got started he couldn't stop. Wasn't a pretty thing to watch, either. You could see in Fitz's face that he knew he was done for before he started, but he wouldn't let up. The booze had him going and he was too proud to back down. Pretty soon he started cussing Mac Strann.

"Well, by that time everybody had cleared out of the saloon, because they knowed that them sort of words meant bullets comin'. But Mac Strann just stood there watchin', and grinnin' in his ugly way—damn his soul black!—and never sayin' a word back. By God, Fatty, he looked sort of hungry. When he grinned, his upper lip went up kind of slow and you could see his big teeth. I expected to see him make a move to sink 'em in the throat of Fitz. But he didn't. Nope, he didn't make a move, and all the time Fitz was ravin' and gettin' worse and worse. Finally Fitz made the move. Yep, he pulled his gun and had it damned near clean on Mac Strann before that devil would stir. But when he *did,* it was jest a flash of light. Both them guns went off, but Mac's bullet hit Fitz's hand and knocked the gun out of it—so of course his shot went wild. But Fitz could see his own blood, and you know what that does to the Scotch-Irish? Makes *some* people quit cold to see their own blood. I remember a kid at school that was a whale at fightin' till his nose got to bleedin', or something, and then he'd quit cold. But you take a Scotch-Irishman and it works just the other way. Show him his own color and he goes plumb crazy.

"That's what happened to Fitz. When he saw the blood on his hand he made a dive at Mac Strann. After that it wasn't the sort of thing that makes a good story. Mac Strann got him around the ribs and I heard the bones crack. God! And him still squeezin', and Fritz beatin' away at Mac's face with his bleedin' hand.

"Will you b'lieve that I stood here and was sort of froze? Yes, Fatty, I couldn't make a move. And I was sort of sick and hollow inside the same way I went one time when I was a kid and seen a big bull horn a yearlin'.

"Then I heard the breath of Fitz comin' hoarse, with a rattle in it—and I heard Mac Strann whining like a dog that's tasted blood and is starvin' for more. A thing to make your hair go up on end, like they say in the storybooks.

"Then Fitz—he was plumb mad—tried to bite Mac Strann. And then Mac let go of him and set his hands on the throat of Fitz. It happened like a flash—I'm here to swear that I could hear the bones crunch. And then Fitz's mouth sagged open and his eyes rolled up to the ceiling, and Mac Strann threw him down on the floor. Just like that! Damn him! And then he stood over poor dead Fitz and kicked him in those busted ribs and turned over to the bar and says to me: 'Gimme!'

"Like a damned beast! He wanted to drink right there with his dead man beside him. And what was worse, I had to give him the bottle. There was a sort of haze in front of my eyes. I wanted to pump that devil full of lead, but I knowed it was plain suicide to try it.

"So there he stood and ups with a glass that was brimmin' full, and downs it at a swallow—gurglin'—like a hog! Fatty, how long will it be before there's an end to Mac Strann?"

But Fatty Matthews shrugged his thick shoulders and poured himself another drink.

"There ain't a hope for Jerry Strann?" cut in Buck Daniels.

"Not one in a million," coughed Fatty, disposing of another formidable potion.

"And when Jerry dies, Mac starts for this Barry?"

"Who's been tellin' you?" queried O'Brien dryly. "Maybe you been readin' minds, stranger?"

Buck Daniels regarded the bartender with a mild and steadfast interest. He was smiling with the utmost good humor, but there was that about him which made big O'Brien flush and look down to his array of glasses behind the bar.

"I been wondering," went on Daniels, "if Mac Strann mightn't come out with Barry about the way Jerry did. Ain't it possible?"

"No," replied Fatty Matthews with calm decision. "It ain't possible. Well, I'm due back in my bear cage. Y'ought to look in on me, O'Brien, and see the mountain lion dyin' and the grizzly lookin' on."

"Will it last long?" queried O'Brien.

"Somewhere about this evening."

Here Daniels started violently and closed his hand hard around his whiskey glass which he had not yet raised toward his lips.

"Are you sure of that, marshal?" he asked. "If Jerry's held on this long ain't there a chance that he'll hold on longer? Can you date him up for tonight as sure as that?"

"I can," said the deputy marshal. "It ain't hard when

you seen as many go west as I've seen. It ain't harder than it is to tell when the sand will be out of an hour glass. When they begin going down the last hill it ain't hard to tell when they'll reach the bottom."

"Ain't you had anybody to spell you, Fatty?" broke in O'Brien.

"Yep. I got Haw-Haw Langley up there. But he ain't much help. Just sits around with his hands folded. Kind of looks like Haw-Haw *wanted* Jerry to pass out."

And Matthews went humming through the swinging door.

15 · Old Gary Peters

FOR some moments after this Buck Daniels remained at the bar with his hand clenched around his glass and his eyes fixed before him in the peculair second-sighted manner which had marked him when he sat so long on the veranda.

"Funny thing," began O'Brien, to make conversation, "how many fellers go west at sunset. Seems like they let go all holts as soon as the dark comes. Hey?"

"How long before sunset now?" asked Buck Daniels sharply.

"Maybe a couple of hours."

"A couple of hours," repeated Daniels, and ground his knuckles across his forehead. "A couple of hours!"

He raised his glass with a jerky motion and downed the contents; the chaser stood disregarded before him and O'Brien regarded his patron with an eye of admiration.

"You long for these parts?" he asked.

"No, I'm strange to this range. Riding up north pretty soon, if I can get someone to tell me the lay of the land. D'you know it?"

"Never been further north than Brownsville."

"Couldn't name me someone that's traveled about, I s'pose?"

"Old Gary Peters knows every rock within three days' riding. He keeps the blacksmith shop across the way."

"So? Thanks; I'll look him up."

Buck Daniels found the blacksmith seated on a box before his place of business; it was a slack time for Gary Peters and he consoled himself for idleness by chewing the stem of an unlighted corn-cob, whose bowl was upside down. His head was pulled down and forward as if by the weight of his prodigious sandy moustache, and he regarded a vague horizon with misty eyes.

"Seen you comin' out of O'Brien's," said the blacksmith, as Buck took possession of a nearby box. "What's the news?"

"Ain't any news," responded Buck dejectedly. "Too much talk; no news."

"That's right," nodded Gary Peters. "O'Brien is the out-talkingest man I ever see. Ain't nobody in Brownsville can get his tongue around so many words as O'Brien."

So saying, he blew through his pipe, picked up a stick of soft pine, and began to whittle it to a point.

"In my part of the country," went on Buck Daniels, "they don't lay much by a man that talks a pile."

Here the blacksmith turned his head slowly, regarded his companion for an instant, and then resumed his whittling.

"But," said Daniels, with a sigh, "if I could find a man that knowed the country north of Brownsville and had a hobble on his tongue I could give him a night's work that'd be worth while."

Gary Peters removed his pipe from his mouth and blew out his dropping moustaches. He turned one wistful glance upon his idle forge; he turned a sadder eye upon his companion.

"I could name you a silent man or two in Brownsville," he said, "but there ain't only one man that knows the country right."

"That so? And who might he be?"

"Me."

"You?" echoed Daniels in surprise. He turned and considered Gary as if for the first time. "Maybe you know the lay of the land up as far as Hawkin's Arroyo?"

"Me? Son, I know every cactus clear to Bald Eagle."

"H-m-m!" muttered Daniels. "I s'pose maybe you could name some of the outfits from here on a line with Bald Eagle—say you put 'em ten miles apart?"

"Nothin' easier. I could find 'em blindfold. First due out they's McCauley's. Then lay a bit west of north and you hit the Circle K Bar—that's about twelve miles from McCauley's. Hit 'er up dead north again, by east, and you come eight miles to Three Roads. Go on to———"

"Partner," cut in Daniels, "I could do business with you."

"Maybe you could."

"My name's Daniels."

"I'm Gary Peters. H'ware you?"

They shook hands.

"Peters," said Buck Daniels, "you look square, and I need you in a square game; but there ain't any questions that go with it. Twenty iron men for one day's riding and one day's silence."

"M'frien'," murmured Peters. "In my day I've gone three months without speakin' to anything in boots; and I wasn't hired for it, neither."

"You know them people up the line," said Daniels. "Do they know you?"

"I'll tell a man they do! Know Gary Peters?"

"Partner, this is what I want. I want you to leave Brownsville inside of ten minutes and start riding for Elkhead. I want you to ride, and I want you to ride like hell. Every ten miles, or so, I want you to stop at some place where you can get a fresh hoss. Get your fresh hoss and leave the one you've got off, and tell them to have the hoss you leave ready for me any time tonight. It'll take you clear till tomorrow night to reach Elkhead, even with relayin' your hosses?"

"Round about that, if I ride like hell. What do I take with me?"

"Nothing. Nothing but the coin I give you to hire someone at every stop to have that hoss you've left ready for me. Better still, if you can have 'em, get a fresh hoss. Would they trust you with hosses that way, Gary?"

"Gimme the coin and where they won't trust me I'll pay cash."

"I can do it. It'll about bust me, but I can do it."

"You going to try for a record between Brownsville and Elkhead, eh? Got a bet up, eh?"

"The biggest bet you ever heard of," said Daniels grimly. "You can tell the boys along the road that I'm tryin' for time. Have you got a fast hoss to start with?"

"Got a red mare that ain't much for runnin' cattle, but she's greased lightnin' for a short bust."

"Then get her out. Saddle her up, and be on your way. Here's my stake—I'll keep back one twenty for accidents. First gimme a list of the places you'll stop for the relays."

He produced an old envelope and a stub of soft pencil with which he jotted down Gary Peters' directions.

"And every second," said Buck Daniels in parting, "that you can cut off your own time will be a second cut off'n mine. Because I'm liable to be on your heels when you ride into Elkhead."

Gary Peters lifted his eyebrows and then restored his pipe. He spoke through his teeth.

"You ain't got a piece of money to bet on that, partner?" he queried softly.

"Ten extra if you get to Elkhead before me."

"They's limits to hoss-flesh," remarked Peters. "What time you ridin' against?"

"Against a cross between a bullet and a nor'easter, Gary. I'm going back to drink to your luck."

A promise which Buck Daniels fulfilled, for he had need of even borrowed strength. He drank steadily until a rattle of hoofs down the street entered the saloon, and then someone came in to say that Gary Peters had started out of town to "beat all hell, on his red mare."

After that, Buck started out to find Dan Barry. His quarry was not in the barn nor in the corral behind the barn. There stood Satan and Black Bart, but their owner was not in sight. But a thought came to Buck while he looked, rather mournfully, at the stallion's promise of limitless speed. "If I can hold him up jest half a minute," murmured Buck to himself, "jest half a minute till I get a start, I've got a rabbit's chance of livin' out the night!"

From the door of the first shed he took a heavy chain with the key in the padlock. This chain he looped about the post and the main timber of the gate, snapped the padlock, and threw the key into the distance. Then he stepped back and surveyed his work with satisfaction. It would be a pretty job to file through that chain, or to knock down those ponderous rails of the fence and make a gap. A smile of satisfaction came on the face of Buck Daniels, then, hitching at his belt, and pulling his sombrero lower over his eyes, he started once more to find Dan Barry.

He was more in haste now, for the sun was dipping behind the mountains of the west and the long shadows moved along the ground with a perceptible speed. When he reached the street he found a steady drift of people toward O'Brien's barroom. They came by ones and twos and idled in front of the swinging doors or slyly peeked through them and then whispered one to the other. Buck accosted one of those by the door and asked what was wrong.

"He's in there," said the other, with a broad and excited grin. "He's in there—waitin'!"

And when Buck threw the doors wide he saw, at the farther end of the deserted barroom, Dan Barry, seated at a table braiding a small horsehair chain. His hat was pushed far back on his head; he had his back to the door. Certainly he must be quite unaware that all Brownsville was waiting, breathless, for his destruction. Behind the bar stood O'Brien, pale under his bristles, and his eyes never leaving the slender figure at the end of his room; but seeing Buck he called with sudden loudness: "Come in, stranger. Come in and have one on the house. There ain't nothing but silence around this place and it's getting on my nerves."

Buck Daniels obeyed the invitation at once, and behind him, stepping softly, some of them entering with their hats in their hands and on tiptoe, came a score of the inhabitants of Brownsville. They lined the bar up and down its length; not a word was spoken; but every head turned as at a given signal toward the quiet man at the end of the room.

16 · The Coming of Night

It was not yet dusk, for the shadows were still swinging out from the mountains and a ghost of color lingered in the west, but midnight lay in the open eyes of Jerry Strann. There had been no struggle, no outcry, no lifting of head or hand. One instant his eyes were closed, and then, indeed, he looked like death; the next instant the eyes opened, he smiled, the wind stirred in his bright hair. He had never seemed so happily alive as in the moment of his death. Fatty Matthews held the mirror close to the faintly parted lips, examined it, and then drew slowly back toward the door, his eyes steady upon Mac Strann.

"Mac," he said, "it's come. I got just this to say: whatever you do, for God's sake stay inside the law!"

And he slipped through the door and was gone.

But Mac Strann did not raise his head or cast a glance after the marshal. He sat turning the limp hand of Jerry back and forth in his own, and his eyes wandered vaguely through the window and down to the roofs of the village.

Night thickened perceptibly every moment, yet still while the eastern slope of every roof was jet black, the western slopes were bright, and here and there at the distance the light turned and waned on upper windows. Sleep was coming over the world, and eternal sleep had come for Jerry Strann.

It did not seem possible.

Some night at sea, when clouds hurtled before the wind across the sky and when the waves leaped up masthigh; when some good ship staggered with the storm, when hundreds were shrieking and yelling in fear or defiance of death; there would have been a death-scene for Jerry Strann.

Or in the battle, when hundreds rush to the attack with one man in front like the edge before the knife—there would have been a death-scene for Jerry Strann. Or while he rode singing, a bolt of lightning that slew and obliterated at once—such would have been a death for Jerry Strann.

It was not possible that he could die like this, with a smile. There was something incompleted. The fury of the death-struggle which had been omitted must take place, and the full rage of wrath and destruction must be vented. Can a bomb explode and make no sound and do no injury?

Yet Jerry Strann was dead and all the world lived on. Someone cantered his horse down the street and called gayly to an acquaintance, and afterward the dust rose, invisible, and blew through the open window and stung the nostrils of Mac Strann. A child cried, faintly, in the distance, and then was hushed by the voice of the mother, making a sound like a cackling hen. This was all!

There should have been wailing and weeping and cursing and praying, for handsome Jerry Strann was dead. Or there might have been utter and dreadful silence and waiting for the stroke of vengeance, for the brightest eye was misted and the strongest hand was unnerved and the voice that had made them tremble was gone.

But there was neither silence nor weeping. Someone in a nearby kitchen rattled her pans and then cursed a dog away from her back door. Not that any of the sounds were loud. The sounds of living are rarely loud, but they run in an endless river—a monotone broken by ugly ripples of noise to testify that men still sleep or waken, hunger or feed. Another ripple had gone down to the sea of darkness, yet all the ripples behind it chased on their way heedlessly and babbled neither louder nor softer.

There should have been some giant voice to peal over the sleeping village and warn them of the coming vengeance—for Jerry Strann was dead!

The tall, gaunt figure of Haw-Haw Langley came on

tiptoe from behind, beheld the dead face, and grinned; a nervous convulsion sent a long ripple through his body, and his Adam's apple rose and fell. Next he stole sideways, inch by inch, so gradual was his cautious progress, until he could catch a glimpse of Mac Strann's face. It was like the open face of a child; there was in it no expression except wonder.

At length a hoarse voice issued from between the grinning lips of Haw-Haw.

"Ain't you goin' to close the eyes, Mac?"

At this the great head of Mac Strann rolled back and he raised his glance to Haw-Haw, who banished the grin from his mouth by a vicious effort.

"Ain't he got to see his way?" asked Mac Strann, and lowered his glance once more to the dead man. As for Haw-Haw Langley, he made a long, gliding step back toward the door, and his beady eyes opened in terror; yet a deadly fascination drew him back again beside the bed.

Mac Strann said: "Kind of looks like Jerry was ridin' the home trail, Haw-Haw. See the way he's smilin'?"

The vulture stroked his lean cheeks and seemed once more to swallow his silent mirth.

"And his hands," said Mac Strann, "is just like life, except that they's gettin' sort of chilly. He don't look changed, none, does he, Haw-Haw? Except that he's seeing something off there—away off there. Looks like he was all wrapped up in it, eh?" He leaned closer, his voice fell to a murmur that was almost soft. "Jerry, what you seein'?"

Haw-Haw Langley gasped in inaudible terror and retreated again toward the door.

Mac Strann laid his giant hand on the shoulder of Jerry. He asked in a raised voice: "Don't you hear me, lad?" Sudden terror caught hold of him. He plunged to his knees beside the bed, and the floor quaked and groaned under the shock. "Jerry, what's the matter? Are you mad at me? Ain't you going to speak to me? Are you forgettin' me, Jerry?"

He caught the dead face between his hands and turned it strongly toward his own. Then for a moment his eyes plumbed the shadows into which they looked. He stumbled back to his feet and said apologetically to Haw-Haw at the door: "I kind of forgot he wasn't livin', for a minute." He stared fixedly at the gaunt cowpuncher. "Speakin' man to man, Haw-Haw, d'you think Jerry will forget me?"

The terror was still white upon the face of Haw-Haw, but something stronger than fear kept him in the room and even drew him a slow step toward Mac Strann; and his eyes moved from the face of the dead man to the face of the living and seemed to draw sustenance from both. He moistened his lips and was able to speak.

"Forget you, Mac? Not if you get the man that fixed him."

"Would you want me to get him, Jerry?" asked Mac Strann. And he waited for an answer.

"I dunno," he muttered, after a moment. "Jerry was always for fightin', but he wasn't never for killin'. He never liked the way I done things. And when he was lyin' here, Haw-Haw, he never said nothin' about me gettin' Barry. Did he?"

Astonishment froze the lips of Haw-Haw. He managed to stammer: "Ain't you going to get Barry? Ain't you goin' to bust him up, Mac?"

"I dunno," repeated the big man heavily. "Seems like I've got no heart for killing. Seems like they's enough death in the world." He pressed his hand against his forehead and closed his eyes. "Seems like they's something dead in me. They's an ache that goes ringin' in my head. They's a sort of hollow feelin' inside me. And I keep thinkin' about times when I was a kid and got hurt and cried." He drew a deep breath. "Oh, my God, Haw-Haw, I'd give most anything if I could bust out cryin' now!"

While Mac Strann stood with his eyes closed, speaking his words slowly, syllable by syllable, like the tolling of a bell, Haw-Haw Langley stood with parted lips—like the spirit of famine drinking deep; joy unutterable was glittering in his eyes.

"If Jerry'd wanted me to get this Barry, he'd of said so," repeated Mac Strann. "But he didn't." He turned toward the dead face. "Look at Jerry now. He ain't thinkin' about killin's. Nope, he's thinkin' about some

quiet place for sleep. I know the place. They's a spring
that come out in a holler between two mountains; and
the wind blows up the valley all the year; and they's a
tree that stands over the spring. That's where I'll put
him. He loved the sound of runnin' water; and the wind'll
be on his face; and the tree'll sort of mark the place. Jerry, lad, would ye like that?"

Now, while Mac Strann talked, inspiration came to
Haw-Haw Langley, and he stretched out his gaunt arms
to it and gathered it in to his heart.

"Mac," he said, "don't you see no reason why Jerry
wouldn't ask you to go after Barry?"

"Eh?" queried Mac Strann, turning.

But as he turned, Haw-Haw Langley glided toward
him, and behind him, as if he found it easier to talk
when the face of Mac was turned away. And while he
talked his hands reached out toward Mac Strann like
one who is begging for alms.

"Mac, don't you remember that Barry beat Jerry to
the draw?"

"What's that to do with it?"

"But he beat him bad to the draw. I seen it. Barry
waited for Jerry. Understand?"

"What of that?"

"Mac, you're blind! Jerry knowed you'd be throwing
yourself away if you went up agin Barry."

At this Mac Strann whirled with a suddenness surprising for one of his bulk. Haw-Haw Langley flattened his
gaunt frame against the wall.

"Mac!" he pleaded, "*I* didn't say you'd be throwin'
yourself away. It was Jerry's idea."

"Did Jerry tell you that?" he asked.

"So help me God!"

"Did Jerry *want* me to get Barry?"

"Why wouldn't he?" persisted the vulture, twisting his
bony hands together in an agony of alarm and suspense.
"Ain't it nacheral, Mac?"

Mac Strann wavered where he stood.

"Somehow," he argued to himself, "it don't seem like
killin' is right, here."

The long hand of Langley touched his shoulder.

He whispered rapidly: "You remember last night

when you was out of the room for a minute? Jerry turned his head to me—jest the way he's lyin' now—and I says: 'Jerry, is there anything I can do for you?' "

Mac Strann reached up and his big fingers closed over those of Haw-Haw.

"Haw-Haw," he muttered, "you was his frien'. I know that."

Haw-Haw gathered assurance.

He said: "Jerry answers to me: 'Haw-Haw, old pal, there ain't nothin' you can do for me. I'm goin' West. But after I'm gone, keep Mac away from Barry."

"I says: 'Why, Jerry?'

" 'Because Barry'll kill him, sure,' says Jerry.

" 'I'll do what I can to keep him away from Barry," says I, 'but don't you want nothin' done to the man what killed you?'

" 'Oh, Haw-Haw,' says Jerry, 'I ain't going to rest easy, I ain't goin' to sleep in heaven—until I know Barry's been sent to hell. But for God's sake don't let Mac know what I want, or he'd be sure to go after Barry and get what I got.' "

Mac Strann crushed the hand of Haw-Haw in a terrible grip.

"Partner," he said, "d'you swear this is straight?"

"So help me God!" repeated the perjurer.

"Then," said Mac Strann, "I got to leave the buryin' to other men what I'll hire. Me—I've got business on hand. Where did Barry run to?"

"He ain't run," cried Haw-Haw, choking with a strange emotion. "The fool—the damned fool!—is waiting right down here in O'Brien's bar for you to come. He's *darin'* you to come!"

Mac Strann made no answer. He cast a single glance at the peaceful face of Jerry, and then started for the door. Haw-Haw waited until the door closed; then he wound his arms about his body, writhed in an ecstasy of silent laughter, and followed with long, shambling strides.

17 · Buck Makes His Getaway

STRAIGHT from the room of the dead man, Fatty Matthews had hurried down to the bar, and there he stepped into the silence and found the battery of eyes all turned upon that calm figure at the end of the room. Upon this man he trotted, breathing hard, and his fat sides jostled up and down as he ran. According to Brownsville, there were only two things that could make Fatty run: a gun or the sight of a drink. But all maxims err. When he reached Barry he struck him on the shoulder with a heavy hand. That is, he struck at the shoulder, but as if the shadow of the falling hand carried a warning before it, at the same time that it dropped Barry swerved around in his chair. Not a hurried movement, but in some mysterious manner his shoulder was not in the way of the plump fist. It struck, instead, upon the back of the chair, and the marshal cursed bitterly.

"Stranger," he said hotly, "I got one thing to say: Jerry Strann has just died upstairs. In ten seconds Mac Strann will be down here lookin' for *you!*"

He stepped back, humming desperately to cover his wheezing, but Barry continued to braid the horsehair with deft fingers.

"I got a double knot that's kind of new," he said. "Want to watch me tie it?"

The deputy sheriff turned on the crowd.

"Boys," he exclaimed, waving his arms, "he's crazy. You heard what he said. You know I've give him fair warning. If we got to dig his grave in Brownsville, is it my fault? It ain't!" He stepped to the bar and pounded upon it. "O'Brien, for God's sake, a drink!"

It was a welcome suggestion to the entire nervous crowd, but while the glasses spun across the bar Buck Daniels walked slowly down the length of the barrom toward Barry. His face was a study which few men could have solved; unless there had been someone present who had seen a man walk to his execution. Beside Dan Barry he stopped and watched the agile hands at work. There was a change in the position of Barry now, for he had taken the chair facing the door and the entire crowd; Buck Daniels stood opposite. The horsehair plied back and forth. And Daniels noted the hands, lean, tapering like the fingers of a girl of sixteen. They were perfectly steady; they were the hands of one who had struggled, in life, with no greater foe than ennui.

"Dan," said Buck, and there was a quiver of excitement in his voice, like the tremor of a piano string long after it has been struck. "Dan, I been thinking about something and now I'm ready to tell you what it is."

Barry looked up in slow surprise.

Now the face of Buck Daniels held what men have called a "deadly pallor," that pallor which comes over one who is cornered and about to fight for his life. He leaned closer, resting one hand upon the edge of the table, so that his face was close to Dan Barry.

"Barry," he said, "I'm askin' you for the last time: Will you get your hoss and ride back to Kate Cumberland with me?"

Dan Barry smiled his gentle, apologetic smile.

"I don't no ways see how I can, Buck."

"Then," said Buck through his teeth, "of all the lyin' hounds in the world you're the lyin'est and meanest and lowest. Which they ain't words to tell you what I think of you. Take this instead!"

And the hand which rested on the table darted up and smote Dan Barry on the cheek, a tingling blow. With the same motion which started his hand for the blow, Buck Daniels turned on his heel and stepped a pace or two toward the center of the room.

There was not a man in the room who had not heard the last words of Buck Daniels, and not a man who had not seen the blow. Every one of them had seen, or heard accurately described, how the slender stranger beat Jerry Strann to the draw and shot him down in that same place. Such a moan came from them as when many men catch their breath with pain, and with a simultaneous movement those who were in line with Buck Daniels and

Barry leaped back against the bar on one side and against the wall on the other. Their eyes, fascinated, held on the face of Barry, and they saw the pale outline which the fingers of Daniels had left on the cheek of the other. But if horror was the first thing they felt, amazement was the next. For Dan Barry sat bolt erect in his chair, staring in an astonishment too great for words. His right hand hung poised and moveless just above the butt of his gun; his whole posture was that of one in the midst of an action, suspended there frozen to stone. They waited for that poised hand to drop, for the slender fingers to clutch the butt of the gun, for the convulsive jerk that would bring out the gleaming barrel, the explosion, the spurt of smoke, and Buck Daniels lurching forward to his face on the floor.

But that hand did not move; and Buck Daniels? Standing there with his back to the suspended death behind him, he drew out Durham and brown papers, without haste, rolled a cigarette, and reached to a hip pocket.

At that move Dan Barry started. His hand darted down and fastened on his gun, and he leaned forward in his chair with the yellow glimmering light flaring up in his eyes. But the hand of Buck Daniels came out from his hip bearing a match. He raised his leg, scratched the match, there was a blue spurt of flame, and Buck calmly lighted his cigarette and started toward the door, sauntering.

The instant the swinging doors closed Barry started from his chair with a strange cry—none of them had ever heard the like from human lips—for there was grief in it, and above all there was a deadly eagerness. So a hungry man might cry out at the sight of food. Down the length of the barroom he darted and was drawing his gun as he whipped through the doors. A common rush followed him, and those who reached the open first saw Buck Daniels leaning far forward in his saddle and spurring desperately into the gloom of the night. Instantly he was only a twinkling figure in the shadows, and the beat of the hoofs rattled back at them. Dan Barry stood with his gun poised high for a second or more. Then he turned, dropped the gun into the holster, and with the same strange, unearthly cry of eagerness, he raced off in the direction of the barns.

There were some who followed him even then, and this is what they reported to incredulous ears when they returned. Barry ran straight for the left hand corral and wrenched at the gate, which appeared to be secured by a lock and chain. Seeing that it would not give way he ran around to the barn, and came out carrying a saddle and bridle. These he tossed over the high fence into the corral. Then he picked up a loose scantling and with it pried and wrenched off the top bar of the fence in one section and vaulted into the enclosure.

The black stallion had whinnied once or twice during this time and the great black, shaggy dog had come snarling and whining about the feet of his master. Now the stranger tossed on the saddle and cinched it with amazing speed, sprang onto his mount, and urged it across to the other side of the corral. Up to that moment no one in the little crowd of watchers had suspected the intention of the rider. For the fence, even after the removal of the top bar, was nearly six feet in height. But when Barry took his horse to the far side of the corral and then swung him about facing the derailed section, it was plain that he meant to attempt to jump at that place. Even then, as O'Brien explained later, and many a time, the thing was so impossible that he could not believe his eyes. There was a dreamlike element to the whole event. And like a phantom in a vision he saw the black horse start into a sharp gallop; saw the great dog sail across the fence first; saw the horse and rider shoot into the air against the stars; heard the click of hoofs against the top rail; heard the thud of hoofs on the near side of the fence, and then the horseman flashed about the corner of the barn and in an instant his hoofs were beating a far distant tattoo.

As for the watchers, they returned in a dead silence to the barroom and they had hardly entered when Mac Strann stalked through the doors behind them; he went straight to O'Brien.

"Somewhere about," he said in his thick, deep voice, "they's a man named Dan Barry. Where is he?"

And O'Brien answered: "Mac, he was sittin' down at

that table until two minutes ago, but where he is now I ain't any idea."

The tall, skeleton form of Haw-Haw Langley materialized behind Mac Strann, and his face was contorted with anger.

"If he was here two minutes ago," he said, "he ain't more than two minutes away."

"Which way?" asked Mac Strann.

"North," answered a score of voices.

O'Brien stepped up to Mac Strann. He said: "Mac, we know what you got in your mind. We know what you've lost, and there ain't any of us that ain't sorry for Jerry—and for you. But, Mac, I can give you the best advice you ever heard in your life: Keep off'n the trail of Barry!"

Haw-Haw Langley added at the ear of Mac Strann: "That was Jerry's advice when he lay dyin'. An' it's my advice, too. Mac, Barry ain't a safe man to foller!"

"Haw-Haw," answered Mac Strann. "Will you gimme a hand saddlin' my hoss? I got an appointment, an' I'm two minutes late already."

18 · Doctor Byrne Analyzes

IN the room which had been assigned to his use Doctor Randall Byrne sat down to an unfinished letter and began to write.

"Dinner has interrupted me, my dear Loughburne. I have dined opposite Miss Cumberland—only the two of us at a great table—with a wide silence around us—and the Chinese cook padding to and from from the kitchen. Have I told you of that room? No, I believe that I have made no more than casual mention of my environment here, for reasons which are patent. But tonight I wished that you might look in upon the scene. Along the walls hangs a rope with which Mr. Cumberland won a roping and tieing contest in his youth—a feat upon which he prides himself highly; at another place hang the six-shooters of a notorious desperado, taken from his dead body; there is the sombrero of a Mexican guerilla chief beside the picture of a prize bull, and an oil painting of Mr. Cumberland at middle age adjoins an immense calendar on which is portrayed the head of a girl in bright colors—a creature with amazing quantities of straw-colored hair. The table itself is of such size that it is said all the guests at a round-up—a festival of note in these barbaric regions—can be easily seated around it. On one side of this table I sat—and on the other side sat the girl, as far away as if an entire room had separated us.

"Before going down to the meal I had laid aside my glasses, for I have observed that spectacles, though often beneficial to the sight, are not always equally commendable in the opinion of women; and it should assuredly be one's endeavor to become agreeable to those about us.

"Be it noted at this point, my dear Loughburne, that I have observed peculiar properties in the eyes of Miss Cumberland. Those of all other humans and animals that have fallen under my observance were remarkable only for their use in seeing, whereas the eyes of Miss Cumberland seem peculiarly designed to be *seen*. This quality I attribute to the following properties of the said eyes. First, they are in size well beyond the ordinary. Secondly, they are of a color restful to behold. It is, indeed, the color of the deep, blue evening sky into which one may stare for an incalculable distance.

"As I have said, then, I noted a glow in these eyes, though they were so immediately lowered that I could not be sure. I felt, however, an extraordinary warmth beneath my collar, the suffusion of blood passing swiftly toward my forehead. I inquired if she had smiled and for what reason; whereat she immediately assured me that she had not, and smiled while making the assurance.

"I was now possessed of an unusual agitation, augmented by the manner in which Miss Cumberland looked at me out of twinkling but not unkindly eyes. What could have caused this perturbation I leave to your scientific keenness in analysis.

"I discovered an amazing desire to sing, which indecorous impulse I, of course, immediately inhibited and transferred the energy into conversation.

" 'The weather,' said I. 'has been uncommonly delightful today.'

"I observed that Miss Cumberland greeted this sentence with another smile.

"Presently she remarked: 'It has seemed a bit windy to me.'

"I recalled that it is polite to agree with ladies and instantly subjoined with the greatest presence of mind: 'Quite right! A most abominably stormy day!'

"At this I was astonished to be greeted by another burst of laughter, even more pronounced than the others.

" 'Doctor Byrne,' she said, 'you are absolutely unique.'

" 'It is a point,' I said earnestly, 'which I shall immediately set about to change.'

"At this she raised both hands in a gesture of protest, so that I could observe her eyes shining behind the slender, brown fingers—observe, Loughburne, that white skin is falsely considered a thing of beauty in women—and she remarked, still laughing: 'Indeed, you must not change!'

"I replied with an adroit change of front. 'Certainly not.'

"For some mysterious reason the girl was again convulsed and broke off her laughter to cry in a voice of music which still tingles through me: 'Doctor Byrne, you are delightful!'

"I should gladly have heard her say more upon this point, but it being one which I could not gracefully dispute with her, and being unwilling that she should lapse into one of her usual silences, I ventured to change the subject from myself to her.

" 'Miss Cumberland,' I said, 'I remark with much pleasure that the anxiety which has recently depressed you seems now in some measure lessened. I presume Mr. Daniels will be successful in his journey, though what the return of Mr. Daniels accompanied by Mr. Barry can accomplish, is, I confess, beyond my computation. Yet you are happier in the prospect of Mr. Barry's return?'

"I asked this question with a falling heart, though I

remain ignorant of the cause to which I can attribute my sudden depression. Still more mysterious was the delight which I felt when the girl shook her head slowly and answered: 'Even if he comes, it will mean nothing.'

"I said: 'Then let us intercept him and send him back!'

"She cried out, as if I had hurt her: 'No, no, no!' and twisted her fingers together in pain. She added at once: 'What of poor Dad?'

" 'Your father,' I confessed, 'had for the moment slipped my mind.'

"It seemed to me, however, that it was not wholly on her father's account that she was grieved. She wished Mr. Barry to return, and yet she dreaded his coming. It was most mysterious. However, I had started Miss Cumberland thinking. She stopped eating and began to stare before her. Presently she said: 'It is strange that we don't hear from Buck. What can have held him so long?'

"I regretted extremely that I had introduced the topic and cast about in my mind for another, but could not find one. I then expressed regret that I had revived her worries, but received in reply a smile in which there was no life: the very color had died out from her cheeks. And she sat during the rest of the meal without speaking a word.

"Afterwards I went in with her to see Mr. Cumberland. His condition was not materially changed. The marvel of it grows upon me more and more. It is a freak which defies medical science. There lies a man at the point of dissolution. His body has died of old age, and yet the life principle remains. He does not eat—at least, the nourishment he takes is wholly negligible. But he still has energy. To be sure, he rarely moves about and his body remains practically inert. But we must never forget that the mind is a muscle and calls for continual rebuilding. And the mind of Mr. Cumberland is never inactive. It works ceaselessly. It will not permit him to sleep. For three days, now, as far as I can tell, he has not closed his eyes. It might be assumed that he is in a state of trance, but by a series of careful experiments,

I have ascertained that he is constantly thinking in the most vigorous fashion.

"What does it mean? There is in the man a flame-like quality; something is burning in him every instant. But on what does the flame feed? I know that material cannot be created and that energy means dissolution of matter: but why does not the life of Joseph Cumberland dissolve?

"The subject possesses me. I dare not ponder it too steadily or my brain begins to whirl. I make no progress toward any reasonable solution. I only feel that I am living in the presence of an astounding mystery.

"Strange thoughts possess me. What is the fire that burns but does not consume Joe Cumberland? What is the thing in the wandering Dan Barry which Kate Cumberland fears and yet waits for? Why was it that Daniels trembled with dread when he started out to find a man who, by his own profession, he holds to be his best friend?

"You see how the mystery assumes shape? It is before me. It is in my hand. And yet I cannot grasp its elements.

"The story of a man, a horse, and a dog. What is the story?

"Today I wandered about the corrals and came to one which was bounded by a fence of extraordinary height. It was a small corral, but all the posts were of great size, and the rails were as large as ordinary posts. I inquired what strange beasts could be kept in such a pen, and the man-of-all-work of whom I asked replied: 'That's Satan's corral.'

"I guessed at some odd story. 'The devil?' I cried. 'Do they fence the devil in a corral?'

"'Oh, ay,' said the fellow, 'he's a devil, right enough. If we'd let him run with the other hosses he'd have cut 'em to ribbons. That's what kind of a devil he is!'

"A story of a man, a horse, and a dog. I think I have seen the great chain which bound the dog. Was that the place where they kept the horse?

"And, if so, what bonds are used for the man? And what sort of man can he be? One of gigantic size, no doubt, to mate his horse and his dog. A fierce and intractable nature, for otherwise Kate Cumberland could not dread him. And yet a man of singular values, for all this place seems to wait for his return. I catch the fire of expectancy. It eats into my flesh. Dreams haunt me night and day. What will be the end?

"Now I am going down to see Mr. Cumberland again. I know what I shall see—the flickering of the fire behind his eyes. The lightning glances, the gentle, rare voice, the wasted face; and by him will be Kate Cumberland; and they both will seem to be listening, listening—for what?

"No more tonight. But, Loughburne, you should be here; I feel that the like of this has never been upon the earth.

"Byrne."

19 · Suspense

HE found them as he had expected, the girl beside the couch, and the old man prone upon it, wrapped to the chin in a gaudy Navajo blanket. But tonight his eyes were closed, a most unusual thing, and Byrne could look more closely at the aged face. For on occasions when the eyes were wide, it was like looking into the throat of a searchlight to stare at the features—all was blurred. He discovered now wrinkled and purple-stained lids under the deep shadow of the brows—and his eyes were so sunken that there seemed to be no pupils there. Over the cheekbones the skin was drawn so tightly that it shone, and the cheeks fell away into cadaverous hollows. But the lips, beneath the shag of gray beard, were tightly compressed. No, this was not sleep. It carried, as Byrne gazed, a connotation of swifter, fiercer thinking, than if the gaunt old man had stalked the floor and poured forth a tirade of words.

The girl came to meet the doctor. She said: "Will you use a narcotic?"

"Why?" asked Byrne. "He seems more quiet than usual."

"Look more closely," she whispered.

And when he obeyed, he saw that the whole body of Joe Cumberland quivered like an aspen, continually. So the finger of the duellist trembles on the trigger of his gun before he receives the signal to fire—a suspense more terrible than the actual face of death.

"A narcotic?" she pleaded. "Something to give him just one moment of full relaxation?"

"I can't do it," said Byrne. "If his heart were a shade stronger, I should. But as it is, the only thing that sustains him is the force of his will power. Do you want me to unnerve the very strength which keeps him alive?"

She shuddered.

"Do you mean that if he sleeps it will be—death?"

"I have told you before," said the doctor, "that there are phases of this case which I do not understand. I predict nothing with certainty. But I very much fear that if your father falls into a complete slumber he will never waken from it. Once let his brain cease functioning and I fear that the heart will follow suit."

They stood on the farther side of the room and spoke in the softest of whispers, but now the deep, calm voice of the old man broke in: "Doc, they ain't no use of worryin'. They ain't no use of medicine. All I need is quiet."

"Do you want to be alone?" asked the girl.

"No, not so long as you don't make no noise. I can 'most hear something, but your whisperin' shuts it off."

They obeyed him, with a glance at each other. And soon they caught the far off beat of a horse in a rapid gallop.

"Is it that?" cried Kate, leaning forward and touching her father's hand. "Is that horse what you hear?"

"No, no!" he answered impatiently. "That ain't what I hear. It ain't no hoss that I hear!"

The hoof-beats grew louder—stopped before the house —steps sounded loud and rattling on the veranda—a door squeaked and slammed—and Buck Daniels stood before them. His hat was jammed down so far that his eyes were almost buried in the shadow of the brim; the bandana at his throat was twisted so that the knot lay over his right shoulder; he carried a heavy quirt in a hand

that trembled so that the long lash seemed alive; a
thousand bits of foam had dried upon his vest and
stained it; the rowels of his spurs were caked and en-
meshed with horsehair; dust covered his face and sweat
furrowed it, and a keen scent of horsesweat passed from
him through the room. For a moment he stood at the
door, bracing himself with legs spread wide apart, and
stared wildly about—then he reeled drunkenly across the
room and fell into a chair, sprawling at full length.

No one else moved. Joe Cumberland had turned his
head; Kate stood with her hand at her throat; the doctor
had placed his hand behind his head, and there it stayed.

"Gimme smoke—quick!" said Buck Daniels. "Run out
of Durham a thousan' years ago!"

Kate ran into the next room and returned instantly
with papers and a fresh sack of tobacco. On these materials Buck seized frantically, but his big fingers were
shaking in a palsy, and the papers tore, one after another, as soon as he started to roll his smoke. "God!"
he cried, in a burst of childish desperation, and collapsed
again in the chair.

But Kate Cumberland picked up the paper and tobacco which he had dashed to the floor and rolled a cigarette with deft fingers. She placed it between his lips
and held the match by which he lighted it. Once, twice,
and again, he drew great breaths of smoke into his
lungs, and then he could open his eyes and look at
them. They were not easy eyes to meet.

"You're hungry, Buck," she said. "I can see it at a
glance. I'll have something for you in an instant."

He stopped her with a gesture.

"I done it!" said Buck Daniels. "He's comin'!"

The doctor flashed his glance upon Kate Cumberland,
for when she heard the words she turned pale and her
eyes and her lips framed a mute question; but Joe Cumberland drew in a long breath and smiled.

"I knowed it!" he said softly.

The wind whistled somewhere in the house and it
brought Buck Daniels leaping to his feet and into the
center of the room.

"He's here!" he yelled. "God help me, where'll I go
now! He's here!"

He had drawn his revolver and stood staring desperately about him as if he sought for a refuge in the solid wall. Almost instantly he recovered himself, however, and dropped the gun back into the holster.

"No, not yet," he said, more to himself than the others. "It ain't possible, even for Dan."

Kate Cumberland rallied herself, though her face was still white. She stepped to Buck and took both his hands.

"You've been working yourself to death," she said gently. "Buck, you're hysterical. What have you to fear from Dan? Isn't he your friend? Hasn't he proved it a thousand times?"

Her words threw him into a fresh frenzy.

"If he gets me, it's blood on your head, Kate. It was for you I done it."

"No, no, Buck. For Dan's sake alone. Isn't that enough?"

"For *his* sake?" Buck threw back his head and laughed—a crazy laughter. "He could rot in hell for all of me. He could foller his wild geese around the world. Kate, it was for you!"

"Hush!" she pleaded. "Buck, dear!"

"Do I care who knows it? Not I! I got an hour—half an hour to live; and while I live the whole damned world can know I love you, Kate, from your spurs to the blue of your eyes. For your sake I brung him, and for your sake I'll fight him, damn him, in spite——"

The wind wailed again, far off, and Buck Daniels cowered back against the wall. He had drawn Kate with him, and he now kept her before him, toward the door.

He began to whisper, swiftly, with a horrible tremble in his voice: "Stand between us, Kate. Stand between me and him. Talk for me, Kate. Will you talk for me?" He drew himself up and caught a long, shuddering breath. "What have I been doin'? What have I been ravin' about?"

He looked about as if he saw the others for the first time.

"Sit here, Buck," said Kate, with perfect quiet. "Give me your hat. There's nothing to fear. Now tell us."

"A whole day and a whole night," he said, "I been

riding with the fear of him behind me. Kate, I ain't
myself, and if I been sayin' things——"

"No matter. Only tell me how you made him follow
you."

Buck Daniels swept his knuckles across his forehead,
as though to rub out a horrible memory.

"Kate," he said in a voice which was hardly more than
a whisper, "why did he follow Jim Silent?"

The doctor slipped into a chair opposite Buck Daniels and watched him with unbelieving eyes. When he
had last seen Buck the man had seemed an army in
himself; but now a shivering, unmanned coward sat before him. Byrne glanced at Kate Cumberland for explanation of the mysterious change. She, also, was transformed with horror, and she stared at Buck Daniels as
at one already among the dead.

"Buck, you didn't—*strike* him?"

Buck Daniels nodded jerkily.

"I'll try to tell you straight from the beginning. I found
Dan in Brownsville. I begged him to come back with
me, but he wouldn't stir. This was why: A gunman had
come to the town lookin' for trouble, and when he run
acrost Dan he found plenty of it. No, don't look like
that, Kate; it was self-defense, pure and simple—they
didn't even arrest Dan for it. But this dyin' man's
brother, Mac Strann, come down from the hills and sat
beside Jerry Strann waitin' for him to go west before he
started out to clean up on Dan. Yesterday evenin' Jerry
was near dead and everybody in Brownsville was waitin'
to see what would happen, because Dan wouldn't
budge till Mac Strann had had his chance to get back
at him. So I sent a feller ahead to fix a relay of hosses
to Elkhead, because I made up my mind I was going to
make Dan Barry chase me out of that town. I walked
into the saloon where Dan was sittin'—braidin' a little
horse-hair strand—my God, Kate, think of him sittin'
there doin' that with a hundred fellers standin' about
waitin' for him to kill or be killed! I went up to him.
I picked a fight, and then I slapped him—in the face."

The sweat started on Daniels' forehead at the thought.

"But you're still alive," cried Kate Cumberland. "Had
you handled his gun first?"

"No. As soon as I hit him I turned my back to him and took a couple of steps away from him."

"Oh, Buck, Buck!" she cried, her face lighting. You knew he wouldn't shoot you in the back!"

"I didn't know nothin'. I couldn't even think—and my body was numb as a dead man's all below the hips. There I stool like I was chained to the floor—you know how it is in a nightmare when something chases you and you can't run? That was the way with me."

"Buck! And he was sitting behind you—while you stood there?"

"Ay, sitting there with my death sittin' on his trigger finger. But I knowed that if I showed the white feather, if I let him see me shake, he'd be out of his chair and on top of me. No gun—he don't need nothin' but his hands—and what was in front of my eyes was a death like—like Jim Silent's!"

He squinted his eyes closed and groaned. Once more he roused himself.

"But I couldn't move a foot without my knees bucklin', so I takes out my makin's and rolls a cigarette. And while I was doin' it I was prayin' that my strength would come back to me before he come back to himself—and started!"

"It was surprise that held him, Buck. To think of you striking him—you who have saved his life and fought for him like a blood brother. Oh, Buck, of all the men in the world you're the bravest and the noblest!"

"They ain't nothin' in that brand of talk," growled Buck, reddening. "Anyway, at last I started for the door. It wasn't farther away than from here to the wall. Outside was my hoss, and a chance for livin'. But that door was a thousand years away, and a thousand times while I walked toward it I felt Dan's gun click and bang behind me and felt the lead go tearin' through me. And I didn't dare to hurry, because I knew that might wake Dan up. So finally I got to the doors and just as they was swingin' to behind me, I heard a sort of a moan behind me——"

"From Dan," whispered the white-faced girl. "I know —a sort of a stifled cry when he's angered! Oh, Buck."

"My first step took me ten yards from that door,"

reminisced Buck Daniels, "and my next step landed me
in the saddle, and I dug them spurs clean into the in-
sides of Long Bess. She started like a watch-spring un-
coilin', and as she spurts down the street I leans clean
over to her mane and looks back and there I seen Dan
standin' in the door with his gun in his hand and the
wind blowin' his hair. But he didn't shoot, because the
next second I was swallowed up in the dark and
couldn't see him no more."

"But it was no use!" cried the girl. "With Black Bart
to trail you and with Satan to carry him, he overtook
you—and then——"

"He didn't," said Buck Daniels. "I'd fixed things so's
he couldn't get started with Satan for some time. And
before he could have Satan on my trail, I'd put a long
stretch behind me because Long Bess was racin' every
step. The lay of the land was with me. It was pretty
level, and on level goin' Long Bess is almost as fast as
Satan; but on rocky goin' Satan is like a goat—nothin'
stops him! And I was ridin' Long Bess like to bust her
heart, straight toward McCauley's. We wasn't more'n a
mile away when I thought—the wind was behind me, you
see—that I heard a sort of far off whistling down the
wind! My God!"

He could not go on for a moment, and Kate Cumberland sat with parted lips, twisting her fingers together
and then tearing them apart once more.

"Well, that mile was the worst in my life. I thought
maybe the man I'd sent on ahead hadn't been able to
leave me a relay at McCauley's, and if he hadn't I knew
I'd die somewhere in the hills beyond. And they looked
as black as dead men, and all sort of grinnin' down at
me.

"But when I got to McCauley's, there stood a hoss
right in front of the house. It didn't take me two seconds
to make the saddle-change. And then I was off agin!"

A sigh of relief came from Byrne and Kate.

"That hoss was a beauty. Not long-legged like Bess,
nor half so fast, but he was jest right for the hills.
Climbed like a goat and didn't let up. Up and up we
goes. The wind blows the clouds away when we gets to
the top of the climb and I looks down into the valley

all white in the moonlight. And across the valley I seen two little shadows slidin', smooth and steady. It was Dan and Satan and Black Bart!"

"Buck!"

"My heart, it stood plumb still! I gives my hoss the spurs and we went down the next slope. And I don't remember nothin' except that we got to the Circle K Bar after a million years, 'most, and when we got there the piebald flops on the ground—near dead. But I made the change and started off agin, and that next hoss was even better than the piebald—a sure goer! When he started I could tell by his gait what he was, and I looked up at the sky——"

He stopped, embarrassed.

"And thanked God, Buck?"

"Kate, I ain't ashamed if maybe I did. But since then I ain't seen or heard Dan, but all the time I rode I was expecting to hear his whistle behind me, close up."

All the life died from her face.

"No, Buck, if he'd a followed all the way he would have caught you in spite of your relay. No, I understand what happened. After a while he remembered that Mac Strann was waiting for him back in Brownsville. And he left your trail to be taken up later and went back to Brownsville. You didn't see him follow you after you left the Circle K Bar?"

"No. I didn't dare look back. But somehow I knew he was comin'.'"

She shook her head.

"He won't come, Buck. He'll go back to meet Mac Strann—and then——" She ran to the chair of Buck swiftly and caught his hands: "What sort of a man is Mac Strann?"

But Buck smiled strangely up into her face.

"Does it make any difference," he said, "to Dan?"

She went slowly back to her place.

"No," she admitted, "no difference."

"If you came by relays for twenty-four hours," said the doctor, numbering his points upon accurate finger tips, "it is humanly impossible that this man could have followed you very closely. It will probably take him another day to arrive."

But here his glance fell upon Joe Cumberland, and found the cattleman smiling faintly to himself.

Buck Daniels was considering the last remark seriously.

"No," he said, "It *ain't* possible. Besides, what Kate says may be true. She ought to know—she says he'll wait for Mac Strann. I didn't think of that; I thought I was savin' Dan from another—well, what a damn fool I been!"

He unknotted his bandana and with it mopped his face to a semblance of cleanliness.

"It was the ridin' that done it," he explained, shamefaced. "You put a man on a hoss for a certain time, and after a while he gets so he can't think. He's sort of nutty. That was the way with me when I come in."

"Open the window on the veranda," said Joe Cumberland. "I want to feel the wind."

The doctor obeyed the instruction, and again he noted that same quiet, contented smile on the lips of the old man. For some reason it made him ill at ease to see it.

"He won't get here for eight or ten hours," went on Buck Daniels, easing himself into a more comfortable position, and raising his head a little higher. "Ten hours more, even if he does come. That'll give me a chance to rest up; right now I'm kind of shaky."

"A condition, you will observe, in which Mr. Barry will also be when he arrives," remarked the doctor.

"Shaky?" grinned Buck Daniels. "M'frien', you don't know that bird!" He sat up, clenching his fist. "And if Dan *does* come, he can't affo'd to press me too far! I'll take so much, and then——" He struck his fist on the arm of the chair.

"Buck!" cried Kate Cumberland. "Are you mad? Have you lost your reason? Would you *face* him?"

Buck Daniels winced, but he then shook his head doggedly.

"He had his chance down in Brownsville," he said. "And he didn't take it. Why? Because my back was turned? Well, he could of got in front of me if he'd been terrible anxious. I've seen Dan in action; he's seen *me* in action! Maybe he's seen too much. They've been stranger things than that, in this world!" He hitched his belt so that the butt of his revolver came farther forward. But now Kate Cumberland advised: "Buck, you're tired out; you don't know what you're saying. Better go up to bed."

He flushed a ruddy bronze.

"D'you think I'm jest talkin' words, Kate, to hear myself talk?"

"Listen!" broke in Joe Cumberland, and raised a bony forefinger for silence.

And the doctor noted a great change in the old man. There was no longer a tremor in his body. There was only a calm and smiling expectation—a certainty. A tinge of color was in his withered face for the first time since Byrne had come to the ranch and now the cattleman raised his finger with such an air of calm authority that at once every voice in the room was stilled.

"D'ye hear?"

They did not. They heard only the faint rushing of the air through the window. The flame danced in the chimney of the lamp and changed the faces in fantastic alteration. One and all, they turned and faced the window. Still there was not a sound audible, but the doctor felt as if the noise were approaching. He knew it as surely as if he could see some far-off object moving near and nearer. And he knew, as clearly, that the others in the room felt the same thing. He turned his glance from the window toward Kate Cumberland. Her face was upturned. There was about it a transparent pallor; the eyes were large and darkly ringed; the lips parted into the saddest and the most patient of smiles; and the slender fingers were interwoven and pressed against the base of her throat.

For the first time he saw how the fire that was so manifest in the old man had been consuming her, also. It left no mark of the coming of death upon her. But it had burned her pure and left her transparent as crystal. Pity swelled in the throat of Byrne as he realized the anguish of her long waiting. Fear mingled with his pity. He felt that something was coming which would seize on her as the wind seizes on the dead leaf, whirling her off into an infinity of storm and darkness into which he could not follow a single pace.

He turned back toward the window. The rush of air played steadily, and then in pulses, upon his face. Then even the wind ceased; as if it, too, were waiting. Not a sound. But silence has a greater voice than discord or music. It seemed to Byrne that he could tell how fast each heart was beating.

The old man had closed his eyes again. And yet the rigid forefinger remained raised, and the faint smile touched at the corners of his mouth. Buck Daniels sat lunging forward in his chair, his knees supporting his elbows, and scowled up at the window with a sort of sullen terror.

Then Byrne heard it—so small a voice that at first he thought it was only a part of the silence. It grew and grew—in a sudden burst it was clear to every ear—the honking of the wild geese!

And Byrne knew the picture they made. He could see them far up in the sky—a dim triangle of winter gray—moving with the beat of lightning wings each in an arrowy flight north, and north, and north. Creatures for sport all the world over; here alone, in all the earth, in the heart of this mountain-desert, they were in some mysterious wise messengers. Once more the far discord showered down upon them, died as they rose, perhaps, to a higher level, and was heard no more.

20 · The Coming

THEN a padding step, light, lighter than the sound of the softest thought. It was passing near; the faint breeze blew the sound to them, around them. Each man felt as if some creature were stalking him, unseen. Next—it appeared by magic against the blue black of the night— the head of a great wolf, quite black, shaggy, with sharply pointed ears. And the eyes stared at them, green eyes with lights that swirled as the flame jumped in the throat of the lamp. For a long moment the horror lasted. Then the head, as it had come, disappeared, and the light, light footfall faded away.

Buck Daniels had risen, now. The sound of his whisper made them start.

"I'm going up—to my room—and lock the door—for God's sake—keep—him away!"

And so he stole soundlessly away, and then they heard the creaks which announced his progress up the stairs.

Not Buck Daniels alone. In the deadly silence Kate rose to her feet; and the old man, the invalid—he with the dead body and the living brain, rose from his couch and stood as erect as a soldier on parade. The doctor was conscious of repeating to himself, hurriedly, a formula something like this: "The thing which is coming is human; it cannot be more than human; as long as it is human it is nothing to fear; the laws of truth are irrevocably fixed; the laws of science will not change." Yet in spite of this formula he was deadly cold, as if a wind were blowing through his naked soul. It was not fear. It was something beyond fear, and he would not have been otherwhere for any reward. All his mind remained poised, expectant, as the astronomer waits for the new star which his calculations have predicted to enter the field of his telescope.

He caught the sound of another horse coming, far different even to his unpracticed ear from the beat of hoofs which announced the coming of Buck Daniels. The rhythm of their fall was slower, as if the stride of the animal were much longer. He pictured a mighty creature with a vast mane blown back against the chest of a giant rider. There was a murmur from Kate: "Dan, my dear, my dear!"

Then he heard a padding footfall, hardly louder than the light, light step of the wolf. The knob of the door turned slowly, without a sound; it opened, and a man stepped in. He was not larger than the doctor; a slender fellow, almost dapper in his dress, with hardly a sign of travel about him, except that the brim of his sombrero was folded back from his face as if from continual pressure of wind. These things Randall Byrne noted vaguely; what he was sharply aware of were the eyes of the man. He had the feeling that he had seen them before; he remembered the yellow light that had swirled in the eyes of the wolf at the window.

The newcomer flashed a glance about the room, yet for all its speed it seemed to linger an instant on each face, and when it crossed the stare of Byrne the doctor shrank.

"Where is Buck?" asked the man. "I've come for him!"

As if in answer, the great, shaggy dog slipped through the entrance past his master and glided across the room. As he passed, Kate held out a hand to him. She called softly: "Bart!" but she was greeted with a silent baring of fangs; and she caught her hand back against her breast, with the tears springing in her eyes. On the other side of the room the black dog paused and looked back to his master, while Byrne realized with a shudder that the door before which it stood was the door through which Buck Daniels had disappeared. Straight to that door Barry stepped, and Byrne realized, with an eerie emotion, that the footfalls made no sound.

Before he reached the door, however, the girl started forward and sprang before him. With her outstretched arms she barred the way. Her skirt brushed almost in the face of the dog, and the beast shrank away not in fear, but crouching in readiness to leap. The sharp ears twitched back; a murderous snarl rolled up from between the wicked teeth. Yet she did not cast a single glance at him; she faced the greater danger.

She was saying: "Whatever Buck did, it wasn't done to hurt you, Dan; it was done for your own sake. And for Dad's sake. You shan't pass here!"

From his position, the doctor could not see the face of Dan Barry, but he guessed at it through the expression of Kate. Such terror and horror were in her eyes as though she were facing a death's head inches away. Then he saw the slender hand of Barry rise and move toward the girl, slowly, tremblingly, as though one fierce impulse urged him to thrust her to one side and as though another held back his arm. The doctor could not watch the girl longer; fear and pity were wringing him as he lowered his glance to the floor.

Then he heard her cry: "Have you forgotten me, like Bart? Like Bart, have you forgotten me, Dan?"

His hand fell to his side and he glided back from her; but now Byrne could see that the eyes of Barry were looking past the girl, as though he stared through the solid wood of the door and found his prey beyond it. The stranger slipped toward the door by which he had entered, with the great dog slinking at his heels. Kate Cumberland leaned heavily against the wall, her arm thrown across her face, but there was no consciousness of her in the face of Barry. Yet at the very door he paused and straightened; Byrne saw that he was staring toward Joe Cumberland; and the old man reached a bony hand out.

"Oh, lad," he said softly, "I been waitin' for you years an' years, seems like!"

Barry crossed the room as noiselessly, as swiftly, as a flying shadow.

"Sit down!" he commanded, and Byrne caught a faint ring in the voice, like the shiver of metal striking steel.

Joe Cumberland obeyed without a word, and then lay back at full length upon the couch—a palsy had seized on him, and the hand which rested on the shoulder of Dan Barry was shaking. By the couch came the tall dog, and crouched, staring up in the master's face; then the younger man turned his face toward Byrne and the girl. Those thin-cut nostrils expanded, the lips compressed, and Byrne dared not look into the flare of the eyes.

"Who done this?" asked Barry, and still the shiver of cold metal rang in his voice. "Who's done this?"

"Steady, lad," said Joe Cumberland faintly. "They ain't no call for fightin'. Steady, Dan, boy. An' don't leave me!"

Byrne caught a signal from Kate and followed her obediently from the room.

"Let them be alone," she said.

"Impossible!" protested the doctor. "Your father is lapsed into a most dangerous condition. The physical inertia which has held him for so long is now broken and I look for a dangerous mental and nervous collapse to accompany it. A sedative is now imperative!"

He laid his hand on the knob of the door to return, but the girl blocked his way.

"Don't go in," she commanded feebly. "I can't explain to you. All I can say is that Dad was the one who found Dan Barry and there's something between them that none of us understand. But I know that he can help Dad. I know Dad is in no danger while Dan is with him."

"A pleasant superstition," nodded the doctor, "but medicine, my dear Miss Cumberland, does not take account of such things."

"Doctor Byrne," she said, rallying a failing strength for the argument, "I insist. Don't ask me to explain."

"In that case," he answered coldly, "I cannot assume responsibility for what may happen."

She made a gesture of surrender, weakly.

"Look back in on them now," she said. "If you don't find father quiet, you may go in to him."

Doctor Byrne obeyed, opening the door softly. He saw Joe Cumberland prone, of course, upon the couch. One hand lay as usual across his breast, but the other was at his side, clasped in the hands of Dan Barry. The old cattleman slept. Yes, there was no doubt that for the first time in many days he slumbered soundly. The lean, narrow chest rose and fell with deep, slow breaths; the eyes were closed, and there was no twitching of muscles to betray ragged nerves or a mind that dreamed fiercely while the body slept. Far over the sleeping man leaned the stranger, as if he were peering closely into the closed eyes of Joe Cumberland. There was a tenseness of watching and waiting in his attitude, like the runner on the mark, or like the burden-bearer lifting a great weight, and Byrne gathered, in some mysterious manner, the impression that Barry sent through his hands and into the body of Cumberland a continual stream of nervous strength—an electric thing. Nonsense, of course. And it was nonsense, also, to think that the huge dog which lay staring up into the face of the master understood all this affair much better than the practiced mind of the physician. Yet the illusion held with Randall Byrne in spite of all his skepticism.

He was certain that he had made not the slightest sound in opening the door, but presently the head of the watcher turned slowly, and Byrne was looking into those same yellow, terrible eyes. At the same instant the sick man moaned faintly. The doctor closed the door as softly as he had opened it and turned a drawn face upon Kate Cumberland.

"I don't understand; it isn't possible!" he whispered.

"No one understands," said the girl, and smiled mirthlessly. "Don't try to, Doctor Byrne. Go to bed, and sleep. If you can. Good night."

"But you," said Byrne, following her, "are almost as ill as your father. Is there nothing I can do for you?"

"You?" she asked, surprised. "No, nothing."

"But there's not the slightest color in your face. And you are trembling, Miss Cumberland!"

She did not seem to hear him.

"Will he stay?" she asked of herself. "Will he leave before the morning?"

"I shall see that he stays," said the doctor. "I will stay here outside the door and see that he does not leave, if you wish."

Once more she smiled in that baffling manner.

"Could you keep the wind from blowing, Doctor Byrne? If I thought that he could be kept——" she stopped. "He has forgotten us. He has forgotten all of us except Dad. And if Dad cannot keep him, nothing will keep him. It's useless for you to wait here. Good night again, Doctor Byrne."

He watched her up the stairs. By the dim light he saw her hand catching at the balustrade as if she were drawing herself up, step by step. When she reached the landing and turned half toward him, he saw that her head was fallen.

"Not a glance, not a thought for me," murmured the doctor. "But if the stranger *does* leave——" Instead of finishing the muttered sentences, he drew a chair back against the wall and sat down with folded hands to wait.

21 • Mac Strann Decides to Keep the Law

It was hours later that night when Haw-Haw Langley and Mac Strann sat their horses on the hill to the south. Before them, on the nearest rise of ground, a clump of tall trees and the sharp triangle of a roof split the sky, while down toward the right spread a wide huddle of sheds and barns.

"That's where the trail ends," said Mac Strann, and started his horse down the slope. Haw-Haw Langley urged his little mount hurriedly alongside the squat bulk of his companion. He looked like the skeleton reality, and Mac Strann the blunt, deformed shadow.

"You ain't going into the house lookin' for him, Mac?" he asked, and he lowered his voice to a sharp whisper in spite of the distance. "Maybe there's a pile of men in that house. It's got room for a whole army. You ain't going in there by yourself, Mac?"

"Haw-Haw," explained the big man quietly, "I ain't going after Barry. I'm going to make him come after me."

Haw-Haw considered this explanation for a dazed moment. It was far too mysterious for his comprehension.

"What you goin' to do?" he asked again.

"Would you know that black hoss agin if you seen him?" asked Mac Strann.

"In a thousand."

"That hoss has had a long ride; and Barry has put him in one of them barns, they ain't no doubt. Most like, the dog is with the hoss."

"It looks a considerable lot like a wolf," muttered Langley. "I wouldn't choose meetin' up with that dog in the dark. Besides, what good is it goin' to do you to find the dog?"

"If you hurt a man's dog," explained Mac Strann calmly, "you're hurting the man, ain't you? I'm going to hurt this man's dog; afterward the dog'll bring the man to me. They ain't no doubt of that. I ain't goin' to kill the dog. I'm goin' to jest nick him so's he'll get well and then hit my trail."

"What sense is they in that?"

"If Barry comes to me, ain't he the one that's breakin' the law? If I kill him then, won't it be in self-defense? I ain't no lawbreaker, Haw-Haw. It ain't any good bein' a lawbreaker. Them lawyers can talk a man right into a grave. They's worse nor poison. I'd rather be caught in a bear trap a hundred miles from my shack than have a lawyer fasten onto my leg right in the middle of Brownsville. No, Haw-Haw, I ain't going to break any law. But I'm going to fix the wolf so's he'll know me; and when he gets well he'll hit my trail, and when he hits my trail he'll have Barry with him. And when Barry sees me, then——" he raised his arms above him in the dark.. "Then!" breathed Mac Strann, "Jerry can start sleepin' sound for the first time!"

Haw-Haw Langley wrapped his long arms about himself.

"An' I'll be there to watch. I'll be there to see fair play, don't you never doubt it, Mac. Why didn't I never go with you before? Why, Jerry never done anything to touch this! But be careful, Mac. Don't make no slip up tonight. If they's trouble—I ain't a fighting man, Mac. I ain't no ways built for it."

"Shut your mouth," said Mac Strann bluntly. "I need quiet now."

For they were now close to the house. Mac Strann brought his horse to a jog trot and cast a semicircle skirting the house and bringing him behind the barns. Here he retreated to a little jutting point of land from behind which the house was invisible, and there dismounted.

Haw-Haw Langley followed example reluctantly. He complained: "I ain't never heard before of a man leavin' his hoss behind him! It ain't right and it ain't policy."

His leader, however, paid no attention to this grumbling. He skirted back behind the barns, walking with a speed which extended even the long legs of Haw-Haw Langley. Most of the stock was turned out in the corrals. Now and then a horse stamped, or a bull snorted from the fenced enclosures, but from the barns they heard not a sound. Now Mac Strann paused. They had reached the largest of the barns, a long, low structure.

"This here," said Mac Strann, "is where that hoss must be. They wouldn't run a hoss like that with others. They'd keep him in a big stall by himself. We'll try this one, Haw-Haw."

But Haw-Haw drew back at the door. The interior was black as the hollow of a throat as soon as Mac Strann rolled back the sliding door, and Haw-Haw imagined evil eyes glaring and twinkling at him along the edges of the darkness.

"The wolf!" he cautioned, grasping the shoulder of his companion. "You ain't goin' to walk onto that wolf, Mac?"

The latter struck down Haw-Haw's hand.

"A wolf makes a noise before it jumps," he whispered, "and that warnin' is all the light I need."

Now their eyes grew somewhat accustomed to the dark and Haw-Haw could make out, vaguely, the posts of the stalls to his right. He could not tell whether or not some animal might be lying down between the posts, but Mac Strann, pausing at every stall, seemed to satisfy himself at a glance. Right down the length of the barn they passed until they reached a wall at the farther end.

"He ain't here," sighed Haw-Haw, with relief. "Mac, if I was you, I'd wait till they was light before I went huntin' that wolf."

"He ought to be here," growled Mac Strann, and lighted a match. The flame spurted in a blinding flash from the head of the match and then settled down into a steady yellow glow. By that brief glow Mac Strann looked up and down the wall. The match burned out against the calloused tips of his fingers.

"That wall," mused Strann, "ain't made out of the same timber as the side of the barn. That wall is whole years newer. Haw-Haw, that *ain't* the end of the barn. They's a holler space beyond it." He lighted another match, and then cursed softly in delight. "Look!" he commanded.

At the farther side of the wall was the glitter of metal —the latch of a door opening in the wooden wall. Mac

Strann set it ajar and Haw-Haw peered in over the big man's shoulder. He saw first a vague and formless glimmer. Then he made out a black horse lying down in the center of a box stall. The animal plunged at once to its feet, and crowding as far as possible away against the wall, turned its head and stared at them with flashing eyes.

"It's him!" whispered Haw-Haw. "It's Barry's black. They ain't another hoss like him on the range. An' the wolf—thank God!—ain't with him."

But Mac Strann closed the door of the stall, frowning thoughtfully, and thought on the face of Strann was a convulsion of pain. He dropped the second match to his feet, where it ignited a wisp of straw that sent up a puff of light.

"Ah-h!" drawled Mac Strann. "The wolf ain't here, but we'll soon have him here. And the thing that brings him here will get rid of the black hoss."

"Are you goin' to steal the hoss?"

"Steal him? He couldn't carry me two mile, a skinny hoss like that. But if Barry ever gets away agin on that hoss I ain't never goin' to catch him. That hoss has got to die."

Haw-Haw Langley caught his breath with a harsh gurgle. For men of the mountain-desert sometimes fall very low indeed, but in their lowest moments it is easier for them to kill a man than a horse. There is the story, for instance, of the cattleman who saw the bullfight in Juarez, and when the bull gored the first horse the cowpuncher rose in the crowd and sent a bullet through the picador to square the deal. So Haw-Haw sighed.

"Mac," he whispered, "has it got to be done? Ain't there any other way? I've seen that hoss. When the sun hits him it sets him on fire, he's that sleek. And his legs is like drawn-iron, they're that fine. And he's got a head that's finer than a man's head, Mac."

"I've seen him close enough," answered Mac Strann grimly. "An' I've follered him for a day and a half, damn near. S'pose Barry finds out I'm on his trail; s'pose he won't foller the wolf when the wolf tries to lead him to me. S'pose he gets on this hoss and cuts away? Can I foller the wind, Haw-Haw? This hoss has got to die!"

From the manger he threw out several armfuls of hay, wrenched down from behind the manger several light boards, and tossed them on the hay. He lighted a match and was approaching the small flame to the pile of inflammables when Haw-Haw Langley cried softly: "Hark, Mac!"

The big man instantly extinguished the match. For a moment they could distinguish nothing, but then they heard the sharp, high chorus of the wild geese flying north. Haw-Haw Langley snickered apologetically.

"That was what I heard a minute ago!" he said. "And it sounded like voices comin'."

A snarl of contempt from Mac Strann; then he scratched another match and at once the flame licked up the side of the hay and cast a long arm up the wooden wall.

"Out of this quick!" commanded Mac Strann and they started hastily down the barn toward the door. The fire behind them, after the puff of flame from the hay, had died away to a ghastly and irregular glow with the crackle of the slowly catching wood. It gave small light to guide them; only enough, indeed, to deceive the eye. The posts of the stalls grew into vast, shadowy images; the irregularities of the floor became high places and pits alternately. But when they were half way to the door Haw-Haw Langley saw a form too grim to be a shadow, blocking their path. It was merely a blacker shape among the shades, but Haw-Haw was aware of the two shining eyes, and stopped short in his tracks.

"The wolf!" he whispered to Mac Strann. "Mac, what're we goin' to do?"

The other had no time to answer, for the shadow at the door of the barn now leaped toward them, silently, without a growl or yelp or snarl. As if to guide the battle, the kindling wood behind them now ignited and sent up a yellow burst of light. By it Haw-Haw Langley saw the great beast clearly, and he leaped back behind the sheltering form of Mac Strann. As for Mac, he did not move or flinch from the attack. His revolver was in his hand, leveled, and following the swift course of Black Bart.

22 · Patience

THERE is one patience greater than the endurance of
the cat at the hole of the mouse or the wolf which waits
for the moose to drop, and that is the patience of the
thinking man; the measure of the Hindoo's moveless con-
templation of Nirvana is not in hours but in weeks or
even in months. Randall Byrne sat at his sentinel post
with his hands folded and his grave eyes steadily fixed
before him, and for hour after hour he did not move.
Though the wind rose, now and again, and whistled
through the upper chambers or mourned down the empty halls, Randall Byrne did not stir so much as an eye-
lash in observance. Two things held him fascinated. One
was the girl who had passed up yonder stairs so wearily
without a single backward glance at him; the other was
the silent battle which went on in the adjoining room.
Now and then his imagination wandered away to secondary pictures. He would see Barry meeting Buck
Daniels, at last, and striking him down as remorselessly
as the hound strikes the hare; or he would see him riding
back toward Elkhead and catch a bright, sad vision of
Kate Cumberland waving a careless adieu to him, and
then hear her singing carelessly as she turned away. Such
pictures as these, however, came up but rarely in the
mind of Byrne. Mostly he thought of the stranger leaning
over the body of old Joe Cumberland, reviving him, stor-
ing him with electric energy, paying back, as it were,
some ancient debt. And he thought of the girl as she
had turned at the landing place of the stairs, her head
fallen; and he thought of her lying in her bed, with her
arm under the mass of bright hair, trying to sleep, very
tired, but remorselessly held awake by that same power
which was bringing Joe Cumberland back from the verge
of death.

It was all impossible. This thing could not be. It was

really as bad as the yarn of the Frankenstein monster. He considered how it would seem in print, backed by his most solemn asseverations, and then he saw the faces of the men who associated with him, pale thoughtful faces striving to conceal their smiles and their contempt. But always he came back, like the desperate hare doubling on his course, upon the picture of Kate Cumberland there at the turning of the stairs, and that bent, bright head with confessed defeat. The man had forgotten her. It made Byrne open his eyes in incredulity even to imagine such a thing. The man had forgotten her! She was no more to him than some withered hag he might ride past on the road.

His ear, subconsciously attentive to everything around him, caught a faint sound from the next room. It was a regular noise. It had the rhythm of a quick footfall, but in its nature it was more like the sound of a heavily beating pulse. Randall Byrne sat up in his chair. A faint creaking attested that it was, indeed, a footfall traversing the room to and fro, steadily.

The stranger, then, no longer leaned over the couch of the old cattleman. He was walking up and down the floor with that characteristic, softly padding step. Of what did he think as he walked? It carried Byrne automatically out into the darkest night, with a wind in his face, and the rhythm of a long striding horse carrying him on to a destination unknown.

Here he heard a soft scratching, repeated, at the door. When it came again he rose and opened the door—at once the tall, shaggy dog slipped through the opening and glided past him. It startled Byrne oddly to see the animal stealing away, as if Barry himself had been leaving. He called to the beast, but he was met by a silent baring of white fangs that stopped him in his tracks. The great dog was gone without a sound, and Byrne closed the door again without casting a look inside. He was stupidly, foolishly afraid to look within.

After that the silence had a more vital meaning. No pictures crowded his brain. He was simply keyed to a high point of expectancy, and therefore, when the door was opened silently, he sprang up as if in acknowledgment of an alarm and faced Barry. The latter closed the door behind him and glided after the big dog. He had almost crossed the big room when Byrne was able to speak.

"Mr. Barry!" he called.

The man hesitated.

"Mr. Barry," he repeated.

And Dan Barry turned. It was something like the act of the wolf the moment before; a swift movement—a flash of the eyes in something like defiance.

"Mr. Barry, are you leaving us?"

"I'm going outside."

"Are you coming back?"

"I dunno."

A great joy swelled in the throat of Doctor Byrne. He felt like shouting in triumph; yet he remembered once more how the girl had gone up the stairs, wearily, with fallen head. He decided that he would do what he could to keep the stranger with them, and though Randall Byrne lived to be a hundred he would never do a finer thing than what he attempted then. He stepped across the room and stood before Barry, blocking the way.

"Sir," he said gravely, "if you go now, you will work a great sorrow in this house."

A glint of anger rose in the eyes of Barry.

"Joe Cumberland is sleepin' soun'," he answered. "He'll be a pile rested when he wakes up. He don't need me no more."

"He's not the only one who needs you," said Byrne. "His daughter has been waiting impatiently for your coming, sir."

The sharp glance of Barry wavered away.

"I'd kind of like to stay," he murmured, "but I got to go."

A dull voice called from the next room.

"It's Joe Cumberland," said Byrne. "You see, he is not sleeping!"

The brow of Barry clouded, and he turned gloomily back.

"Maybe I better stay," he agreed.

Yet before he made a step Byrne heard a far-away honking of the wild geese, that musical discord carrying for uncounted miles through the windy air. The sound worked like magic on Barry. He whirled back.

"I got to go," he repeated.

And yet Byrne blocked the way. It required more courage to do that than to do anything he had ever attempted in his life. The sweat poured out from under his armpits as the stranger stepped near; the blood rushed from his face as he stared into the eyes of Barry—eyes which now held an uncanny glimmer of yellow light.

"Sir," said Byrne huskily, "you must not go! Listen! Old Cumberland is calling to you again! Does that mean nothing? If you have some errand out in the night, let me go for you."

"Partner," said the soft voice of Barry, "stand aside. I got no time, I'm wanted!"

Every muscle of Randall Byrne's body was set to repulse the stranger in any effort to pass through that door, and yet, mysteriously, against his will, he found himself standing to one side, and saw the other slip through the open door.

"Dan! Are ye there?" called a louder voice from the room beyond.

There was no help for it. He, himself, must go back and face Joe Cumberland. With a lie, no doubt. He would say that Dan had stepped out for a moment and would be back again. That might put Cumberland safely to sleep. In the morning, to be sure, he would find out the deception—but let every day bury its dead. Here was enough trouble for one night. He went slowly, but steadily toward the door of what had now become a fatal room to the doctor. In that room he had seen his dearest doctrines cremated. Out of that room he had come bearing the ashes of his hopes in his hands. Now he must go back once more to try to fill, with science, a gap of which science could never take cognizance.

He lingered another instant with his hand on the door; then he cast it wide bravely enough and stepped in. Joe Cumberland was sitting up on the edge of his couch. There was color in the old man's face. It almost seemed, to the incredulous eyes of Byrne, that the face was filled out a trifle. Certainly the fire of the old cattleman's glance was less unearthly.

"Where's Dan?" he called. "Where'd he go?"

It was no longer the deep, controlled voice of the stoic;

it was the almost whining complaint of vital weakness.

"Is there anything I can do for you?" parried Byrne. "Anything you need or wish?"

"Him!" answered the old man explosively. "Damn it, I need Dan! Where is he? He was here. I *felt* him here while I was sleepin'. *Where is he?*"

"He has stepped out for an instant," answered Byrne smoothly. "He will be back shortly."

"He—has—stepped—out?" echoed the old man slowly. Then he rose to the full of his gaunt height. His white hair, his triangle of beard and pointed mustache gave him a detached, a mediaeval significance; a portrait by Van Dyck had stepped from its frame.

"Doc, you're lyin' to me! Where has he gone?"

A sudden, almost hysterical burst of emotion swept Doctor Byrne.

"Gone to heaven or hell!" he cried with startling violence. "Gone to follow the wind and the wild geese— God knows where!"

Like a period to his sentence, a gun barked outside, there was a howl of demoniac pain and rage, and then a scream that would tingle in the ear of Doctor Randall Byrne till his dying day.

23 • How Mac Strann Kept the Law

FOR when the dog sprang, Mac Strann fired, and the wolf was jerked up in the midst of his leap by the tearing impact of the bullet. It was easy for Strann to dodge the beast, and the great black body hurtled past him and struck heavily on the floor of the barn. It missed Mac Strann, indeed, but it fell at the very feet of Haw-Haw Langley, and a splash of blood flirted across his face. He was too terrified to shriek, but fell against the wall of the barn, gasping. There he saw Black Bart struggle to regain his feet, vainly, for both of the animal's forelegs seemed paralyzed. Now the yellow light of the fire rose brightly, and by it Haw-Haw marked the terrible eyes and the lolling, slavering tongue of the great beast, and the fangs like ivory daggers. It could not regain its feet, but it thrust itself forward by convulsive efforts of the hind legs toward Mac Strann.

Haw-Haw Langley stared for a single instant in white faced fear, but when he realized that Black Bart was helpless as a toothless old dog, the tall cowpuncher twisted his lean fingers with a silent joy. Once more Bart pushed himself toward Mac Strann, and then Haw-Haw Langley stepped forward, and with all the force of his long leg smashed his heavy riding boot into the face of the dog. Black Bart toppled back against the base of the manger, struggled vainly to regain his poise, and it was then that he pointed his nose up, and wailed like a lost soul, wailed with the fury of impotent hate. Mac Strann caught Haw-Haw by the arm and dragged him back toward the door.

"I don't want to *kill* the dog," he repeated. "Get out of here, Haw-Haw. Barry'll be comin' any minute."

He could have used no sharper spur to urge on the laggard. Haw-Haw Langley raced out of the barn with a full stride before Mac Strann. They hurried together to the little rise of ground behind which they had left their horses, and as they ran the scream which had curdled the blood of Randall Byrne rang through the night. In a thousand years he could never have guessed from what that yell issued; his nearest surmise would have been a score of men screaming in unison under the torture. But Mac Strann and Haw-Haw Langley knew the sound well enough.

When they mounted their saddles they could look over the top of the little hill and observe everything easily without being seen; for the hill-top commanded a range of the corrals and a view of the fronts of the barns and sheds which opened upon the fenced enclosures. The largest and longest of these buildings was now plainly visible, for a long arm of fire reached above the roof on one side of the low shed and by this growing light the other barns, the glimmering-eyed horses and cattle of the corrals, the trees about the house, the house itself, were in turn visible, though vaguely, and at times, as the flames lapsed, all were lost in a flood of swift darkness. Once more that unhuman shriek echoed from hill to hill and from building to building. It was Satan in his box stall. The flames were eating through the partition, and the stallion was mad with fear.

Lights flashed, here and there, in the big ranch house; and from the bunkhouse on the farther side of the corrals rose a volley of curses and yells of dismay. The cattle began milling blindly, bellowing and stamping, and the horses ranged at a mad gallop back and forth across their corrals, wild-eyed with terror. It was like the tumult of a battle, and sharper than a trumpet a new sound cut through the din—it was a short, high whistle, twice repeated. An answer came from the burning barn—the long, strong neighing of the stallion.

"D'ye hear?" muttered Mac Strann. "It's the hoss talkin' to his master!"

"And there he comes!" said Haw-Haw Langley. "Runnin' like the wind!"

The flame, picked up by the gale, tore for itself a wider breathing space through the roof and sent up an audibly roaring column of blinding red. By that light, Mac Strann, following Haw-Haw's directing arm, saw a lithe figure vault over the fence on the farther side of the corral and dart forward among the milling cattle.

Now, when cattle begin to mill it takes a brave man on a brave, well-trained horse to trust his chances in the midst of that ocean of tossing horns. But this man ventured it on foot. Mac Strann could follow him easily, for the man's hat was off, and the fire-light glittered on his black hair. That glimmering head darted here and there among the circling cattle. Now it was lost, swamped, to all appearances, under a score of trampling hooves. Again it reappeared on the further side. Mac Strann could see the runner in a comparatively open space, racing like a trained sprinter, and he headed straight toward a wall of tossing horns. They were longhorns, and one sway of those lowered heads could drive the hard, sharp point through and through the body of a man. Yet straight at this impassable wall the stranger rushed, like a warrior in his berserk madness leaping naked upon a hedge of spears. At the verge of the danger the man sprang high into the air. Two leaps, from back to back among the herd, and he was across the thickest of danger, down once more on the ground, and dodging past the outskirts of the bellowing cows. Over the nearer fence he vaulted and disappeared into the smoke which vomited from the mouth of the burning barn.

"God A'mighty," groaned Haw-Haw Langley, "can he get the hoss out?"

"It ain't possible," answered Mac Strann. "All hosses goes mad when they gets in a fire—even when they sees a fire. Look at them fools over yonder in the corral."

Indeed, in the horse-corral a score of frantic animals were attempting to leap the high rails in the direction of the burning barn. Their stamping and snorting came volleying up the hill to the watchers.

"All hosses goes mad," concluded Mac Strann, "an' Barry'll get tramped under the feet of his own hoss even if he gets to the stall—which he won't. Look there!"

Out of the rush of fire and smoke at the door of the barn Dan Barry stumbled, blindly, and fell back upon the ground. Haw-Haw Langley began to twist his cold hands together in an ecstasy.

"The hoss is gone and the wolf is gone, and Barry is beat!" he chuckled to himself. "Mac, I wouldn't of missed this for a ten days' ride. It's worth it. But see the gal and that new gent, Mac!"

For when the clamor rose outside the house Buck Daniels had run to the window. For many reasons he had not taken off his clothes this night, but had lain down on the bed and folded his hands behind his head to wait. With the first outcry he was at the window and there he saw the flames curling above the roof of the barn, and next, by that wild light, how Dan Barry raced through the dangerous corral, and then he heard the shrill neighing of Satan, and saw Dan disappear in the smoking door of the barn.

Fear drew Buck Daniels one way but a fine impulse drew him another. He turned away from the window with a curse; he turned back to it with a curse, and then, muttering; "He went through hell for me; and him

and me together, we'll go through hell again!" he ran
from the room and thundered down the crazy stairs.

As he left the house he found Kate Cumberland and
they went on together, running without a word to each
other. Only, when he came beside her, she stopped
short and flashed one glance at him. By that glance he
knew that she understood why he was there, and that
she accepted his sacrifice.

They hurried around the outer edge of the corrals, and
as they approached the flaming barn from one side the
men from the bunkhouse rushed up from the other. It
was Buck Daniels who reached Dan as the latter stumbled back from the door of the bar surrounded by a
following cloud of smoke, and fell stumbling to the
ground. And Buck raised him.

The girl was instantly beside them.

She had thrown on a white dressing gown when she
rose from bed. It was girded high across her breast, and
over it showered her bright hair, flashing like liquid
gold in growing light. She, now, received the semi-
conscious burden of Dan Barry, and Buck Daniels
stepped forward, close to the smoke. He began to shout
directions which the two watchers behind the hill could
not hear, though they saw his long arms point and ges-
ticulate and they could see his speaking lips. But wild
confusion was on the crowd of cowpunchers. They ran
here and there. One or two brought buckets of water and
tossed the contents uselessly into the swirling, red-stained
hell of smoke. But most of them ran here and there, ac-
complishing nothing.

"An' all this come from one little match, Mac," cried
Haw-Haw ecstatically at the ear of Mac Strann. "All
what we're seein'! Look at the gal, Mac! She's foolin'
about Barry, doin' no good."

A gust of smoke and fire must have met Barry face
to face when he entered the barn, for he seemed now as
helpless as if he were under a strong narcotic influence.
He leaned heavily back into the arms of the girl, his
head rolling wildly from side to side. Then, clearer than
before, dominating all the confusion of noise, and with a
ringing, trumpet note of courage in it, the black stallion
neighed again from his burning stall. It had a magic ef-

fect upon Barry. He stood up and tore himself from the arms of the girl. They saw her gesture and cry to the surrounding men for help, and a dozen hands were stretched out to keep the madman from running into the fire. They might better have attempted to hold a wild horse with their naked hands. He slipped and broke through their grips, and a second later had leaped into the inferno of smoke, running bent close to the ground where the pure air, if there were any, was sure to be.

"The gal's sick!" said Haw-Haw Langley. "Look, Mac!"

And he began to laugh in that braying voice which had given him his nickname. Yet even in his laughter his eyes were brightly observant; not a single detail of misery or grief was lost upon him; he drank it in; he fed his famine-stricken soul upon it. Kate Cumberland had buried her face in her arms; Buck Daniels, attempting to rush in after Dan Barry, had been caught beneath the arms by Doctor Byrne and another and was now borne struggling back.

From the very heart of the burning barn the sharp single whistle burst and over the rolling smoke and flaming fire rose the answering neigh. A human voice could not have spoken more intelligibly: "I wait in trust!"

After that neigh and whistle, a quiet fell over the group at the barn door. There was nothing to do. There was not enough wind to blow the flames from this barn to one of the neighboring sheds; all they could do was stand still and watch the progress of the conflagration.

The deep, thick voice of Mac Strann broke in: "Start prayin', Haw-Haw, that the hoss don't kill Barry when he gets to him. Start prayin' that Barry is left for me to finish."

He must have meant his singular request more as a figure of speech than a real demand, but an hysteria was upon Haw-Haw Langley. He stretched up his vast, gaunt arms to the dim spot of red in the central heavens above the fire, and Haw-Haw prayed for the first and last time in his life.

"O Lord, gimme this one favor. Bring Barry safe out of the barn. Bring him out even if you got to bring the damned hoss with him. Bring him out and save him for

Mac Strann to meet. And, God A'mighty, let me be
around somewheres when they meet!"

This strange exhibition Mac Strann watched with a
glowering eye.

"But it ain't possible," he said positively. "I been in
fires. Barry can't live through the fire; an' if he does,
the hoss will finish him. It ain't possible for him to come
out!"

From half the roof of the shed flames now poured, but
presently a great shower of sparks rose at the farther end
of the barn, and then Haw-Haw heard the sound of a
beating and crashing.

"Hei!" he screamed, "Barry's reached the black hoss
and the black hoss is beating him into the floor!"

"You fool!" answered Mac Strann calmly, "Barry has
got a beam or something and he's smashing down the
burning partition of the box stall. That's what he's doing; listen!"

High over the fire, once again rose the neighing of
the black horse, a sound of unspeakable triumph.

"You're right," groaned Haw-Haw, downcast. "He's
reached the hoss!"

He had hardly finished speaking when Mac Strann
said: "Anyway, he'll never get out. This end of the barn
is fallin' in."

Indeed, the outer wall of the barn, nearest the door,
was wavering in a great section and slowly tottering in.
Another moment or two it would crash to the floor and
block the way of Dan Barry, coming out, with a flaming
ruin. Next the watchers saw a struggle among the
group which watched. Three men were struggling with
Buck Daniels, but presently he wrenched his arms free,
struck down two men before him with swinging blows of
his fists, and leaped into the smoke.

"He's gone nutty, like a crazy hoss with the sight of
the fire," said Mac Strann quietly.

"He ain't! He ain't!" cried Haw-Haw Langley, wild
with excitement. "He's holdin' back the burnin' wall to
keep the way clear, damn him!"

Indeed, the tottering wall, not having leaned to a
great angle, was now pushed back by some power from
the inside of the barn and kept erect. Though now and

again it swayed in, as though the strength which held it was faltering under the strain.

Now the eyes of the watchers were called to the other end of the barn by a tremendous crashing. The entire section of that part of the roof fell in, and a shower of sparks leaped up into the heart of the sky, lighting the distant hills and drawing them near like watchers of the horror of the night.

"That's the end," said Mac Strann. "Haw-Haw, they wasn't any good in your prayer."

"I ain't a professional prayin' man," answered Haw-Haw defensively, "but I done my best. If———"

He was cut short by a chorused cry from the watchers near the door of the barn, and then, through the vomited smoke and the fire, leaped the unsaddled body of Satan bearing on his back the crouched figure of Dan Barry, and in the arms of Barry, limp, his head hanging down loosely, was the body of the great black dog, Bart.

A fearful picture. The smoke swept following around the black stallion, and a great tongue of flame licked hungrily after the trio. But the stallion stood with head erect, and ears flattened, pawing the ground. With that cloud of destruction blowing him he stood like the charger which the last survivor might ride through the ruin of the universe in the Twilight of the Gods.

At the same instant, another smoke-clad figure lunged from the door of the barn, his hands outstretched as though he felt and fumbled his way through utter darkness. It was Buck Daniels, and as he cleared the door the section of tottering wall which he had upheld to keep the way clear for the Three, wavered, sagged, and then sank in thunder to the floor, and the whole barn lay a flame-tossed mass of ruin.

The watchers had scattered before the plunge of Satan, but he came to a sliding halt, as if his rider had borne heavily back upon the reins. Barry slipped from the stallion's back with the wounded dog, and kneeled above the limp figure.

"It ain't the end," growled Mac Strann, "that hoss will go runnin' back into the fire. It ain't hoss nature to keep from goin' mad at the sight of a fire!"

In answer to him, the stallion whirled, raised his head

high, and, with flaunting mane and tail, neighed a ringing defiance at the rising flames. Then he turned back
and nuzzled the shoulder of his master, who was
working with swift hands over the body of Black Bart.

"Anyway," snarled Haw-Haw Langley, "the damned
wolf is dead."

"I dunno," said Mac Strann. "Maybe—maybe not.
They's quite a pile that we dunno."

"If you want to get rid of the hoss," urged Haw-Haw,
writhing in the glee of a new inspiration, "now's the time
for it, Mac. Get out your gun and pot the black. Before
the crowd can get us, we'll be miles away. They ain't
a saddled hoss in sight. Well, if you don't want to do
it, I will!"

But Mac Strann reached across and dragged the muzzle down.

"We done all we're goin' to do tonight. Seems like
God's been listenin' pretty close, around here!"

He turned his horse, and Haw-Haw, reluctantly, followed suit. Still, as they trotted slowly away from the
burning barn, Haw-Haw kept his glance fixed behind
him until a final roaring crash and a bellying cloud of
fire that smote the zenith announced the end of the
barn. Then Haw-Haw turned his face to his companion.

"Now what?" he demanded.

"We go to Elkhead and sit down and wait," answered
Mac Strann. "If the dog gets well he'll bring Barry to us.
Then all I've got to do is defend myself."

Haw-Haw Langley twisted up his face and laughed,
silently, to the red-stained sky.

24 • Doctor Byrne Looks into the Past

THE black head of Barry, the brown head of Randall Byrne, the golden head of Kate Cumberland, were all bowed around the limp body of Black Bart. Buck Daniels, still gasping for breath, stood reeling nearby.

"Let me attempt to resuscitate the animal," offered the doctor.

He was met by a blank look from Barry. The hair of the man was scorched, his skin was blistered and burned. Only his hands remained uninjured, and these continued to move over the body of the great dog. Kate Cumberland was on her knees over the brute.

"Is it fatal, Dan?" she asked. "Is there no hope for Bart?"

There was no answer from Barry, and she attempted to raise the fallen, lifeless head of the animal; but instantly a strong arm darted out and brushed her hands away. Those hands fell idly at her sides and her head went back as though she had been struck across the face. She found herself looking up into the angry eyes of Randall Byrne. He reached down and raised her to her feet; there was no color in her face, no life in her limbs.

"There's nothing more to be done here, apparently," said the doctor coldly. "Suppose we take your father and go back to the house."

She made neither assent or dissent. Dan Barry had finished a swift, deft bandage and stopped the bleeding of the dog's wounds. Now he raised his head and his glance slipped rapidly over the faces of the doctor and the girl and rested on Buck Daniels. There was no flash of kindly thanks, no word of recognition. His right hand raised to his cheek, and rested there, and in his eyes came that flare of yellow hate. Buck Daniels shrank back until he was lost in the crowd. Then he turned and stumbled back toward the house.

Instantly, Barry began to work at expanding and depressing the lungs of the huge animal as he might have worked to bring a man back to life.

"Watch him!" whispered the doctor to Kate Cumberland. "He is closer to that dog—that wolf, it looks like —than he has ever been to any human being!"

She would not answer, but she turned her head quickly from the man and his beast.

"Are you afraid to watch?" challenged Byrne, for his anger at Barry's blunt refusals still made his blood hot. "When your father lay at death's door was he half so anxious as he is now? Did he work so hard, by half? See how his eyes are fixed on the muzzle of the beast as if he were studying a human face?"

"No, no!" breathed the girl.

"I tell you, look!" commanded the doctor. "For there's the solution of the mystery. No mystery at all. Barry is simply a man who is closer akin to the brute forces in nature. See! By the eternal heavens, he's dragging that beast—that dumb beast—back from the door of death!"

Barry had ceased his rapid manipulations, and turned the big dog back upon its side. Now the eyes of Black Bart opened, and winked shut again. Now the master kneeled at the head of the beast and took the scarred, shaggy head between his hands.

"Bart!" he commanded.

Not a stir in the long, black body. The stallion edged a pace closer, dropped his velvet muzzle, and whinnied softly at the very ear of the dog. Still, there was not an answering quiver.

"Bart!" called the man again, and there was a ring of wild grief—of fear—in his cry.

"Do you hear?" said Byrne savagely, at the ear of the girl. "Did you ever use such a tone with a human being? Ever?"

"Take me away!" she murmured. "I'm sick—sick at heart. Take me away!"

Indeed, she was scarcely sure of her poise, and tottered where she stood. Doctor Byrne slipped his arm about her and led her away, supporting half her weight. They went slowly, by small, soft steps, toward the house, and before they reached it, he knew that she was weep-

ing. But if there was sadness in Byrne, there was also a
great joy. He was afire, for there is a flamelike quality
in hope.

Loss of blood and the stifling smoke, rather than a
mortal injury or the touch of fire, had brought Black
Bart close to death, but now that his breathing was restored, and almost normal, he gained rapidly. One instant he lingered on the border between life and death;
the next, the brute's eyes opened and glittered with dim
recognition up toward Dan, and he licked the hand
which supported his head. At Dan's direction, a blanket
was brought, and after Dan had lifted Black Bart upon
it, four men raised the corners of the blanket and carried the burden toward the house. One of the cowpunchers went ahead bearing a light. This was the sight
which Doctor Byrne and Kate Cumberland saw from
the veranda of the ranch-house as they turned and
looked back before going in.

"A funeral procession," suggested the doctor.

"No," she answered positively. "If Black Bart were
dead, Dan wouldn't allow any hands save his own to
touch the body. No, Black Bart is alive! Yet, it's impossible."

The word "impossible," however, was gradually dropping from the vocabulary of Randall Byrne. True, the
wolf dog had seemed dead past recovery and across the
eyes of Byrne came a vision of the dead rising from
their graves. Yet he merely shook his head and said
nothing.

"Ah!" she broke in. "Look!"

The procession drew nearer, heading toward the back
of the big house, and now they saw that Dan Barry
walked beside the body of Black Bart, a smile on his
lifted face. They disappeared behind the back of the
house.

Byrne heard the girl murmuring, more to herself than
to him: "Once he was like that all the time."

"Like what?" he asked bluntly.

She paused, and then her hand dropped lightly on
his arm. He could not see more than a vague outline of
her in the night, only the dull glimmer of her face as

she turned her head, and the faint whiteness of her hand.

"Let's say good night," she answered, at length. "Our little worlds have toppled about our heads tonight—all your theories, it seems, and, God knows, all that I have hoped. Why should we stay here and make ourselves miserable by talk?"

"But because we have failed," he said steadily, "is that the reason we should creep off and brood over our failure in silence? No, let's talk it out, man to man."

"You have a fine courage," said the girl. "But what is there we can say?"

He answered: "For my part, I am not so miserable as you think. For I feel as if this night had driven us closer together, you see; and I've caught a perspective on everything that has happened here."

"Tell me what you know."

"Only what I think I know. It may be painful to hear."

"I'm very used to pain."

"Well, a moment ago, when Barry was walking beside his dog, smiling, you murmured that he once was like that always. It gave me light. So I'd say that there was a time when Dan Barry lived here with you and your father. Am I right?"

"Yes, for years and years."

"And in those times he was not greatly different from other men. Not on the surface."

"No."

"You came to be very fond of him."

"We were to marry," answered Kate Cumberland, and Byrne winced.

He went on: "Then something happened—suddenly— that took him away from you, and you did not see him again until tonight. Am I right?"

"Yes. I thought you must have heard the story—from the outside. I'll tell you the truth. My father found Dan Barry wandering across the hills years ago. He was riding home over the range and he heard a strange and beautiful whistling, and when he looked up he saw on the western ridge, walking against the sky, a tattered figure of a boy. He rode up and asked the boy his name. He learned it was Dan Barry—Whistling Dan, he was called. But the boy could not, or would not, tell how he came to be there in the middle of the range without a horse. He merely said that he came from 'over there,' and waved his hand to the south and east. That was all. He didn't seem to be alarmed because he was alone, and yet he apparently knew nothing of the country; he was lost in this terrible country where a man could wander for days without finding a house, and yet the boy was whistling as he walked! So Dad took him home and sent out letters all about—to the railroad in particular—to find out if such a boy was missing.

"He received no answer. In the meantime he gave Dan a room in the house; and I remember how Dan sat at the table the first night—I was a very little girl then—and how I laughed at his strange way of eating. His knife was the only thing he was interested in and he made it serve for knife, fork and spoon, and he held the meat in his fingers while he cut it. The next morning he was missing. One of Dad's range riders picked up Dan several miles to the north, walking along, whistling gayly. The next morning he was missing again and was caught still farther away. After that Dad had a terrible scene with him—I don't know exactly what happened—but Dan promised to run away no more, and ever since then Dad has been closer to Dan than anyone else.

"So Dan grew up. From the time I could first distinctly remember, he was very gentle and good-natured, but he was different, always. After a while he got Black Bart, you know, and then he went out with a halter and captured Satan. Think of capturing a wild mustang with nothing but a halter! He played around with them so much that I was jealous of them. So I kept with them until Bart and Satan were rather used to me. Bart would even play with me now and then when Dan wasn't near. And so finally Dan and I were to be married.

"Dad didn't like the idea. He was afraid of what Dan might become. And he was right. One day, in a saloon that used to stand on that hill over there, Dan had a fight—his first fight—with a man who had struck him across the mouth for no good reason. That man was Jim Silent. Of course you've heard of him?"

"Never."

"He was a famous long-rider—an outlaw with a very black record. At the end of that fight he struck Dan down with a chair and escaped. I went down to Dan when I heard of the fight—Black Bart led me down, to be exact—but Dan would not come back to the house, and he'd have no more to do with anyone until he had found Jim Silent. I can't tell you everything that happened. Finally he caught Jim Silent and killed him—with his bare hands. Buck Daniels saw it. Then Dan came back to us, but on the first night he began to grow restless. It was last Fall—the wild geese were flying south—and while they were honking in the sky Dan got up, said good-bye, and left us. We have never seen him again until tonight. All we knew was that he had ridden south—after the wild geese."

A long silence fell between them, for the doctor was thinking hard.

"And when he came back," he said, "Barry did not know you? I mean, you were nothing to him?"

"You were there," said the girl, faintly.

"It is perfectly clear," said Byrne. "If it were a little more commonplace it might be puzzling, but being so extraordinary it clears itself up. Did you really expect the dog, the wolf dog, Black Bart, to remember you?"

"I may have expected it."

"But you were not surprised, of course!"

"Naturally not."

"Yet you see that Dan Barry—Whistling Dan, you call him—was closer to Black Bart than he was to you?"

"Why should I see that?"

"You watched him a moment ago when he was leaning over the dog."

He watched her draw her dressing gown closer about her, as though the cold bit more keenly then.

She said simply: "Yes, I saw."

"Don't you see that he is simply more in tune with the animal world? And it's really no more reasonable to expect Black Bart to remember you than it is to expect Dan Barry to remember you? It's quite plain. When you go back to the beginning man was simply an animal, without the higher senses, as we call them. He was simply a brute, living in trees or in caves. Afterward he grew into the thing we all know. But why not imagine a throw-back into the earlier instincts? Why not imagine the creature devoid of the impulses of mind, the thing which we call man, and see the splendid animal? You saw in Dan Barry simply a biological sport—the freak—the thing which retraces the biological progress and comes close to the primitive. But of course you could not realize this. He seemed a man, and you accepted him as a man. In reality he was no more a man than Black Bart is a man. He had the face and form of a man, but his instincts were as old as the ages. The animal world obeys him. Satan neighs in answer to his whistle. The wolf dog licks his hand at the point of death. There is the profound difference, always. You try to reconcile him with other men; you give him the attributes of other men. Open your eyes; see the truth: that he is no more akin to man than Black Bart is like a man. And when you give him your affection, Miss Cumberland, *you are giving your affection to a wild wolf!* Do you believe me?"

He knew that she was shaken. He could feel it, even without the testimony of his eyes to witness. He went on, speaking with great rapidity, lest she should escape from the influence which he had already gained over her.

"I felt it when I first saw him—a certain nameless kinship with elemental forces. The wind blew through the open door—it was Dan Barry. The wild geese called from the open sky—for Dan Barry. These are the things which lead him. These the forces which direct him. You have loved him; but is love merely a giving? No, you have seen in him a man, but I see in him merely the animal force."

She said after a moment: "Do you hate him—you plead against him so passionately?"

He answered: "Can you hate a thing which is not human? No, but you can dread it. It escapes from the laws which bind you and which bind me. What standards govern it? How can you hope to win it? Love? What beauty is there in the world to appeal to such a creature except the beauty of the marrow-bone which his teeth have the strength to snap?"

"Ah, listen!" murmured the girl. "Here is your answer!"

And Doctor Randall Byrne heard a sound like the muted music of the violin, thin and small and wonderfully penetrating. He could not tell, at first what it might be. For it was as unlike the violin as it was like the bow and the rosined strings. Then he made out, surely, that it was the whistling of a human being.

It followed no tune, no reasoned theme. The music was beautiful in its own self. It rose straight up like the skylark from the ground, sheer up against the white light of the sky, and there it sang against heaven's gate. He had never heard harmony like it. He would never again hear such music, so thin and yet so full that it went through and through him, until he felt the strains take a new, imitative life within him. He would have whistled the strains himself, but he could not follow them. They escaped him, they soared above him. They followed no law or rhythm. They flew on wings and left him far below. The girl moved away from him as if led by an invisible hand, and now she stood at the extremity of the porch. He followed her.

"Do you hear?" she cried, turning to him.

"What is it?" asked the doctor.

"It is he! Don't you understand?"

"Barry? Yes! But what does the whistling mean; is it for his wolf dog?"

"I don't know," she answered quickly. "All I understand is that it is beautiful. Where are your theories and explanations now, Doctor Byrne?"

"It *is* beautiful—God knows!—but doesn't the wolf dog understand it better than either you or I?"

She turned and faced Byrne, standing very close, and when she spoke there was something in her voice which was like a light. In spite of the dark he could guess at every varying shade of her expression.

"To the rest of us," she murmured, "Dan has nothing but silence, and hardly a glance. Buck saved his life tonight, and yet Dan remembered nothing except the blow which had been struck. And now—now he pours out all the music in his soul for a dumb beast. Listen!"

He saw her straighten herself and stand taller.

"Then through the wolf—I'll conquer through the dumb beast!"

She whipped past Byrne and disappeared into the house; at the same instant the whistling, in the midst of a faint, high climax, broke, shivered, and was ended. There was only the darkness and the silence around Byrne, and the unsteady wind against his face.

25 · Werewolf

DOCTOR BYRNE, pacing the front veranda with his thoughtful head bowed, saw Buck Daniels step out with his quirt dangling in his hand, his cartridge belt buckled above his waist, and a great red silk bandana knotted at his throat.

He was older by ten years than he had been a few days before, when the doctor first saw him. To be sure, his appearance was not improved by three days' growth of beard. It gave his naturally dark skin a dirty cast, but even that rough stubble could not completely shroud the new hollows in Daniels' cheeks. His long, black uncombed hair sagged down raggedly across his forehead, hanging almost into his eyes; the eyes themselves were sunk in such formidable cavities that Byrne caught hardly more than two points of light in the shadows. All the devil-may-care insouciance of Buck Daniels was quite, quite gone. In its place was a dogged sullenness, a hang-dog air which one would not care to face of a dark night or in a lonely place. His manner was that of a man whose back is against the wall, who, having fled some keen pursuit, has now come to the end of his tether and prepares for desperate, even if hopeless, battle. There was that about him which made the doctor hesitate to address the cowpuncher.

At length he said: "You're going out for an outing, Mr. Daniels?"

Buck Daniels started violently at the sound of this

voice behind him, and whirled upon the doctor with
such a set and contorted expression of fierceness that
Byrne jumped back.

"Good God, man!" cried the doctor, "What's up with
you?"

"Nothin'," answered Buck, gradually relaxing from his
first show of suspicion. "I'm beating it, that's all."

"Leaving us?"

"Yes."

"Not really!"

"D'you think I ought to stay?" asked Buck, with something of a sneer.

The doctor hesitated, frowning in a puzzled way. At
length he threw out his hands in a gesture of mute
abandonment.

"My dear fellow," he said with a faint smile, "I've
about stopped trying to think."

At this Buck Daniels grinned mirthlessly.

"Now you're talkin' sense," he nodded. "They ain't no
use in thinking."

"But why do you leave so suddenly?"

Buck Daniels shrugged his broad shoulders.

"I am sure," went on Byrne, "that Miss Cumberland
will miss you."

"She will not," answered the big cowpuncher. "She's
got her hands full with—*him*."

"Exactly. But if it is more than she can do, if she
makes no headway with that singular fellow—she may
need help——"

He was interrupted by a slow, long-drawn, deep-
throated curse from Buck Daniels.

"Why in hell should I help her with—*him?*"

"There is really no reason," answered the doctor,
alarmed, "except, I suppose, old friendship——"

"Damn old friendship!" burst out Buck Daniels.
"There's an end to all things and my friendship is worn
out—on both sides. It's done!"

He turned and scowled at the house.

"Help her to win *him* over? I'd rather stick the muzzle
of my gun down my throat and pull the trigger. I'd
rather see her marry a man about to hang. Well—to hell
with this place. I'm through with it. S'long, doc."

But Doctor Byrne ran after him and halted him at the foot of the steps down from the veranda.

"My dear Mr. Daniels," he urged, touching the arm of Buck. "You really mustn't leave so suddenly as this. There are a thousand questions on the tip of my tongue."

Buck Daniels regarded the professional man with a hint of weariness and disgust.

"Well," he said, "I'll hear the first couple of hundred. Shoot!"

"First: the motive that sends you away."

"Dan Barry."

"Ah—ah—fear of what he may do?"

"Damn the fear. At least, it's him that makes me go."

"It seems an impenetrable mystery," sighed the doctor. "I saw you the other night step into the smoking hell of that barn and keep the way clear for this man. I knew, before that, how you rode and risked your life to bring Dan Barry back here. Surely those are proofs of friendship!"

Buck Daniels laughed unpleasantly. He laid a large hand on the shoulder of the doctor and answered: "If them was the only proofs, doc, I wouldn't feel the way I do. Proofs of friendship? Dan Barry has saved me from the—rope!—and he's saved me from dyin' by the gun of Jim Silent. He took me out of a rotten life and made me a man that could look honest men in the face!"

He paused, swallowing hard, and the doctor's misty, overworked eyes lighted with some comprehension. He had felt from the first a certain danger in this big fellow, a certain reckless disregard of laws and rules which commonly limit the actions of ordinary men. Now part of the truth was hinted at. Buck Daniels, on a time, had been outside the law; and Barry had drawn him back to the ways of men. That explained some of the singular bond that lay between them.

"That ain't all," went on Buck. "Blood is thick, and I've loved him better nor a brother. I've gone to hell and back for him. For him I took Kate Cumberland out of the hands of Jim Silent, and I left myself in her place. I took her away and all so's she could go to him. Damn him! And now on account of him I got to leave this place."

His voice rose to a ringing pitch.

"D'you think it's easy for me to go? D'you think it ain't like tearing a fingernail off'n the flesh for me to go away from Kate? God knows what she means to me! God knows, but if He does, He's forgotten me!"

Anguish of spirit set Buck Daniels shaking, and the doctor looked on in amazement. He was like one who reaches in his pocket for a copper coin and brings out a handful of gold pieces.

"Kind feelin's don't come easy to me," went on Buck Daniels. "I been raised to fight. I been raised to hard ridin' and dust in the throat. I been raised on whiskey and hate. And then I met Dan Barry, and his voice was softer'n a girl's voice, and his eyes didn't hold no doubt of me. Me that had sneaked in on him at night and was goin' to kill him in his sleep—because my chief had told me to! That was the Dan Barry what I first knew. He give me his hand and give me the trust of his eyes, and after he left me I sat down and took my head between my hands and my heart was like to bust inside me. It was like the clouds had blowed away from the sun and let it shine on me for the first time in my life. And I swore that if the time come I'd repay him. For every cent he give me I'd pay him back in gold. I'd foller to the end of the world to do what he bid me do."

His voice dropped suddenly, choked with emotion.

"Oh, doc, they was tears come in my eyes; and I felt sort of clean inside, and I wasn't ashamed of them tears! That was what Dan Barry done for me!

"And I *did* pay him back, as much as I could. I met Kate Cumberland and she was to me among girls what Dan Barry was to me among men. I ain't ashamed of sayin' it. I loved her till they was a dryness like ashes inside me, but I wouldn't even lift up my eyes to her, because she belonged to him. I follered her around like a dog. I done her bidding. I asked no questions. What she wanted—that was law to me, and all the law I wanted. All that I done for the sake of Dan Barry. And then I took my life in my hands for him—not once, but day after day.

"Then he rode off and left her and I stayed behind. D'you think it's been easy to stay here? Man, man, I've had to hear her talkin' about Dan Barry day after day, and never a word for me. And I had to tell her stories about Dan and what he used to do, and she'd sit with her eyes miles away from me, listenin' and smilin' and me there hungerin' for just one look out of her eyes—hungerin' like a dyin' dog for water. And then for her and Joe I rode down south and when I met Dan Barry d'you think they was any light in his eyes when he seen me?

"No, he'd forgotten me the way even a hoss won't forget his master. Forgot me after a few months—and after all that'd gone between us! Not even Kate—even she was nothin' to him. But still I kept at it and I brought him back. I had to hurt him to do it, but God knows it wasn't out of spite that I hit him—God knows!

"And when I seen Dan go into that burnin' barn I says to myself: 'Buck, if nothin' is done that wall will fall and there's the end of Dan Barry. There's the end of him, that ain't any human use, and when he's finished after a while maybe Kate will get to know that they's other men in the world besides Dan.' I says that to myself, deep and still inside me. And then I looked at Kate standin' in that white thing with her yaller hair all blowin' about her face—and I wanted her like a dyin' man wants heaven! But then I says to myself again: 'No matter what's happened, he's been my friend. He's been my pal. He's been my bunkie.'

"Doc, you ain't got a way of knowin' what a partner is out here. Maybe you sit in the desert about a thousand miles from nowhere, and across the little mesquite fire, there's your pal, the only human thing in sight. Maybe you go months seein' only him. If you're sick he takes care of you. If you're blue he cheers you up. And that's what Dan Barry was to me. So I stands sayin' these things to myself, and I says: 'If I keep that wall from fallin' Dan'll know about it, and they won't be no more of that yaller light in his eyes when he looks at me.' That's what I says to myself, poor fool!

"And I went into the fire and I fought to keep that wall from fallin'. You know what happened. When I come out, staggerin' and blind and three parts dead, Dan Barry looks up to me and touches his face where

I'd hit him, and the yaller comes up glimmerin' and blazin' in his eyes. Then I went back to my room and I fought it out.

"And here's where I stand now. If I stay here, if I see that yaller light once more, they won't be no waitin'. Him and me'll have to have it out right then. Am I a dog, maybe, that I got to stand around and jump when he calls me?"

"My dear fellow—my dear Mr. Daniels!" cried the horrified Doctor Byrne. "Surely you're wrong. He wouldn't go so far as to make a personal attack upon you!"

"Wouldn't he? Bah! Not if he was a man, no. I tell you, he ain't a man; he's what the Canucks up north call a werewolf! There ain't no mercy or kindness in him. The blood of a man means nothin' to him. The world would be better rid of him. Oh, he can be soft and gentle as a girl. Mostly he is. But cross him once and he forgets all you done for him. Give him a taste of blood and he jumps at your throat. I tell you, I've seen him do it!"

He broke off with a shudder.

"Doc," he said, in a lower and solemn voice. "Maybe I've said too much. Don't tell Kate nothin' about why I'm goin'. Let her go on dreamin' her fool dream. But now hear what I'm sayin': If Dan Barry crosses me once more, one of us two dies, and dies damned quick. It may be me, it may be him, but I've come to the end of my rope. I'm leavin' this place till Barry gets a chance to come to his senses and see what I've done for him. That's all. I'm leavin' this place because they's a blight on it, and that blight is Dan Barry. I'm leavin' this place because—doc—because I can smell the comin' of bloodshed in it. They's a death hangin' over it. If the lightnin' was to hit and burn it up, house and man, the range would be better for it!"

26 · The Battle

THE chain which fastened Black Bart had been passed around the trunk of a tree that stood behind the ranch house, and there the great dog lay tethered. Doctor Byrne had told Whistling Dan, with some degree of horror, that the open air was in the highest degree dangerous to wounds, but Whistling Dan had returned no answer. So Black Bart lay all day in the soft sand, easing himself from time to time into a new position, and his thoughtful eyes seemed to be concentrated on the desire to grow well. Beside him was the chair in which Dan Barry sat for many an hour of the day and even the night.

Kate Cumberland watched the animal from the shadow of the house; his eyes were closed, and the long, powerful head lay inert on the sand, yet she knew that the wolf dog was perfectly aware of her presence. Day after day since he lay there, she had attempted to approach Black Bart, and day after day he had allowed her to come within reaching distance of him, only to drive her back at the last moment by a sudden display of the murderous, long fangs; or by one of those snarls which came out of the black depths of his heart. Now, a dog snarls from not far down in its throat, but the noise of an angered wild beast rolls up out of its very entrails—a passion of hate and defiance. And when she heard that sound, or when she saw the still more terrible rage of the beast, Kate Cumberland's spirit failed, and she would shrink back again to a safe distance.

She was not easily discouraged. She had that grim resolution which comes to the gambler after he has played at the same table night after night, night after night, and lost, lost, lost, until, playing with the last of his money, he begins to mutter through his set teeth: "The luck *must* change!" So it was with Kate Cumberland. For in Black Bart she saw the only possible clue to Whistling Dan. There was the stallion, to be sure, but she knew Satan too well. Nothing in the wide world could induce that wild heart to accept more than one master—more than one friend. For Satan there was in the animal world Black Bart, and in the world of men, Dan Barry. These were enough. For all the rest he kept the disdainful speed of his slender legs or the terror of his teeth and trampling hoofs. Even if she could have induced the stallion to eat from her hand she could never have made him willing to trust himself to her guidance. Some such thing she felt that she must accomplish with Black Bart. To the wild beast with the scarred and shaggy head she must become a necessary, an accepted thing.

One repulse did not dishearten her. Again and again she made the trial. She remembered having read that no animal can resist the thoughtful patience of thinking man, and hour after hour she was there, until a new light in the eye of the wolf dog warned her that the true master was coming.

Then she fled, and from a post of vantage in the house she would watch the two. An intimacy surpassing the friendships and devotions of human beings existed between them. She had seen the wolf lie with his great head on the foot of his master and the unchanging eyes fixed on Barry's face—and so for an hour at a stretch in mute worship. Or she had watched the master go to the great beast to change the dressing—a thing which could not be done too often during the day. She had seen the swift hands remove the bandages and she had seen the cleansing solution applied. She knew what it was; it stung even the unscratched skin, and to a wound it must be torture, but the wolf lay and endured —not even shuddering at the pain.

It had seemed to her that this was the great test. If she could make the wolf lie like this for her, then, truly, she might feel herself in some measure admitted to that mystic fellowship of the three—the man, the stallion, and the wolf. If she could, with her own unaided hands, remove the bandages and apply that solution, then she could know many things, and she could feel that she was nearer to Whistling Dan than ever before.

So she had come, time and again, with the basin and the roll of cloth in her arm, and she had approached with infinite patience, step by step, and then inch by inch. Once it had taken a whole hour for her to come within a yard of the beast. And all that time Black Bart had lain with closed eyes. But at the critical instant always there was the silent writhing up of the lips and the gleam of hate—or the terrible snarl while the eyes fastened on her throat. Her heart had stopped in midbeat; and that day she ran back into the house and threw herself on her bed, and would not come from her room till the following morning.

Now, as she watched from the shadow of the house, with the basin of antiseptic under her arm, the gambler's desperation rose stronger and stronger. She came out, at length, and walked steadily toward Black Bart. She had grown almost heedless of fear at this moment, but when she was within a pace, once more the head reared back; the teeth flashed. And the heart of Kate Cumberland, as always, stopped. Yet she did not retreat this time. All the color left her face, so that her eyes seemed amazingly blue and wide. One foot drew back, tremblingly ready to spring to safety; yet she held her place. She moved —and it was toward Black Bart.

At that came a snarl that would have made the heart of a lonely grizzly quake and leave his new-found nuts. One further pace she made—and the beast plunged up, and braced itself with its one strong foreleg. A devil of yellow-green gleamed in either eye, and past the grinning fangs she saw the hot, red throat, and she saw the flattened ears, the scars on the bony forehead, the muscles that bulged on the base of the jaw. Ay, strength to drive those knife-like teeth through flesh and bone at a single snap. More—she had seen their effect, and the throat of a bull cut at a single slash. And yet—she sank on her knees beside the monster.

His head was well nigh as high as hers, then; if he attacked there could be no dream of escape for her. Or she might drag herself away from the tearing teeth—a disfigured horror forever. Think not that an iota of all these terrors missed her mind. No, she felt the fangs buried in her throat and heard the snarl of the beast stifled with blood. Yet—she laid her hand on the bandage across the shoulder of Black Bart.

His head whirled. With those ears flattened, with that long, lean neck, it was like the head of a striking snake. Her sleeve was rolled up to the elbow, and over the bare skin the teeth of the wolf dog were set. The snarl had grown so deep and hideous that the tremor of it fairly shook her, and she saw that the jaws of the beast slavered with hunger. She knew—a thousand things about Black Bart, and among the rest that he had tasted human blood. And there is a legend which says that once a wild beast has tasted the blood of man he will taste it a second time before he dies. She thought of that—she dared not turn her head lest she should encounter the hellfire of Bart's eyes. Yet she had passed all ordinary fear. She had reached that exquisite frenzy of terror when it becomes one with courage. The very arm over which the wolf's teeth were set moved—raised —and with both hands she untied the knot of the bandage.

The snarling rose to a pitch of maniacal rage; the teeth compressed—if they broke the skin it was the end; the first taste of blood would be enough!—and drew away her arm. If she had started then, all the devil in the creature would be loosed, for her terror taught her that. And by some mysterious power that entered her at that moment she was able to turn her head, slowly, and look deep into those terrible eyes.

Her arm was released.

But Black Bart crouched and the snakelike head lowered; he was quivering throughout that steel-muscled body to throw himself at her throat. The finger was on the hair-trigger; it needed a pressure not greater than a bodiless thought. And still she looked into the eyes of the wolf dog; and her terror had made her strangely light of body and dizzy of mind. Then the change came, suddenly. The yellow-green changed, swirled in the eyes of Black Bart; the eyes themselves wavered, and at last looked away; the snarl dropped to a sullen growl. And Black Bart lay down as he had been before.

His head was still turned toward her, to be sure. And the teeth were still bared, as with rapid, deft fingers she undid the bandage; and from instant to instant, as the bandage in spite of her care pressed against the wound, the beast shivered and wicked glances flashed up at her face. The safe-blower who finds his "soup" cooling and dares not set it down felt as Kate Cumberland felt then.

She never knew what kept her hands steady, but steady they were. The cloth was removed, and now she could see the red, angry wound, with the hair shaven away to a little distance on every side. She dipped her cloth into the antiseptic; it stung her fingers! She touched the cloth lightly against the wound; and to her astonishment the wolf dog relaxed every muscle and let his head fall to the ground; also the growl died into a soft whine, and this in turn ended.

She had conquered! Ay, when the wound was thoroughly cleansed and when she started to wind the bandage again, she had even the courage to touch Black Bart's body and make him rise up so that she could pass the cloth freely. At her touch he shuddered, to be sure, as a man might shudder at the touch of an unclean thing, but there was no snarl, and the teeth were not bared.

As she tied the knot which secured the bandage in its place she was aware that the eyes of Bart, no longer yellow-green, watched her; and she felt some vague movement of the wonder that was passing through the brute mind. Then the head of the wolf dog jerked up; he was staring at something in the distance, and there was nothing under heaven that Bart would raise his head to look at in this manner except one thing. The fingers of Kate grew stiff, and trembled. Slowly, in a panic, she finished the knot, and then she was aware of someone who had approached without sound and now stood behind her.

She looked up, at length, before she rose to her feet.

Thankfulness welled up warm in her heart to find her voice steady and commonplace when she said: "The wound is much better. Bart will be well in a very few days now."

Whistling Dan did not answer, and his wondering eyes glanced past her own. She saw that he was staring at a double row of white indentations on her forearm, where the teeth of Black Bart had set. He knew those marks, and she knew he knew. Strength was leaving her, and weakness went through her—water where blood should have been. She dared not stay. In another moment she would be hopelessly in the grip of hysteria.

So she rose, and passed Dan without a word, and went slowly toward the house. She tried to hurry, indeed, but her legs would not quicken their pace. Yet at length she had reached shelter and no sooner was she past the door of the house than her knees buckled; she had to steady herself with both hands as she dragged herself up the stairs to her room. There, from the window, she looked down and saw Whistling Dan standing as she had left him, staring blankly at the wolf dog.

27 · The Conquest

THERE was no star-storming confidence in Kate Cumberland after that first victory. Rather she felt as the general who deploys his skirmishers and drives in the outposts of an enemy. The advantage is his, but it has really only served to give him some intimation of the strength of the enemy. At the supper table this night she found Whistling Dan watching her—not openly, for she could never catch his eye—but subtly, secretly, she knew that he was measuring her, studying her; whether—in hostility, amity, or mere wonder, she could not tell. Finally a vast uneasiness overtook her and she turned to the doctor for relief. Doctor Randall Byrne held a singular position in the attention of Kate. Since the night of the fire and her open talk with him, the doctor knew "everything," and women are troubled in the presence of a man who knows the details of the past.

The shield behind which they hide in social intercourse is a touch of mystery—or at least a hope of mystery. The doctor, however, was not like other men; he was more similar to a precocious child and she comforted herself in his obvious talent for silence. If he had been alert, strong, self-confident, she might have hated him because he knew so much about her; but when she noted the pale, thoughtful face, the vast forehead outbalancing the other features, and the wistful, uncertain eyes, she felt nothing toward him stronger than pity.

It is good for a woman to have something which she may pity, a child, an aged parent, or a house-dog. It provides, in a way, the background against which she acts; so Kate, when in doubt, turned to the doctor, as on this night. There was a certain cruelty in it, for when she smiled at him the poor doctor became crimson, and when she talked to him his answers stumbled on his tongue; and when she was silent and merely looked at him that was worst of all, for he became unable to manage knife and fork and would sit crumbling bread and looking frightened. Then he was apt to draw out his glasses and make a move to place them on his nose, but he always caught and checked himself in time—which added to his embarrassment.

These small maneuvers had not lasted long before the girl became aware that the silent attention of Whistling Dan had passed from her to the doctor—and held steadily upon him. She did not go so far as to call it jealousy, but certainly it was a grave and serious consideration that measured the doctor up and down and back again; and it left her free to examine the two men in contrast. For the first time it struck her that they were much alike in many ways. Physically, for instance, there was the same slenderness, the same delicacy with which the details were finished; the same fragile hands, for instance. The distinction lay in a suggestion of strength and inexhaustible reserve of energy which Dan Barry possessed. The distinction lay still more in their faces. That of Byrne was worn and pallid from the long quest and struggle for truth; the body was feeble; the eyes were uncertain; but within there was a powerful machine which could work infallibly from the small to the large and the large to the small. With Whistling Dan there was no suggestion at all of mental care. She could not imagine him worrying over a problem. His knowledge was not even communicable by words; it was more impalpable than the instinct of a woman; and there was about him the wisdom and the coldness of Black Bart himself.

The supper ended too soon for Kate. She had been rallying Randall Byrne, and as soon as he could graciously leave, the poor fellow rose with a crimson face and left the room; and behind him, sauntering apparently in the most casual manner, went Whistling Dan. As for Kate Cumberland, she could not put all the inferences together—she dared not; but when she lay in her bed that night it was a long time before she could sleep, for there was a voice inside her, singing.

She chose her time the next day. Dan alternated between Black Bart and old Joe Cumberland during most of the day, and no sooner had he left the wolf dog in the morning than she went out to Bart.

As always, Black Bart lay with his head flattened against the sand, dreaming in the sun, and not an eyelid quivered when she approached, yet she understood perfectly that the animal knew every move she made. She would have attempted to dress the wound again, but the memory of the ordeal of yesterday was too terrible. She might break down in the midst of her effort, and the first sign of weakness, she knew, was the only spur which Black Bart needed. So she went, instead, to the chair where Dan often sat for hours near the dog, and there she took her place, folded her hands on her lap, and waited. She had no particular plan in mind, more than that she hoped to familiarize the great brute with the sight of her. Once he had known her well enough, but now he had forgotten all that passed before as completely, no doubt, as Whistling Dan himself had forgotten.

While she sat there, musing, she remembered a scene that had occurred not many a month before. She had been out walking one fall day, and had gone from the house down past the corrals where a number of cattle newly driven in from the range were penned. They were to be driven off for shipment the next day. A bellowing caught her ear from one of the enclosures and

she saw two bulls standing horn to horn, their heads
lowered, and their puffing and snorting breaths knocking
up the dust while they pawed the sand back in clouds
against their flanks. While she watched, they rushed together, bellowing, and for a moment they swayed back
and forth. It was an unequal battle, however, for one of
the animals was a hardened veteran, scarred from many
a battle on the range, while the other was a young three-
year-old with a body not half so strong as his heart.
For a short time he sustained the weight of the larger
bull, but eventually his knees buckled, and then dropped
heavily against the earth. At that the older bull drew
back a little and charged again. This time he avoided
the long horns of his rival and made the unprotected
flank of the animal his target. If he had charged squarely
the horns would have been buried to the head; but
striking at an angle only one of them touched the target
and delivered a long, ripping blow. With the blood
streaming down his side, the wounded bull made off into a group of cows, and when the victor pursued him
closely, he at length turned tail and leaped the low
fence—for the corral was a new one, hastily built for the
occasion. The conquerer raised his head inside the fence
and bellowed his triumph, and outside the fence the
other commenced pawing up the sand again, switching
his tail across his bleeding side, and turning his little red
eyes here and there. They fixed, at length, upon Kate
Cumberland, and she remembered with a start of horror
that she was wearing a bright red blouse. The next instant the bull was charging. She turned in a hopeless
flight. Safety was hundreds of yards away in the house;
the skirts tangled about her legs; and behind her the
dull impacts of the bull's hoofs swept close and closer.
Then she heard a snarl in front, a deep-throated, murderous snarl, and she saw Black Bart racing toward her.
He whizzed by her like a black thunderbolt; there was
a roar and bellow behind her, and at the same time she
stumbled over a fence-board and fell upon her knees.
But when she cast a glance of terror behind her she
saw the bull lying on its side with lolling tongue and
glazing eyes and the fangs of Black Bart were buried in
its throat.

When she reached this point in her musings her glance naturally turned toward the wolf dog, and she started violently when she saw that Bart was slinking toward her, trailing the helpless leg. The moment he felt her eyes upon him, Bart dropped down, motionless, with a wicked baring of his teeth; his eyes closed, and he seemed, as usual, dreaming in the sun.

Was the brute stalking her? It was worse, in a way, than the ordeal of the day before, this stealthy, noiseless approach. And in her panic she first thought of springing from her chair and reaching a distance which the chain would keep him from following. Yet it was very strange. Black Bart in his wildest days after Dan brought him to the ranch had never been prone to wantonly attack human beings. Infringe upon his right, come suddenly upon him, and then, indeed, there was a danger to all saving his master. But this daylight stalking was stranger than words could tell.

She forced her eyes to look straight ahead and sat with a beating heart, waiting. Then, by slow degrees, she let her glance travel cautiously back toward Bart without turning her head. There was no doubt about it! The great wolf dog was slinking toward her on his belly, still trailing the wounded foreleg. There was something snake-like in that slow approach, so silent and so gradual.

And yet she waited, moving neither hand nor foot.

A sort of nightmare paralysis held her, as when we flee from some horror in our dreams and find that our limbs have grown numb. Behind us races the deadly thing, closer and closer; before us is the door of safety—only a step to reach it—and yet we cannot move a foot!

It was not all pure terror. There was an incredible excitement as well—her will against the will of the dumb brute—which would conquer?

She heard a faint rustling of the sand beside her and could hardly keep from turning her head again. But she succeeded. Waves of coldness broke on her mind; her whole body would have shuddered had not fear chilled her into motionlessness. All reason told her that it was madness to sit there with the stealthy horror sliding closer; even now it might be too late. If she rose the shaggy form might spring from the ground at her. Perhaps the wolf had treasured up the pain from the day before and now—

A black form did, indeed, rise from the ground, but slowly. And standing on three legs, Bart stood a moment and stared in the face of the girl. The fear rushed out of her heart; and her face flushed hotly with relief. There was no enmity in the steady stare of the wolf dog. She could feel that even though she did not look. Something that Whistling Dan had said long before came to her: "Even a hoss and a dog, Kate, can get terrible lonesome."

Black Bart moved until he faced her directly. His ears were pricking in eagerness; she heard a snarl, but so low and muffled that there was hardly a threat in it; could it be a plea for attention? She would not look down to the sharp eyes, until a weight fell on her knees —it was the long, scarred head of the wolf! The joy that swelled in her was so great that it pained her like a grief.

She stretched out her hand, slowly, slowly toward that head. And Black Bart shrank and quivered, and his lips writhed back from the long, deadly teeth, and his snarl grew to a harsher, hoarser threat; still he did not remove his head, and he allowed the hand to touch him between the eyes and stroke the fur back to between the ears. Only one other hand had ever touched that formidable head in such a manner! The teeth no longer showed; the keen, suspicious eyes grew dim with pleasure; the snarl sank to a murmur and then died out.

"Bart!" commanded the girl, sharply.

The head jerked up, but the questing eyes did not look at her. He glanced over his shoulder to find the danger that had made her voice so hard. And she yearned to take the fierce head in her arms; there were tears she could have wept over it. He was snarling again, prepared already to battle, and for her sake.

"Bart!" she repeated, more gently. "Lie down!"

He turned his head slowly back to her and looked with the unspeakable wistfulness of the dumb brutes into her eyes. But there was only one voice in which Bart could speak, and that was the harsh, rattling snarl which would have made a mountain lion check itself in mid-leap and slink back to its lair. In such a voice he answered Kate, and then sank down, gradually. And he lay still.

So simply, and yet so mysteriously, she was admitted to the partnership. But though one member of that swift, grim trio had accepted her, did it mean that the other two would take her in?

A weight sank on her feet and when she looked down she saw that Black Bart had lowered his head upon them, and so he lay there with his eyes closed dreaming in the sun.

28 · The Trail

BANDAGES and antiseptics and constant care by themselves could not have healed Black Bart so swiftly, but nature took a strong hand. The wound closed with miraculous speed. Three days after he had laid his head on the feet of Kate Cumberland, the wolf dog was hobbling about on three legs and tugging now and again at the restraining chain; and the day after that the bandages were taken off and Whistling Dan decided that Bart might run loose. It was a brief ceremony, but a vital one. Doctor Byrne went out with Barry to watch the loosing of the dog; from the window of Joe Cumberland's room he and Kate observed what passed. There was little hesitancy in Black Bart. He merely paused to sniff the foot of Randall Byrne, snarl, and then trotted with a limp toward the corrals.

Here, in a small enclosure with rails much higher than the other corrals, stood Satan, and Black Bart made straight for the stallion. He was seen from afar, and the black horse stood waiting, his head thrown high in the air, his ears pricking forward, the tail flaunting, a picture of expectancy. So under the lower rail Bart slunk and stood under the head of Satan, growling terribly. Of this display of anger the stallion took not the slightest notice, but lowered his beautiful head until his velvet nose touched the cold muzzle of Bart. There was something ludicrous about the greeting—it was such an odd shade close to the human. It was as brief as it was strange, for Black Bart at once whirled and trotted away toward the barns.

By the time Doctor Byrne and Whistling Dan caught up with him, the wolf dog was before the heaps and ashes which marked the site of the burned barn. Among these white and gray and black heaps he picked his way, sniffing hastily here and there. In the very center of the place he sat down suddenly on his haunches, pointed his nose aloft, and wailed with tremendous dreariness.

"Now," murmured the doctor to Dan, "that strikes me as a singular manifestation of intelligence in an animal—he has found the site of the very barn where he was hurt—upon my word! Even fire doesn't affect his memory!"

Here he observed that the face of Whistling Dan had grown grim. He ran to Bart and crouched beside him, muttering; and Byrne heard.

"That's about where you was lyin'," said Dan, "and you smell your own blood on the ground. Keep tryin', Bart. They's something else to find around here."

The wolf dog looked his master full in the face with pricking ears, whined and then started off sniffling busily at the heaps of ashes.

"The shooting of the dog is quite a mystery," said Byrne, by way of conversation. "Do you suppose that one of the men from the bunkhouse could have shot him?"

But Dan seemed no longer aware of the doctor's presence. He slipped here and there with the wolf dog among the ash-heaps, pausing when Bart paused, talking to the brute continually. Sometimes he pointed out to Bart things which the doctor did not perceive and Bart whined with a terrible, slavering blood-eagerness.

The wolf dog suddenly left the ash-heaps and now darted in swiftly entangled lines here and there among the barns. Dan Barry stood thoughtfully still, but now and then he called a word of encouragement.

And Black Bart stayed with his work. Now he struck
out a wide circle, running always with his nose close to
the ground. Again he doubled back sharply to the barn-
site, and began again in a new direction. He ran swiftly,
sometimes putting his injured leg to the ground with
hardly a limp, and again drawing it up and running on
three feet. In a moment he passed out of sight behind
a slight rise of ground to the left of the ash-heaps, and
at some little distance. He did not reappear. Instead, a
long, shrill wail came wavering toward the doctor and
Dan Barry. It raised the hair on the head of the doctor
and sent a chill through his veins; but it sent Whistling
Dan racing toward the place behind which Black Bart
had disappeared. The doctor hurried after as fast as he
might and came upon the wolf dog making small, swift
circles, his nose to the ground, and then crossing to and
fro out of the circles. And the face of the master was
black while he watched. He ran again to Bart and began talking swiftly.

"D'you see?" he asked, pointing. "From behind this
here hill you could get a pretty good sight of the barn—
and you wouldn't be seen, hardly, from the barn. Someone must have waited here. Look about, Bart, you'll be
findin' a pile of signs, around here. It means that them
that done the shootin' and the firin' of the barn stood
right here behind this hilltop and watched the barn
burn—and was hopin' that Satan and you wouldn't ever
come out alive. That's the story."

He dropped to his knees and caught Bart as the big
dog ran by.

"Find 'em, Bart!" he whispered. "Find 'em!"

And he struck sharply on the scar where the bullet
had ploughed its way into Bart's flesh.

The answer of Bart was a yelp too sharp and too
highly pitched to have come from the throat of any
mere dog. Once more he darted out and ran here and
there, and Doctor Byrne heard the beast moaning as
it ran. Then Bart ceased circling and cut down the
slope away from the hill at a sharp trot.

A cry of inarticulate joy burst from Dan, and then:
"You've found it! You have it!" and the master ran
swiftly after the dog. He followed the latter only for a

short distance down the slope and then stood still and whistled. He had to repeat the call before the dog turned and ran back to his master, where he whined eagerly about the man's feet. There was something uncanny and horrible about it; it was as if the dumb beast was asking for a life, and the life of a man. The doctor turned back and walked thoughtfully to the house.

At the door he was met by Kate and a burst of eager questions, and he told, simply, all that he had seen.

"You'll get the details from Mr. Barry," he concluded.

"I know the details," answered the girl. "He's found the trail and he knows where it points, now. And he'll want to be following it before many hours have passed. Doctor Byrne, I need you now—terribly. You must convince Dan that if he leaves us it will be a positive danger to Dad. Can you do that?"

"At least," said the doctor, "there will be little deception in that. I will do what I can to persuade him to stay."

"Then," she said hurriedly, "sit here, and I shall sit here. We'll meet Dan together when he comes in."

They had hardly taken their places when Barry entered, the wolf at his heels; at the door he paused to flash a glance at them and then crossed the room. On the farther side he stopped again.

"I might be tellin' you," he said in his soft voice, "that now's Bart's well I got to be travelin' again. I start in the morning."

The pleading eyes of Kate raised Byrne to his feet.

"My dear Mr. Barry!" he called. The other turned again and waited. "Do you mean that you will leave us while Mr. Cumberland is in this critical condition?"

A shadow crossed the face of Barry.

"I'd stay if I could," he answered. "But it ain't possible!"

"What takes you away is your affair, sir," said the doctor. "My concern is Mr. Cumberland. He is in a very precarious condition. The slightest nerve shock may have—fatal—results."

Dan Barry sighed.

"Seemed to me," he answered, "that he was buckin' up considerable. Don't look so thin, doc."

"His body may be well enough," said the doctor calmly, "but his nerves are wrecked. I am afraid to prophesy the consequences if you leave him."

It was apparent that a great struggle was going on in Barry. He answered at length: "How long would I have to stay? One rain could wipe out all the sign and make me like a blind man in the desert. Doc, how long would I have to stay?"

"A few days," answered Byrne, "may work wonders with him."

The other hesitated.

"I'll go up and talk with him," he said, "and what he wants I'll do."

29 · Talk

HE was long in getting his answer. The hours dragged on slowly for Kate and the doctor, for if Joe Cumberland could hold Dan it was everything to the girl, and if Barry left at once there might be some root for the hope which was growing stronger and stronger every day in the heart of Randall Byrne. Before evening a not unwelcome diversion broke the suspense somewhat.

It was the arrival of no less a person than Marshal Jeff Calkins. His shoulders were humped and his short legs bowed from continual riding, and his head was slung far forward on a gaunt neck; so that when he turned his head from one to another in speaking it was with a peculiar pendulum motion. The marshal had a reputation which was strong over three hundred miles and more of a mountain-desert. This was strange, for the marshal was a very talkative man, and talkative men are not popular on the desert; but it had been discovered that on occasion his six-gun could speak as rapidly and much more accurately than his tongue. So Marshal Calkins waxed in favor.

He set the household at ease upon his arrival by announcing that "they hadn't nothin' for him there." All he wanted was a place to bunk in, some chow, and a feed for the horse. His trail led past the Cumberland Ranch many and many a dreary mile.

The marshal was a politic man, and he had early in life discovered that the best way to get along with any man was to meet him on his own ground. His opening blast of words at Doctor Byrne was a sample of his art.

"So you're a doc, hey? Well, sir, when I was a kid I had a colt that stuck its foreleg in a hole and busted it short and when that colt had to be shot they wasn't no holdin' me. No, sir, I could of cleaned up on the whole family. And ever since then I've had a hankerin' to be a doc. Something about the idea of cuttin' into a man that always sort of tickled me. They's only one main thing that holds me back—I don't like the idea of knifin' a feller when he ain't got a chance to fight back! That's me!"

To this Doctor Randall Byrne bowed, rather dazed, but returned no answer.

"And how's your patient, doc?" pursued the irresistible marshal. "How's old Joe Cumberland? I remember when me and Joe used to trot about the range together. I was sort of a kid then; but think of old Joe bein' down in bed—sick! Why, I ain't never been sick a day in my life. Sick? I'd laugh myse'f plumb to death if anybody ever wanted me to go to bed. What's the matter with him, anyway?"

"His nerves are a bit shaken about," responded the doctor. "To which I might add that there is superimposed an arterial condition——"

"Cut it short, doc," cried the marshal goodnaturedly. "I ain't got a dictionary handy. Nerves bad, eh? Well, I don't wonder about that. The old man's had enough trouble lately to make anybody nervous. I wouldn't like to go through it myself. No, sir! What with that Dan Barry—I ain't steppin' on any corns, Kate, am I?"

She smiled vaguely, but the marshal accepted the smile as a strong dissent.

"They was a time not so long ago when folks said that

you was kind of sweet on Dan. Glad to hear they ain't
nothin' in it. 'S a matter of fact——"

But here Kate interrupted with a raised hand. She
said: "I think that was the supper gong. Yes, there it is.
We'll go in now, if you wish."

"They's only one sound in the world that's better to
me than a dinner gong," said the profuse marshal, as
they seated themselves around the big dinner table, "and
that was the sound of my wife's voice when she said
'I will.' Queer thing, too. Maria ain't got a very soft
voice, most generally speakin', but when she busted up
in front of that preacher and says 'I will,' why, God
A'mighty—askin' your pardon, Kate—they was a change
come in her voice that was like a bell chimin' down in
her throat—a bell ringin' away off far, you know, so's you
only kind of guess at it! But comin' back to you and
Dan, Kate——"

It was in vain she plied the marshal with edibles. His
tongue wagged upon roller-bearings and knew no stop-
ping. Moreover, the marshal had spent some portion of
his life in a boarding house and had mastered the
boarding-house art of talking while he ate.

"Comin' back to you and Dan, we was all of us saying
that you and Dan kind of had an eye for each other.
I s'pose we was all wrong. You see, that was back in
the days before Dan busted loose. When he was about
the range most usually he was the quietest man I ever
sat opposite to barrin' one—and that was a feller that
went west with a bum heart at the chuck table! Ha,
ha, ha!" The marshal's laughter boomed through the big
room as he recalled this delightful anecdote. He went
on: "But after that Jim Silent play we all changed our
minds, some. D'you know, doc, I was in Elkhead the
night that Dan got our Lee Haines?"

"I've never heard of the episode," murmured the doctor.

"You ain't? Well, I be damned!—askin' your pardon,
Kate——But you sure ain't lived in these parts long!
Which you wouldn't think one man could ride into a
whole town, go to the jail, knock out two guards that
was proved men, take the keys, unlock the irons off'n
the man he wanted, saddle a hoss, and ride through a

whole town—full of folks that was shootin' at him. Now, would you think that was possible?"

"Certainly not."

"And it *ain't* possible, I'm here to state. But they was something different about Dan Barry. D'you ever notice it, Kate?"

She was far past speech.

"No, I guess you never would have noticed it. You was livin' too close to him all the time to see how different he was from other fellers. Anyway, he done it. They say he got plugged while he was ridin' through the lines and he bled all the way home, and he got there unconscious. Is that right, Kate?"

He waited an instant and then accepted the silence as an affirmative.

"Funny thing about that, too. The place where he come to was Buck Daniels' house. Well, Buck was one of Jim Silent's men, and they say Buck had tried to plug Dan before that. But Dan let him go that time, and when Buck seen Dan ride in all covered with blood he remembered that favor and he kept Dan safe from Jim Silent and safe from the law until Dan was well. I seen Buck this morning over to Rafferty's place, and——"

Here the marshal noted a singular look in the eyes of Kate Cumberland, a look so singular that he turned in his chair to follow it. He saw Dan Barry in the act of closing the door behind him, and Marshal Calkins turned a deep and violent red, varied instantly by a blotchy yellow which in turn faded to something as near white as his tan permitted.

"Dan Barry!" gasped the marshal, rising, and he reached automatically toward his hip before he remembered that he had laid his belt and guns aside before he entered the dining room, as etiquette is in the mountain-desert. For it is held that shooting at the table disturbs the appetite.

"Good evenin'," said Dan quietly. "Was it Buck Daniels that you seen at Rafferty's place, Marshal Calkins?"

"Him," nodded the marshal, hoarsely. "Yep, Buck Daniels."

And then he sank into his chair, silent for the first time. His eyes followed Barry as though hypnotized.

"I'm kind of glad to know where I can find him," said Barry, and took his place at the table.

The silence continued for a while, with all eyes focused on the newcomer. It was the doctor who had to speak first.

"You've talked things over with Mr. Cumberland?" he asked.

"We had a long talk," nodded Dan. "You was wrong about him, doc. He thinks he can do without me."

"What?" cried Kate.

"He thinks he can do without me," said Dan Barry. "We talked it all over."

The silence fell again. Kate Cumberland was staring blankly down at her plate, seeing nothing; and Doctor Byrne looked straight before him and felt the pulse drumming in his throat. His chance, then, was to come. By this time the marshal had recovered his breath.

He said to Dan: "Seems like you been away some time, Dan. Where you been hangin' out?"

"I been ridin' about," answered Dan vaguely.

"Well," chuckled the marshal, "I'm glad they ain't no more Jim Silents about these parts—not while you're here and while I'm here. You kept things kind of busy for Glasgow, Dan."

He turned to Kate, who had pushed back her chair.

"What's the matter, Kate?" he boomed. "You ain't lookin' any too tip-top. Sick?"

"I may be back in a moment," said the girl, "but don't delay supper for me."

She went out of the room with a step poised well enough, but the moment the door closed behind her she fairly staggered to the nearest chair and sank into it, her head fallen back, her eyes dim, and all the strength gone from her body and her will. Several minutes passed before she roused herself, and then it was to drag herself slowly up the stairs to the door of her father's room. She opened it without knocking, and then closed it and stood with her back against it, in the shadow.

30 • The Voice of Black Bart

HER father lay propped high with pillows among which his head lolled back. The only light in the room was near the bed and it cast a glow upon the face of Joe Cumberland and on the white linen, the white hair, the white, pointed beard. All the rest of the room swam in darkness. The chairs were blotches, indistinct, uncertain; even the foot of the bed trailed off to nothingness. It was like one of those impressionistic, very modern paintings, where the artist centers upon one point and throws the rest of his canvas into dull oblivion. The focus here was the face of the old cattleman. The bedclothes, never stirred, lay in folds sharply cut out with black shadows, and they had a solid seeming, as the mort-cloth rendered in marble over the effigy. That suggested weight exaggerated the frailty of the body beneath the clothes. Exhausted by that burden, the old man lay in the arms of a deadly languor, so that there was a kinship of more than blood between him and Kate at this moment. She stepped to the side of the bed and stood staring down at him, and there was little gentleness in her expression.

So cold was that settled gaze that her father stirred, at length, shivered, and without opening his eyes, fumbled at the bedspread and drew it a little more closely about his shoulders. Even that did not give him rest; and presently the wrinkled eyelids opened and he looked up at his daughter. A film of weariness heavier than sleep at first obscured his sight, but this in turn cleared away; he frowned a little to clear his vision, and then wagged his head slowly from side to side.

"Kate," he said feebly, "I done my best. It simply wasn't good enough."

She answered in a voice as low as his, but steadier: "What could have happened? Dad, what happened to make you give up every hold on Dan? What was it? You were the last power that could keep him here. You knew it. Why did you tell him he could go?"

The monotone was more deadly than any emphasis of a raised word.

"If you'd been here," pleaded Joe Cumberland, "you'd have done what I done. I couldn't help it. There he sat on the foot of the bed—see where them covers still kind of sag down—after he told me that he had something to do away from the ranch and that he wanted to go now that Black Bart was well enough to travel in short spells. He asked me if I still needed him."

"And you told him no?" she cried. "Oh Dad, you know it means everything to me—but you told him no?"

He raised a shaking hand to ward off the outburst and stop it.

"Not at first, honey. Gimme a chance to talk, Kate. At first I told him that I needed him—and God knows that I *do* need him. I dunno why—not even Doc Byrne knows what there is about Dan that helps me. I told Dan all them things. And he didn't say nothin', but jest sat still on the foot of the bed and looked at me.

"It ain't easy to bear his eyes, Kate. I lay here and tried at first to smile at him and talk about other things —but it ain't easy to bear his eyes. You take a dog, Kate. It ain't supposed to be able to look you in the eye for long; but s'pose you met up with a dog that could. It'd make you feel sort of queer inside. Which I felt that way while Dan was lookin' at me. Not that he was threatenin' me. No, it wasn't that. He was only thoughtful, but I kept gettin' more nervous and more fidgety. I felt after a while like I couldn't stand it. I had to crawl out of bed and begin walkin' up and down till I got quieter. But I seen that wouldn't do.

"Then I begun to think. I thought of near everything in a little while. I thought of what would happen s'pose Dan should stay here. Maybe you and him would get to like each other again. Maybe you'd get married. Then what would happen?

"I thought of the wild geese flyin' north in the spring o' the year and the wild geese flyin' south in the fall o' the year. And I thought of Dan with his heart follow-in' the wild geese—God knows why!—and I seen a picture of him standin' and watchin' them, with you nearby and not able to get one look out of him. I seen that, and it made my blood chilly, like the air on a frosty night.

"Kate, they's something like the power of prophecy that comes to a dyin' man!"

"Dad!" she cried. "What are you saying?"

She slipped to her knees beside the bed and drew his cold hands toward her, but Joe Cumberland shook his head and mildly drew one hand away. He raised it, with extended forefinger—a sign of infinite warning; and with the glow of the lamp full upon his face, the eyes were pits of shadow with stirring orbs of fire in the depths.

"No, I ain't dead now," he said, "but I ain't far away from it. Maybe days, maybe weeks, maybe whole months. But I've passed the top of the hill, and I know I'm ridin' down the slope. Pretty soon I'll finish the trail. But what little time I've got left is worth more'n everything that went before. I can see my life behind me and the things before like a cold mornin' light was over it all—you know before the sun begins to beat up the waves of heat and the mist gets tanglin' in front of your eyes? You know when you can look right across a thirty mile valley and name the trees, a'most the other side? That's the way I can see now. They ain't no feelin' about it. My body is all plumb paralyzed. I jest see and know—that's all.

"And what I see of you and Dan—if you ever marry— is plain—hell! Love ain't the only thing they is between a man and a woman. They's something else. I dunno what it is. But it's a sort of a common purpose; it's havin' both pairs of feet steppin' out on the same path. That's what it is. But your trail would go one way and Dan's would go another, and pretty soon your love wouldn't be nothin' but a big wind blowin' between two mountains—and all it would do would be to freeze up the blood in your hearts.

"I seen all that, while Dan was sittin' at the foot of the bed. Not that I don't want him here. When I see him I see the world the way it was when I was under thirty. When there wasn't nothin' I wouldn't try once, when all

I wanted was a gun and a hoss and a song to keep me from tradin' with kings. No, it ain't goin' to be easy for me when Dan goes away. But what's my tag-end of life compared with yours? You got to be given a chance; you got to be kept away from Dan. That's why I told him, finally, that I thought I could get along without him."

"Whether or not you save me," she answered, "you signed a death warrant for at least two men when you told him that."

"Two men? They's only one he's after—and Buck Daniels has had a long start. He can't be caught!"

"That Marshal Calkins is here tonight. He saw Buck at Rafferty's, and he talked about it in the hearing of Dan at the table. I watched Dan's face. You may read the past and see the future, Dad, but I know Dan's face. I can read it as the sailor reads the sea. Before tomorrow night Buck Daniels will be dead; and Dan's hands will be red."

She dropped her head against the bedclothes and clasped her fingers over the bright hair.

When she could speak again she raised her head and went on in the same swift, low monotone: "And besides, Black Bart has found the trail of the man who fired the barn and shot him. And the body of Buck won't be cold before Dan will be on the heels of the other man. Oh, Dad, two lives lay in the hollow of your hand. You could have saved them by merely asking Dan to stay with you; but you've thrown them away."

"Buck Daniels!" repeated the old man, the horror of the thing dawning on him only slowly. "Why didn't he get farther away? Why didn't he ride night and day after he left us? He's got to be warned that Dan is coming!"

"I've thought of that. I'm going into my room now to write a note and send it to Buck by one of our men. But at the most he'll have less than a day's start—and what is a day to Satan and Dan Barry?"

"I thought it was for the best," muttered old Joe. "I couldn't see how it was wrong. But I can send for Dan and tell him that I've changed my mind." He broke off in a groan. "No, that wouldn't be no good. He's set his mind on going by this time, and nothing can keep him back. But—Kate, maybe I can delay him. Has he gone up to his room yet?"

"He's in there now. Talk softly or he'll hear us. He's walking up and down, now."

"Ay, ay, ay!" nodded old Joe, his eyes widening with horror, "and his footfall is like the padding of a big cat. I could tell it out of a thousand steps. And I know what's going on inside his mind!"

"Yes, yes; he's thinking of the blow Buck Daniels struck him; he's thinking of the man who shot down Bart. God save them both!"

"Listen!" whispered the cattleman. "He's raised the window. I heard the rattle of the weights. He's standing there in front of the window, letting the wind of the night blow in his face!"

The wind from the window, indeed, struck against the door communicating with Joe Cumberland's room, and shook it as if a hand were rattling at the knob.

The girl began to speak again, as swiftly as before, her voice the barely audible rushing of a whisper: "The law will trail him, but I won't give him up. Dad, I'm going to fight once more to keep him here—and if I fail, I'll follow him around the world." Such words should have come loudly, ringing. Spoken so softly, they gave a terrible effect; like the ravings of delirium, or the monotone of insanity. And with the white light against her face she was more awe-inspiring than beautiful. "He loved me once; and the fire must still be in him; such fire *can't* go out, and I'll fan it back to life, and then if it burns me—if it burns us both—the fire itself cannot be more torture than to live on like this!"

"Hush, lass!" murmured her father. "Listen to what's coming!"

It was a moan, very low pitched, and then rising slowly, and gaining in volume, rising up the scale with a dizzy speed, till it burst and rang through the house—the long-drawn wail of a wolf when it hunts on a fresh trail.

31 · The Message

BUCK DANIELS opened his eyes and sat bolt-upright in bed. He had dreamed the dream again, and this time, as always, he awakened before the end. He needed no rubbing of eyes to rouse his senses. If a shower of cold water had been dashed upon him he could not have rallied from sound slumber so suddenly. His first movement was to snatch his gun from under his mattress, not that he dreamed of needing it, but for some reason the pressure of the butt against his palm was reassuring. It was better than the grip of his friend—a strong man.

It was the first gray of dawn, a light so feeble that it served merely to illuminate the darkness, so to speak. It fell with any power upon one thing alone, the bit of an old, dusty bridle that hung against the wall, and it made the steel glitter like a watchful eye. There was a great dryness in the throat of Buck Daniels; and his whole big body shook with the pounding of his heart.

He was not the only thing that was awake in the gray hour. For now he caught a faint and regular creaking of the stairs. Someone was mounting with an excessively cautious and patient step, for usually the crazy stairs that led up to this garret room of the Rafferty house creaked and groaned a protest at every footfall. Now the footfall paused at the head of the stairs, as when one stops to listen.

Buck Daniels raised his revolver and levelled it on the door; but his hand was shaking so terribly that he could not keep his aim—the muzzle kept veering back and forth across the door. He seized his right hand with his left, and crushed it with a desperate pressure. Then it was better. The quivering of the two hands counteracted each other and he managed to keep some sort of a bead.

Now the step continued again, down the short hall. A hand fell on the knob of the door and pressed it slowly open. Against the deeper blackness of the hall beyond, Buck saw a tall figure, hatless. His finger curved about the trigger, and still he did not fire. Even to his hysterical brain it occurred that Dan Barry would be wearing a hat—and moreover the form was tall.

"Buck!" called a guarded voice.

The muzzle of Daniels' revolver dropped; he threw the gun on his bed and stood up.

"Jim Rafferty!" he cried, with something like a groan in his voice. "What in the name of God are you doin' here at this hour?"

"Someone come here and banged on the door a while ago. Had a letter for you. Must have rid a long ways and come fast; while he was givin' me the letter at the door I heard his hoss pantin' outside. He wouldn't stay, but went right back. Here's the letter, Buck. Hope it ain't no bad news. Got a light here, ain't you?"

"All right, Jim," answered Buck Daniels, taking the letter. "I got a lantern. You get back to bed."

The other replied with a noisy yawn and left the room while Buck kindled the lantern. By that light he read his name upon the envelope and tore it open. It was very brief.

"Dear Buck,
    Last night at supper Dan found out where you are. In the morning he's leaving the ranch and we know that he intends to ride for Rafferty's place; he'll probably be there before noon. The moment you get this, saddle your horse and ride. Oh, Buck, why did you stay so close to us?
    Relay your horses. Don't stop until you're over the mountains. Black Bart is well enough to take the trail and Dan will use him to follow you. You know what that means.
    Ride, ride, ride!

                                        Kate."

He crumpled up the paper and sank back upon the bed.

"Why did you stay so close?"

He had wondered at that, himself, many times in the

past few days. Like the hunted rabbit, he expected to find safety under the very nose of danger. Now that he was discovered it seemed incredible that he could have followed so patently foolish a course. In a sort of daze he uncrumpled the note again and read the wrinkled writing word by word. He had leaned close to read by the uncertain light, and now he caught the faintest breath of perfume from the paper. It was a small thing, smaller among scents than a whisper is among voices, but it made Buck Daniels drop his head and crush the paper against his face. It was a moment before he could uncrumple the paper sufficiently to study the contents of the note thoroughly. At first his dazed brain caught only part of the significance. Then it dawned on him that the girl thought he had fled from the Cumberland Ranch through fear of Dan Barry.

Ay, there had been fear in it. Every day at the ranch he had shuddered at the thought that the destroyer might ride up on that devil of black silken grace, Satan. But every day he had convinced himself that even then Dan Barry remembered the past and was cursing himself for the ingratitude he had shown his old friend. Now the truth swept coldly home to Buck Daniels. Barry was as fierce as ever upon the trail; and Kate Cumberland thought that he—Buck Daniels—had fled like a cur from danger.

He seized his head between his hands and beat his knuckles against the corrugated flesh of his forehead. She had thought that!

Desire for action, action, action, beset him like thirst. To close with this devil, this wolf-man, to set his big fingers in the smooth, almost girlish throat, to choke the yellow light out of those eyes—or else to die, but like a man proving his manhood before the girl.

He read the letter again and then in an agony he crumpled it to a ball and hurled it across the room. Catching up his hat and his belt he rushed wildly from the room, thundered down the crazy stairs, and out to the stable.

Long Bess, the tall, bay mare which had carried him through three years of adventure and danger and never failed him yet, raised her aristocratic head above the side of the stall and whinnied. For answer he shook his fist at her and cursed insanely.

The saddle he jerked by one stirrup leather from the wall and flung it on her back, and when she cringed to the far side of the stall, he cursed her again, bitterly, and drew up the cinch with a lunge that made her groan. He did not wait to lead her to the door before mounting, but sprang into the saddle.

Here he whirled her about and drove home the spurs. Cruel usage, for Long Bess had never denied him the utmost of her speed and strength at the mere sound of his voice. Now, half mad with fear and surprise, she sprang forward at full gallop, slipped and almost sprawled on the floor, and then thundered out of the door.

At once the soft sandy soil received and deadened the impact of her hoofs. Off she flew through the gray of the morning, soundless as a racing ghost.

Long Bess—there was good blood in her. She was as delicately limbed as an antelope, and her heart was as strong as the smooth muscles of her shoulders and hips. Yet to Buck Daniels her fastest gait seemed slower than a walk. Already his thoughts were flying far before. Already he stood before the ranch house calling to Dan Barry. Ay, at the very door of the place they should meet and one of them must die. And better by far that the blood of him who died should stain the hands of Kate Cumberland.

32 · Victory

THE gray light which Buck Daniels saw that morning hardly brightened as the day grew, for the sky was overcast with sheeted mist and through it a dull evening radiance filtered to the earth. Wung Lu, his celestial, slant eyes now yellow with cold, built a fire on the big hearth in the living room. It was a roaring blaze, for the wood was so dry that it flamed as though soaked in oil, and tumbled a mass of yellow fire up the chimney. So bright was the fire, indeed, that its light quite overshadowed the meager day which looked in at the window, and every chair cast its shadow away from the hearth. Later on Kate Cumberland came down the backstairs and slipped into the kitchen.

"Have you seen Dan?" she asked of the cook.

"Wung Lu make nice fire," grinned the Chinaman. "Misser Dan in there."

She thought for an instant.

"Is breakfast ready, Wung?"

"Pretty soon quick," nodded Wung Lu.

"Then throw out the coffee or the eggs," she said quickly. "I don't want breakfast served yet; wait till I send you word."

As the door closed behind her, the eyebrows of Wung rose into perfect Roman arches.

"Ho!" grunted Wung Lu, "O ho!"

In the hall Kate met Randall Byrne coming down the stairs. He was dressed in white and he had found a little yellow wildflower and stuck it in his buttonhole. He seemed ten years younger than the day he rode with her to the ranch, and now he came to her with a quick step, smiling.

"Doctor Byrne," she said quietly, "breakfast will be late this morning. Also, I want no one to go into the living room for a while. Will you keep them out?"

"He hasn't gone, yet?" he queried.

"Not yet."

The doctor sighed and then, apparently following an impulse, he reached his hand to her.

"I hope something comes of it," he said.

Even then she could not help a wan smile.

"What do you mean by that, doctor?"

The doctor sighed again.

"If the inference is not clear," he said, "I'm afraid that I cannot explain. But I'll try to keep everyone from the room."

The doctor was instantly gone.

She nodded her thanks, and went on; but passing the mirror in the hall the sight of her face made her

stop abruptly. There was no vestige of color in it; and
the shadow beneath her eyes made them seem in-
humanly large and deep. The bright hair, to be sure,
waved over her head and coiled on her neck, but it was
like a futile shaft of sunlight falling on a dreary moor
in winter. She went on thoughtfully to the door of the
living room but there she paused again with her hand
upon the knob; and while she stood there she remembered herself as she had been only a few months before, with the color flushing in her face and a continual
light in her eyes. There had been little need for thinking then. One had only to let the wind and the sun
strike on one, and live. Then, in a quiet despair, she said
to herself: "As I am—I must win or lose—as I am!" and
she opened the door and stepped in.

She had been cold with fear and excitement when
she entered the room to make her last stand for happiness, but once she was in, it was not so hard. Dan
Barry lay on the couch at the far end of the room with
his hands thrown under his head, and he was smiling
in a way which she well knew; it had been a danger
signal in the old days, and when he turned his face and
said good morning to her, she caught that singular glimmer of yellow which sometimes came up behind his eyes.
In reply to his greeting she merely nodded, and then
walked slowly to the window and turned her back to
him.

It was a one-tone landscape. Sky, hills, barns, earth,
all was a single mass of lifeless gray; in such an atmosphere old Homer had seen the wraiths of his dead he-
roes play again at the things they had done on earth.
She noted these things with a blank eye, for a thousand thoughts were leaping through her mind. Something
must be done. There he lay in the same room with her.
He had turned his head back, no doubt, and was staring at the ceiling as before, and the yellow glimmer was
in his eyes again. Perhaps, after this day, she should
never see him again; every moment was precious beyond
the price of gold, and yet there she stood at the window, doing nothing. But what *could* she do?

Should she go to him and fall on her knees beside
him and pour out her heart, telling him again of the old

days. No, it would be like striking on a wooden bell; no echo would rise; and she knew beforehand the deadly blackness of his eyes. So Black Bart lay often in the sun, staring at infinite distance and seeing nothing but his dreams of battle. What were appeals and what were words to Black Bart? What were they to Dan Barry? Yet once, by sitting still—the thought made her blood leap with a great, joyous pulse that set her cheeks tingling.

She waited till the first impulse of excitement had subsided, and then turned back and sat down in a chair near the fire. From a corner of her eye she was aware that Whistling Dan had turned his head again to await her first speech. Then she fixed her gaze on the wall of yellow flame. The impulse to speak to him was like a hand tugging to turn her around, and the words came up and swelled in her throat, but still she would not stir.

In a moment of rationality she felt in an overwhelming wave of mental coldness the folly of her course, but she shut out the thought with a slight shudder. Silence, to Dan Barry, had a louder voice and more meaning than any words.

Then she knew that he was sitting up on the couch. Was he about to stand up and walk out of the room? For moment after moment he did not stir; and at length she knew, with a breathless certainty, that he was staring fixedly at her! The hand which was farthest from him, and hidden, she gripped hard upon the arm of the chair. That was some comfort, some added strength.

She had now the same emotion she had had when Black Bart slunk toward her under the tree—if a single perceptible tremor shook her, if she showed the slightest awareness of the subtle approach, she was undone. It was only her apparent unconsciousness which could draw either the wolf dog or the master.

She remembered what her father had told her of hunting young deer—how he had lain in the grass and thrust up a leg above the grass in sight of the deer and how they would first run away but finally come back step by step, drawn by an invincible curiosity, until at length they were within range for a point blank shot.

Now she must concentrate on the flames of the fireplace, see nothing but them, think of nothing but the swiftly changing domes and walls and pinnacles they made. She leaned a little forward and rested her cheek upon her right hand—and thereby she shut out the sight of Dan Barry effectually. Also it made a brace to keep her from turning her head toward him, and she needed every support, physical and mental.

Still he did not move. Was he in truth looking at her, or was he staring beyond her at the gray sky which lowered past the window? The faintest creaking sound told her that he had risen, slowly, from the couch. Then not a sound, except that she knew, in some mysterious manner, that he moved, but whether toward her or toward the door she could not dream. But he stepped suddenly and noiselessly into the range of her vision and sat down on a low bench at one side of the hearth. If the strain had been tense before, it now became terrible; for there he sat almost facing her, and looking intently at her, yet she must keep all awareness of him out of her eyes. In the excitement a strong pulse began to beat in the hollow of her throat, as if her heart were rising. She had won, she had kept him in the room, she had brought him to a keen thought of her. A Pyrrhic victory, for she was poised on the very edge of a cliff of hysteria. She began to feel a tremor of the hand which supported her cheek. If that should become visible to him he would instantly know that all her apparent unconsciousness was a sham, and then she would have lost him truly!

Something sounded at one of the doors—and then the door opened softly. She was almost glad of the interruption, for another instant might have swept away the last reserve of her strength. So this, then, was the end.

But the footfall which sounded in the apartment was a soft padding step, with a little scratching sound, light as a finger running on a frosty window pane. And then a long, shaggy head slipped close to Whistling Dan. It was Black Bart!

A wave of terror swept through her. She remembered another scene, not many months before, when Black Bart had drawn his master away from her and led him south, south, after the wild geese. The wolf dog had come again like a demoniac spirit to undo her plans!

Only an instant—the crisis of a battle—then the great beast turned slowly, faced her, slunk with his long stride closer, and then a cold nose touched the hand which gripped the arm of her chair. It gave her a welcome excuse for action of some sort; she reached out her hand, slowly, and touched the forehead of Black Bart. He winced back, and the long fangs flashed; her hand remained tremulously poised in air, and then the long head approached again, cautiously, and once more she touched it, and since it did not stir, she trailed the tips of her fingers backwards toward the ears. Black Bart snarled again, but it was a sound so subdued as to be almost like the purring of a great cat. He sank down, and the weight of his head came upon her feet. Victory!

In the full tide of conscious power she was able to drop her hand from her face, raise her head, turn her glance carelessly upon Dan Barry; she was met by ominously glowing eyes. Anger—at least it was not indifference.

He rose and stepped in his noiseless way behind her, but he reappeared instantly on the other side, and reached out his hand to where her fingers trailed limp from the arm of the chair. There he let them lie, white and cool, against the darkness of his palm. It was as if he sought in the hand for the secret of her power over the wolf dog. She let her head rest against the back of the chair and watched the nervous and sinewy hand upon which her own rested. She had seen those hands fixed in the throat of Black Bart himself, once upon a time. A grim simile came to her; the tips of her fingers touched the paw of the panther. The steel-sharp claws were sheathed, but suppose once they were bared, and clutched. Or she stood touching a switch which might loose, by the slightest motion, a terrific voltage. What would happen?

Nothing! Presently the hand released her fingers, and Dan Barry stepped back and stood with folded arms, frowning at the fire. In the weakness which overcame her, in the grip of the wild excitement, she dared not stay near him longer. She rose and walked into the dining room.

"Serve breakfast now, Wung," she commanded, and at once the gong was struck by the cook.

Before the long vibrations had died away the guests were gathered around the table, and the noisy marshal was the first to come. He slammed back a chair and sat down with a grunt of expectancy.

"Mornin', Dan," he said, whetting his knife across the tablecloth, "I hear you're ridin' this mornin'? Ain't going my way, are you?"

Dan Barry sat frowning steadily down at the table. It was a moment before he answered.

"I ain't leavin'," he said softly, at length. "Postponed my trip."

33 • Doctor Byrne Shows the Truth

On this day of low-lying mists, this day so dull that not a shadow was cast by tree or house or man, there was no graver place than the room of old Joe Cumberland; even lamp light was more merciful in the room, for it left the corners of the big apartment in obscurity, but this meager daylight stripped away all illusion and left the room naked and ugly. Those colors of wall and carpet, once brighter than spring, showed now as faded and lifeless as foliage in the dead days of late November when the leaves have no life except what keeps them clinging to the twig, and when their fallen fellows are lifted and rustled on the ground by every faint wind, with a sound like breathing in the forest. And like autumn, too, was the face of Joe Cumberland, with a color neither flushed nor pale, but a dull sallow which foretells death. Beside his bed sat Doctor Randall Byrne and kept the pressure of two fingers upon the wrist of the rancher.

When he removed the thermometer from between the lips of Cumberland the old man spoke, but without lifting his closed eyelids, as if even this were an effort which he could only accomplish by a great concentration of the will.

"No fever today, doc?"

"You feel a little better?" asked Byrne.

"They ain't no feelin'. But I ain't hot; jest sort of middlin' cold."

Doctor Byrne glanced down at the thermometer with a frown, and then shook down the mercury.

"No," he admitted, "there is no fever."

Joe Cumberland opened his eyes a trifle and peered up at Byrne.

"You ain't satisfied, doc?"

Doctor Randall Byrne was of that merciless modern school which believes in acquainting the patient with the truth.

"I am not," he said.

"H-m-m!" murmured the sick man. "And what might be wrong?"

"Your pulse is uneven and weak," said the doctor.

"I been feelin' sort of weak since I seen Dan last night," admitted the other. "But that news Kate brought me will bring me up! She's kept him here, lad, think of that!"

"I am thinking of it," answered the doctor coldly. "Your last interview with him nearly—killed you. If you see him again I shall wash my hands of the case. When he first came you felt better at once—in fact, I admit you *seemed* to do better both in body and mind. But the thing could not last. It was a false stimulus, and when the first effects had passed away, it left you in this condition. Mr. Cumberland, you must see him no more!"

But Joe Cumberland laughed long and softly.

"Life," he murmured, "ain't worth that much! Not half!"

"I can do no more than advise," said the doctor, as reserved as before. "I cannot command."

"A bit peeved, doc?" queried the old man. "Well, sir, I know they ain't much longer for me. Lord, man, I can feel myself going out like a flame in a lamp when the oil runs up. I can feel life jest makin' its last few jumps in me like the flame up the chimney. But listen to me——" he reached out a long, large knuckled, claw-like hand and drew the doctor down over him, and his eyes were earnest—"I got to live till I see 'em standin' here before me, hand in hand, doc!"

The doctor, even by that dim light, had changed color. He passed his hand slowly across his forehead.

"You expect to see that?"

"I expect nothin'. I only hope!"

The bitterness of Byrne's heart came up in his throat.

"It will be an oddly suited match," he said, "if they marry. But they will not marry."

"Ha!" cried Cumberland, and starting up in bed he braced himself on a quaking elbow. "What's that?"

"Lie down!" ordered the doctor, and pressed the ranchman back against the pillows.

"But what d'you mean?"

"It would be a long story—the scientific explanation."

"Doc, where Dan is concerned I got more patience than Job."

"In brief, then, I will prove to you that there is no mystery in this Daniel Barry."

"If you can do that, doc, you're more of a man than I been guessing you for. Start now!"

"In primitive times," said Doctor Randall Byrne, "man was nearly related to what we now call the lower animals. In those days he could not surround himself with an artificial protective environment. He depended on the unassisted strength of his body. His muscular and sensory development, therefore, was far in advance of that of the modern man. For modern man has used his mind at the expense of his body. The very *quality* of his muscles is altered; and the senses of sight and hearing, for instance, are much blunted. For in the primitive days the ear kept guard over man even when he slept in terror of a thousand deadly enemies, each stronger than he; and the eye had to be keenly attuned to probe the shadows of the forest for lurking foes.

"Now, sir, there is in biology the thing known as the sport. You will have heard that all living organisms undergo gradual processes of change. Season by season and year by year, environment affects the individual; yet these gradual changes are extremely slow. Between steps of noticeable change there elapse periods many times longer than the life of historic man. All speed in changes such as these comes in what we call 'sports.' That is, a particular plant, for instance, gradually tends to have fewer leaves and a thicker bark, but the change is slight from age to age until suddenly a single instance occurs of a plant which realizes suddenly in a single step the 'ideal' toward which the species has been striving. In a word, it has very, very few leaves, and an extraordinarily thick bark.

"For a particular instance, one species of orange tended to have few and fewer seeds. But finally came an orange tree whose fruit had no seeds at all. That was the origin of the navel orange. And that was a typical 'sport.'

"Now, there is the reverse of the sport. Instead of jumping a long distance ahead, an individual may lapse back toward the primitive. That individual is called an atavism. For instance, in this mountain-desert there has, for several generations, been a pressure of environment calling for a species of man which will be able to live with comparative comfort in a waste region—a man, in a word, equipped with such powerful organisms that he will be as much at home in the heart of the desert as an ordinary man would be in a drawing room. You gather the drift of my argument.

"I have observed this man Barry carefully. I am thoroughly convinced that he is such an atavism. Among other men he seems strange. He is different and therefore he seems mysterious. As a matter of fact, he is quite a common freak. I could name you others like him in differing from common men, though not differing from them in exactly the same manner.

"You see the result of this? Daniel Barry is a man to whom the desert is necessary, because he was made for the desert. He is lonely among crowds—you have said it yourself—but he is at home in a mountain wilderness with a horse and a dog."

"Doc, you talk well," broke in Joe Cumberland, "but if he ain't human, why do humans like him so much? Why does he mean so much to me—to Kate?"

"Simply because he is different. You get from him what you could get from no other man in the world, perhaps, and you fail to see that the fellow is really more akin to his wolf dog than he is to a man."

"Supposin' I said you was right," murmured the old man, frowning, "how d'you explain why he likes other folks? According to you, the desert and the mountains and animals is what he wants. Then how is it that he took so much care of me when he come back this time? How is it that he likes Kate enough to give up a trail of blood to stay here with her?"

"It is easy to explain the girl's attraction," said the doctor. "All animals wish to mate, Mr. Cumberland, and an age old instinct is now working out in Dan Barry. But while you and Kate may please him, you are not necessary to him. He left you once before and he was quite happy in his desert. And I tell you, Mr. Cumberland, that he will leave you again. You cannot tame the untameable. It is not habit that rules this man. It is instinct a million years old. The call which he will hear is the call of the wilderness, and to answer it he will leave father and wife and children and ride out with his horse and his dog!"

The old man lay quite motionless, staring at the ceiling.

"I don't want to believe you," he said slowly, "but before God I think you're right. Oh, lad, why was I bound up in a tangle like this one? And Kate—what will she do?"

The doctor was quivering with excitement.

"Let the man stay with her. In time she will come to see the brute nature of Daniel Barry. That will be the end of him with her."

"Brute. Doc. They ain't nobody as gentle as Dan!"

"Till he tastes blood, a lion can be raised like a house-dog," answered the doctor.

"Then she mustn't marry him? Ay, I've felt it—jest what you've put in words. It's livin' death for Kate if she marries him! She's kept him here today. Tomorrow something may cross him, and the minute he feels the pull of it, he'll be off on the trail—the blow of a man, the hollering out of the wild geese—God knows what it'll take to start him wild again and forget us all—jest the way a child forgets its parents!"

A voice broke in upon them, calling far away: "Dan! Dan Barry!"

34 · The Acid Test

IN the living room below they heard it, Dan and Kate Cumberland. All day she had sat by the fire which still blazed on the hearth, replenished from time to time by the care of Wung Lu. She had taken up some sewing, and she worked at it steadily. Some of that time Dan Barry was in the room, sitting through long intervals, watching her with lynx-eyed attention. Very rarely did he speak—almost never, and she could have numbered upon her two hands the words he had spoken—ay, and she could have repeated them one by one. Now and again he rose and went out, and the wolf dog went with him each time. But toward the last Black Bart preferred to stay in the room, crouched in front of her and blinking at the fire, as if he knew that each time his master would return to the fire. Then, why leave the pleasant warmth for the chilly grayness of the day outside?

There he remained, stirring only now and then to lift a clumsy paw and brush it across his eyes in an oddly human gesture. Once or twice, also, he lifted the great, scarred head and slid it on her knees, looking curiously from her busy hands to her face, and from her face back again to her work, until, having apparently assured himself that all was well, he dropped his head again and lay once more motionless. She could see him open a listless eye when the master entered the room again. And with each coming of Dan Barry she felt again surrounded as if by invisible arms. Something was prying at her, striving to win a secret from her.

As the day wore on, a great, singing happiness rose in her throat, and at about the same time she heard a faint sound, impalpable, from the farther side of the room where Dan Barry sat. He was whistling.

A simple thing for a man to do, to be sure, but the astonishment of it nearly stopped the heart of Kate Cumberland. For in all her life she had never before heard him whistle except when he was in the open, and preferably when he was astride of the strength and the speed of Satan, with Black Bart scouting swiftly and smoothly ahead. But now he whistled here by the warmth of the fire. To be sure the sound was small and thin, but there was such music in it as she had never heard before. It was so thin that it was almost ghostly, as if the soul of wild Paganini played here on a muted violin. No tune that might be repeated, but as always when she heard it, a picture rose before the eyes of Kate. It wavered at first against the yellow glow of the firelight. Then it quite shut out all else.

It was deep night, starry night. The black horse and his rider wound up a deep ravine. To one side a bold mountain tumbled up to an infinite height, bristling with misshapen trees here and there, and losing its head against the very stars. On the other side were jagged hills, all carved in the solid rock. And down the valley, between the mountains and the stars, blew a soft wind; as if that wind made the music. They were climbing up, up, up, and now they reached—the music rising also to a soft but triumphant outburst—a high plateau. They were pressed up against the heart of the sky. The stars burned low, and low. Around them the whole earth seemed in prospect at their feet. The moon burst through a mass of clouds, and she saw, far off, a great river running silver through the night.

Happy? Ay, and he was happy too, and his happiness was one with hers. He was not even looking out the window while he whistled, but his eyes were fixed steadily, unchangingly, upon her face.

It was then that they heard it: "Dan! Dan Barry! Come out!"

A hoarse, ringing cry, as of one who is shouting against a great wind: "Dan! Dan Barry! Come out!"

Dan Barry was on his feet and gliding to the wall, where he took down his belt from a nail and buckled it swiftly around him. And Kate ran to the window with the wolf dog snarling beside her and saw standing in front of the house, his hat off, his black hair wildly tumbled, and two guns in his hands, Buck Daniels! Behind him the tall bay mare shook with her panting and glistened with the sweat of the long ride.

She heard a scratching next and saw the wolf dog rear up and paw at the door. Once through that door and he would be at the throat of the man outside, she knew. Nor he alone, for Dan Barry was coming swiftly across the room with that strange, padding step. He had no eye for her. He was smiling, and she had rather have seen him in a cursing fury than to see this smile. It curled the upper lip with something like a sneer; and she caught the white glint of his teeth; the wolf dog snarled back over his shoulder to hurry his master. It was the crisis which she had known all day was coming, sooner or later. She had only prayed that it might be delayed for a little time. And confronting the danger was like stepping into the path of runaway horses. Fear ruled her with an iron hand, and she swayed back against the wall and supported herself with an outstretched hand.

What was there to be done? If she stepped in between him and his man, he would brush her aside from his path and out of his life forever. If he went on to his vengeance he would no less be started on the path which led around the world away from her. The law would be the hound which pursued him and relentlessly nipped at his heels—an eternal terror and unrest. No thought of Buck Daniels who had done so much for her. She cast his services out of her mind with the natural cruelty of woman. Her whole thought was, selfishly, for the man before her, and for herself.

He was there—his hand was upon the knob of the door. And then she remembered how the teeth of Black Bart had closed over her arm—and how they had not broken even the skin. In an instant she was pressed against the door before Dan Barry—her arms outstretched.

He fell back the slightest bit before her, and then he came again and brushed her slowly, gently, to one side, with an irresistible strength. She had to meet his eyes

now—there was no help for it—and she saw there that
swirl of yellow light—that insatiable hunger. And she
knew, fully and bitterly, that she had failed. With the
wolf dog, indeed, she had conquered, but the man escaped her. If time had been granted her she would have
won, she knew, but the hand of Buck Daniels, so long
her ally, had destroyed her chances. It was his hand now
which shook the knob of the door, and she turned with
a sob of despair to face the new danger.

In her wildest dreams she had never visioned Buck
Daniels transformed like this. She knew that in his past,
as one of those long-riders who roam the mountain-
desert, their hands against the hands of every man, Buck
Daniels had been known and feared by the strongest.
But all she had seen of Buck Daniels had been gentleness itself. Yet what faced her as the door flew wide
was a nightmare thing with haggard face and shadow-
buried, glittering eyes—unshaven, unkempt of hair, his
shirt open at the throat, his great hands clenched for
the battle. The wolf dog, at that familiar sight, whined
a low greeting, but with a glance at his master knew
that there was a change—the old alliance was broken—
so he bared his white teeth and changed his whine to
a snarl of hate.

Then a strange terror struck Kate Cumberland. She
had never dreamed that she could fear for Dan Barry
at the hands of any man, but now the desperate resolve
which breathed from every line of Buck Daniels chilled
her blood at the heart. She sprang back before Dan
Barry. Facing him, she saw that demoniac glitter of yellow rising momently brighter in his eyes, and he was
smiling. No execration or loud voiced curse could have
contained the distilled malignancy of that smile. All this
she caught in a single glimpse. The next instant she had
whirled and stood before Dan, shielding him with outspread arms and facing Buck Daniels. The latter thrust
back into the holster the gun which he had drawn when
he entered the room.

"Stand away from him, Kate," he commanded, and
his eyes went past her to dwell on the face of Barry.
"Stand away from him. It's been comin' for a long time,
and now it's here. Barry, I'm takin' no start on you. Stand

away from the girl and pull your gun—and I'll pump you full of lead."

The softest of soft voices murmured behind her: "I been waitin' for you, Buck, days and days and days. I ain't never been so glad to see anybody!"

And she felt Barry slip shadowlike to one side. She sprang in front of him again with a wild cry.

"Buck!" she begged, "don't shoot!"

Laughter, ringing and unhuman, filled the throat of Buck Daniels.

"Is it him you're beggin' for?" he sneered at her. "Is it him you got your fears for? Ain't you got a word of pity for poor Buck Daniels that sneaked off like a whipped puppy? Bah! Dan Barry, the time is come. I been leadin' the life of a houn' dog for your sake. But it's ended. Pull your gun and get out from behind the skirts of that girl!"

As long as they faced each other with the challenge in their eyes, nothing on earth could avert the fight, she knew, but if she could delay them for one moment—she felt that swift moving form behind her slipping away from behind her—she could follow Barry's movements by the light in Daniels' eyes.

"Buck!" she cried, "for God's sake—for my sake turn away from him—and—roll another cigarette!"

For she remembered the story—how Daniels had turned under the very nose of danger and done this insane thing in the saloon at Brownsville and in her despair she could think of no other appeal.

It was the very strangeness of it that gave it point. Buck Daniels turned on his heel.

"It's the last kindness I do you, Dan," he said, with his broad back to them. "But before you die you got to know why I'm killin' you. I'm going to roll one cigarette and smoke it and while I smoke it I'm goin' to tell you the concentrated truth about your worthless self and when I'm done smokin' I'm goin' to turn around and drop you where you stand. D'ye hear?"

"They's no need of waitin'," answered the soft voice of Barry. "Talkin' don't mean much."

But Kate Cumberland turned and faced him. He was fairly a-quiver with eagerness and the hate welled and blazed and flickered in his eyes; his face was pale—very pale—and it seemed to her that she could make out in the pallor the print of the fingers of Buck Daniels and that blow those many days before. And she feared him as she had never feared him before—yet she blocked his way still with the outspread arms.

They could hear the crinkle of the cigarette paper as Buck rolled his smoke.

"No," said Buck, his voice suddenly altered to an almost casual moderation, "talk don't mean nothin' to you. Talk is human, and nothin' human means nothin' to you. But I got to tell you why you ought to die, Barry.

"I started out this mornin' hatin' the ground you walked on, but now I see that they ain't no use to hate you. Is they any use hatin' a mountain lion that kills calves? No, you don't hate it, but you get a gun and trail it and shoot it down. And that's the way with you."

They heard the scratch of his match.

"That's the way with you. I got my back to you right now because if I looked you in the eye I couldn't let you live no more'n I could let a mountain lion live. I know you're faster with your gun than I am and stronger than I am, and made to fight. But I know I'm going to kill you. You've done your work—you've left hell on all sides of you—it's your time to die. I know it! You been lyin' like a snake in the rocks with your poison ready for any man that walks past you. Now your poison is about used up."

He paused, and then when he spoke again there was a ring of exultation in his voice: "I tell you, Dan, I don't fear you, and I know that the bullet in this gun here on my hip is the one that's goin' to tear your heart out. I *know* it!"

Something like a sob came from the lips of Dan Barry. His hands moved out toward Buck Daniels as though he were plucking something from the empty air.

"You've said enough," he said. "You said plenty. Now turn around and fight!"

And Kate Cumberland stepped back, out of line of the two. She knew that in what followed she could not play the part of the protector or the delayer. Here they stood, hungry for battle, and there was no power in her

weak hands to separate them. She stood far back and
fumbled with her hands at the wall for support. She
tried to close her eyes, but the fascination of the horror
forced her to watch against her strongest will. And the
chief part of that dreadful suspense lay in the even, calm
voice of Buck Daniels as he went on: "I'll turn around
and fight soon enough. But Kate asked me to smoke another cigarette. I know what she means. She wants me
to leave you the way I done in the saloon that day. I
ain't goin' to leave, Dan. But I'm glad she asked me
to turn away, because it gives me a chance to tell you
some things you got to know before you go west.

"Dan, you been like a fire that burns every hand that
touches you." He inhaled a long breath of smoke and
blew it up toward the ceiling. "You've busted the heart
of the friend that follered you; you've busted the heart
of the girl that loves you."

He paused again, for another long inhalation, and Kate
Cumberland, staring in fearful suspense, waiting for the
instant when Buck should at last turn and when the shots
should explode, saw that the yellow glow was now somewhat misted in the eyes of Barry. He frowned, as one
bewildered.

"Think of her, Dan!" went on Buck Daniels. "Think of
her wasting herself on a no-good houn' dog like you—
a no-good wild *wolf!* My God A'mighty, she might of
made some good man happy—some man with a soul
and a heart—but instead of that God sent you like a
blast across her—you with your damned soul of wind
and your heart of stone! Think of it! When you see what
you been, Barry, I wonder you don't go out and take
your own gun and blow off your head."

"Buck," called Dan Barry, "so help me God, if you
don't turn your face to me—I'll shoot you through the
back!"

"I knew," said the imperturbable Daniels, "that you'd
come to that in the end. You used to fight like a man,
but now you're followin' your instincts, and you fight
like a huntin' wolf. Look at the brute that's slinkin' up
to me there! That's what you are. You kill for the sake
of killin'—like the beasts.

"If you was a man, could you treat me like you've

done? Your damned cold heart and your yaller eyes and all would of burned up in the barn the other night—you and your wolf and your damned hoss. Why didn't I let you burn? Because I was a fool. Because I still thought they was something of the man in you. But I seen afterwards what you was, and I rode off to get out of your way—to keep your hands from gettin' red with my blood. And then you plan on follerin' me—damn you!—on follerin' *me!*

"So that, Dan, is why I've come to put you out of the world—as I'm goin' to do now! Once you hated to give pain, and if you hurt people it was because you couldn't help it. But now you live on torturin' others. Barry, pull your gun!"

And as he spoke, he whirled, the heavy revolver leaping into his hand.

Still Kate Cumberland could not close her eyes on the horror. She could not even cry out; she was frozen.

But there was no report—no spurt of smoke—no form of a man stumbling blindly toward death. Dan Barry stood with one hand pressed over his eyes and the other dangled at his side, harmless, while he frowned in bewilderment at the floor.

He said slowly, at length: "Buck, I kind of think you're right. They ain't no use in me. I been rememberin', Buck, how you sent Kate to me when I was sick."

There was a loud clatter; the revolver dropped from the hand of Buck Daniels.

The musical voice of Dan Barry murmured again: "And I remember how you stood up to Jim Silent, for my sake. Buck, what's come between us since them days? You hit me a while back, and since then I been wantin' your blood—but hearin' you talk now, somehow —I feel sort of lost and lonesome—like I'd thrown somethin' away that I valued most."

Buck Daniels threw out his great arms and his voice was broken terribly.

"Oh, God A'mighty, Dan," he cried, "jest take one step back to me and I'll come all the way around the world to meet you!"

He stumbled across the floor and grasped at the hand of Barry, for a mist had half-blinded his eyes.

"Dan," he pleaded, "ain't things as they once was? D'you forgive me?"

"Why, Buck," murmured Dan Barry, in that same bewildered fashion, "seems like we was bunkies once."

"Dan," muttered Buck Daniels, choking, "Dan——" but he dared not trust his voice further, and turning, he fairly fled from the room.

The dazed eyes of Dan Barry followed him. Then they moved until they encountered the face of Kate Cumberland. A shock, as if of surprise, widened the lids. For a long moment they stared in silence, and then he began to walk, very slowly, a step at a time, toward the girl. Now, as he faced her, she saw that there was no longer a hint of the yellow in his eyes, but he stepped closer and closer; he was right before her, watching her with an expression of mute suffering that made her heart grow large.

He said, more to himself than to her: "Seems like I been away a long time."

"A very long time," she whispered.

He drew a great breath.

"Is it true, what Buck said? About you?"

"Oh, my dear, my dear!" she cried. "Don't you see?"

He started a little, and taking both her hands he made her face the dull light from the windows.

"Seems like you're kind of pale, Kate."

"The color went while I waited for you, Dan."

"But there comes a touch of red—like morning—in your throat, and runnin' up your cheeks."

"Don't you see? It's because you've come back!"

He closed his eyes and murmured: "I remember we was close—closer than this. We were sittin' here—in this room—by a fire. And then something called me out and I follered it."

"The wild geese—yes."

"Wild geese?" he repeated blankly, and then shook his head. "How could wild geese call me? But things happened. I was kept away. Sometimes I wanted to come back to you, but somehow I could never get started. Was it ten years ago that I left?"

"Months—months longer than years."

"What is it?" he asked. "I been watchin' you, and

waitin' to find out what was different in you. Black Bart seen something in you. I dunno what. Today I sort of guessed what it is. I can feel it now. It's something like a pain. It starts sort of in the stomach, Kate. It's like bein' away from a place where you want to be. Queer, ain't it? I ain't far from you. I've got your hands in mine, but somehow you don't feel near. I want to walk—a long ways—closer. And the pain keeps growin'."

His voice fell away to a murmur, and now a deadly silence lay between them, and it seemed as if lights were varying upon their faces, so swift and subtle were the changes of expression. And they drew closer by imperceptible degrees. So his arms, fumbling, found their away about her, drew her closer, till her head drooped back, and her face was close beneath his.

"Was it true," he whispered, "what Buck said?"

"There's nothing true except that we're together."

"But your eyes are brimful of tears!"

"The same pain you feel, Dan; the same loneliness and the hurt."

"But it's going now. I feel as if I'd been riding three days without more'n enough water to moisten my tongue every hour; with the sand white hot, and my hoss staggerin', and the sun droppin' closer and closer till the mountains are touched with white fire. Then I come, in the evenin', to a valley with cool shadows beginning to slip across from the western side, and I stand in the shadow and feel the red-hot blood go smashin', smashin', smashin' in my temples—and then—a sound of runnin' water somewhere up the hillside. Runnin', cool, fresh, sparkling water whispering over the rocks. Ah, God, that's what it means to me to stand here close to you, Kate!

"And it's like standin' up in the mornin' on the top of a high hill and seein' the light jump up quick in the east, and there lies all the world at my feet, mile after mile of it—they's a river like silver away off yonder—and they's range after range walkin' off into a blue nothing. That's what it's like to stand here and look down into them blue eyes of yours, Kate—miles and miles into 'em, till I feel as if I seen your heart beneath. And they's the rose of the mornin' on your cheeks, and the breath of the mornin' stirrin' between your lips, and the light of the risin' sun comes flarin' in your eyes. And I own the world—I own the world.

"Two burnin' pieces of wood, that's you and me, and when I was away from you the fire went down to a smolder; but now that we're close a wind hits us, and the flames come together and rise and jump and twine together. Two pieces of burnin' wood, but only one flame—d'you feel it?—Oh, Kate, our bodies is ashes and dust, and all that's worth while is that flame blowin' up from us, settin' the world on fire!"

35 · Pale Annie

EVEN in Elkhead there were fires this day. In the Gilead saloon one might have thought that the liquid heat which the men imbibed would serve in place of stoves, but the proprietor, "Pale Annie," had an eye to form, and when the sky was gray he always lighted the stove.

"Pale Annie" he was called because his real name was Anderson Hawberry Sandringham. That name had been a great aid to him when he was an undertaker in Kansas City; but Anderson Hawberry Sandringham had fallen from the straight and narrow path of good undertakers some years before and he had sought refuge in the mountain-desert, where most things prosper except sheriffs and grass. He was fully six inches more than six feet in height and his face was so long and pale that even Haw-Haw Langley seemed cheerful beside the ex-undertaker. In Kansas City this had been much prized, for that single face could lend solemnity to any funeral. In Elkhead it was hardly less of an asset.

People came out of curiosity to see Pale Annie behind the bar with his tall silk hat—which he could never bring himself to lay aside—among the cobwebs of the rafters. They came out of curiosity and they remained to drink—which is a habit in the mountain-desert. A traveling drummer or a patent medicine man had offered Pale Annie a handsome stake to simply go about with him and lend the sanction of his face to the talk of the drummer, but Pale Annie had discovered a veritable philosopher's stone in Elkhead and he was literally turning whiskey into gold.

This day was even more prosperous than usual for Pale Annie, for the gray weather and the chilly air made men glad of the warmth, both external and internal, which Pale Annie possessed in his barroom. His dextrous hands were never for a moment still at the bar, either setting out drinks or making change, except when he walked out and threw a fresh feed into the fire, and stirred up the ruddy depths of the stove with a tall poker. It was so long, indeed, that it might have served even Pale Annie for a cane and it was a plain untapered bar of iron which the blacksmith had given him as the price of a drink, on a day. He needed a large poker, however, for there was only the one stove in the entire big room, and it was a giant of its kind, as capacious as a hogshead. This day Pale Annie kept it red hot, so that the warmth might penetrate to the door on the one hand and to the rear of the room where the tables and chairs were, on the other.

Since Pale Annie's crowd took little exercise except for bending their elbows now and again, and since the majority of them had been in the place fully half the day, by ten in the evening sounds of hilarity began to rise from the saloon. Solemn-faced men who had remained in their places for hour after hour, industriously putting away the redeye, now showed symptoms of life. Some of them discovered hitherto hidden talents as singers, and they would rise from their places, remove their hats, open their bearded mouths, and burst into song. An antiquarian who had washed gold in '49 and done nothing the rest of his life save grow a prodigious set of pure white whiskers, sprang from his place and did a hoe-down that ravished the beholders. Thrice he was compelled to return to the floor; and in the end his performance was only stopped by an attack of sciatica. Two strong men carried him back to his chair and wept over him, and there was another drink all around.

In this scene of universal joy there were two places of shadow. For at the rear end of the room, almost out of reach of the lantern-light, sat Haw-Haw Langley and Mac Strann. The more Haw Haw Langley drank the more cadaverous grew his face, until in the end it was almost as solemn as that of Pale Annie himself; as for Mac Strann, he seldom drank at all.

A full hour had just elapsed since either of them spoke, yet Haw-Haw Langley said, as if in answer to a remark: "He's heard too much about you, Mac. He ain't no such fool as to come to Elkhead."

"He ain't had time," answered the giant.

"Ain't had time? All these days?"

"Wait till the dog gets well. He'll follow the dog to Elkhead."

"Why, Mac, the trail's been washed out long ago. That wind the other day would of knocked out any trail less'n a big wagon."

"It won't wash out the trail for *that* dog," said Mac Strann calmly.

"Well," snarled Haw-Haw, "I got to be gettin' back home pretty soon. I ain't rollin' in coin the way you are, Mac."

The other returned no answer, but let his eyes rove vacantly over the room, and since his head was turned the other way, Haw-Haw Langley allowed a sneer to twist at his lips for a moment.

"If I had the price," he said, "we'd have another drink."

"I ain't drinkin'," answered the giant monotonously.

"Then I'll go up and bum one off'n Pale Annie. About time he come through with a little charity."

So he unfurled his length and stalked through the crowd up to the bar. Here he leaned and confidentially whispered in the ear of Pale Annie.

"Partner, I been sprinklin' dust for a long time in here, and there ain't been any reward. I'm dry, Annie."

Pale Annie regarded him with grave disapproval.

"My friend," he said solemnly, "liquor is the real root of all evil. For my part, I quench my thirst with water. They's a tub over there in the corner with a dipper handy. Don't mention it."

"I didn't thank you," said Haw-Haw Langley furiously. "Damn a tightwad, say I!"

The long hand of Pale Annie curled affectionately around the neck of an empty bottle.

"I didn't quite gather what you said?" he remarked courteously, and leaned across the bar—within striking distance.

"I'll tell you later," remarked Haw-Haw sullenly, and turned his shoulder to the bar.

As he did so two comparatively recent arrivals came up beside him. They were fresh from a couple of months of range-finding, and they had been quenching a concentrated thirst by concentrated effort. Haw-Haw Langley looked them over, sighed with relief, and then instantly produced Durham and the brown papers. He paused in the midst of rolling his cigarette and offered them to the nearest fellow.

"Smoke?" he asked.

Now a man of the mountain-desert knows a great many things, but he does not know how to refuse. The proffer of a gift embarrasses him, but he knows no way of avoiding it; also he never rests easy until he has made some return.

"Sure," said the man, and gathered in the tobacco and papers. "Thanks!"

He covertly dropped the cigarette which he had just lighted, and stepped on it. then he rolled another from Haw-Haw's materials. The while, he kept an uneasy eye on his new companion.

"Drinkin'?" he asked at length.

"Not jest now," said Haw-Haw carelessly.

"Always got room for another," protested the other, still more in earnest as he saw his chance of a return disappearing.

"All right, then," said Haw-Haw. "Jest one more."

And he poured a glass to the brim, waved it gracefully toward the other without spilling a drop, and downed it at a gulp.

"Been in town long?" he asked.

"Not long enough to find any action," answered the other.

The eye of Haw-Haw Langley brightened. He looked

over the two carefully. The one had black hair and the other red, but they were obviously brothers, both tall, thick shouldered, square jawed, and pug-nosed. There was Irish blood in that twain; the fire in their eyes could have come from only one place on earth. And Haw-Haw grinned and looked down the length of the room to where Mac Strann sat, a heavy, inert mass, his fleshy forehead puckered into a half-frown of animal wistfulness.

"You ain't the only ones," he said to his companion at the bar. "They's a man in town who says they don't turn out any two men in this range that could give him action."

"The hell!" grunted he of the red hair. And he looked down to his blunt-knuckled hands.

" 'S matter of fact," continued Haw-Haw easily, "he's right here now!"

He looked again toward Mac Strann and remembered once more the drink which Mac might so easily have purchased for him.

"It ain't Pale Annie, is it?" asked the black-haired man, casting a dubious glance up and down the vast frame of the undertaker.

"Him? Not half!" grinned Haw-Haw. "It's a fat feller down to the end of the bar. I guess he's been drinkin-some. Kind of off his nut."

He indicated Mac Strann.

"He looks to me," said the red-haired man, setting his jaw, "like a feller that ain't any too old to learn one more thing about the range in these parts."

"He looks to me," chimed in the black-haired brother, "like a feller that might be taught something right here in Pale Annie's barroom. Anyway, he's got room at his table for two more."

So saying the two swallowed their drinks and rumbled casually down the length of the room until they came to the table where Mac Strann sat. Haw-Haw Langley followed at a discreet distance and came within earshot to hear the deep voice of Mac Strann rumbling: "Sorry, gents, but that chair is took."

The black-haired man sank into the indicated chair. "You're right," he announced calmly. "Anybody could

see with half an eye that you ain't a fool. It's took by
me!"

And he grinned impudently in the face of Mac Strann.
The latter, who had been sitting with slightly bent head,
now raised it and looked the pair over carelessly; there
was in his eye the same dumb curiosity which Haw-Haw
Langley had seen many a time in the eye of a bull,
leader of the herd.

The giant explained carefully: "I mean, they's a friend
of mine that's been sittin' in that chair."

"If I ain't your friend," answered the black-haired
brother instantly, "it ain't any fault of mine. Lay it up
to yourself, partner!"

Mac Strann stretched out his hand on the surface of
the table.

He said: "I got an idea you better get out of that
chair."

The other turned his head slowly on all sides and then
looked Mac Strann full in the face.

"Maybe they's something wrong with my eyes," he
said, "but I don't see no reason."

The little dialogue had lasted long enough to focus all
eyes on the table at the end of the room, and therefore
there were many witnesses to what followed. The arm
of Mac Strann shot out; his hand fastened in the collar
of the black-haired man's shirt, and the latter was raised
from his seat and propelled to one side by a convulsive
jerk. He probably would have been sent crashing into
the bar had not his shirt failed under the strain. It
ripped in two at the shoulders, and the seeker after action, naked to the waist, went reeling back to the middle of the room, before he gained his balance. After him
went Mac Strann with an agility astonishing in that
squat, formless bulk. His long arms were outstretched
and his fingers tensed, and in his face there was an uncanny joy; his lip had lifted in that peculiarly disheart-
ening sneer.

He was not a pace from him of the black hair when
a yell of rage behind him and the other brother
leaped through the air and landed on Mac Strann's
back. He doubled up, slipped his arms behind him, and
the next instant, without visible reason, the red-headed

man hurtled through the air and smashed against the bar with a jolt that set the glassware shivering and singing. Then he relaxed on the floor, a twisted and foolish looking mass.

As for the seeker after action, he had at first reached after his revolver, but he changed his mind at the last instant and instead picked up the great poker which leaned against the stove. It was a ponderous weapon and he had to wield it in both hands. As he swung it around his head there was a yell from men ducking out of the way, and Pale Annie curled his hand again around his favorite empty bottle. He had no good opportunity to demonstrate its efficiency, however. Mac Strann, crouching in the position from which he had catapulted the red-haired man, cast upwards a single glance at the other brother, and then he sprang in. The poker hissed through the air with the vigor of a strong man's arms behind it and it would have cracked the head of Mac Strann like an empty eggshell if it had hit its mark. But it was heaved too high, and Mac Strann went in like a football player rushing the line, almost doubled up against the floor as he ran. His shoulders struck the other hardly higher than the knees, and they went down together, but so doing the head of Mac Strann's victim cracked against the floor, and he also was still.

The exploit was greeted by a yell of applause and then someone proposed a cheer, and it was given. It died off short on the lips of the applauders, however, for it was seen that Mac Strann was not yet done with his work, and he went about it in a manner which made men sober suddenly and exchange glances.

First the stranger dragged the two brothers together, laying one of them face down on the floor. The second he placed over the first, back to back. Next he picked up the long poker from the floor and slipped it under the head and down to the neck of the first man. The bystanders watched in utter silence, with a touch of horror coming now in their eyes.

Now Mac Strann caught the ends of the iron and began to twist up on them. There was no result at first. He refreshed his hold and tried again. The sleeves of his shirt were seen to swell and then grow hard and

taut with vast play of muscle beneath. His head bowed
lower between his shoulders, and those shoulders trembled, and the muscles over them quivered like heat-waves
rising of a spring morning. There was a creaking, now,
and then the iron was seen to shiver and then bend,
slowly, and once it was wrenched out of the horizontal,
the motion was more and more rapid. Until, when the
gaint was done with his labor, the ends of the iron
overlapped around the necks of the two luckless brothers.
Mac Strann stepped back and surveyed his work; the
rest of the room was in silence, saving that the red-
headed man was coming back to consciousness and now
writhed and groaned feebly. He could not rise; that was
manifest, for the thick band of iron tied his neck to the
neck of his brother.

Upon this scene Mac Strann gazed with a thoughtful
air and then stepped to the side of the room where
stood a bucket of dirty water, recently used for mopping
behind the bar. This he caught up, returned, and dashed
the black, greasy water over the pair.

If it had been electricity it could not have operated
more effectively. The two awoke with one mind, and
with a tremendous spluttering and cursing struggled to
regain their feet. It was no easy thing, however, for
when one stood up the other slipped and in his fall in-
volved the brother. In the meantime it made a jest exactly suited to the mind of Elkhead, and shrieks of hysterical laughter rewarded their struggles. Until at length
they sat solemnly, back to back, easing the pressure of the
iron as best they might with their hands. Assembled
Elkhead reeled about the room, drunken with laughter.
But Mac Strann went quietly back to his table and paid
no attention to the scene.

There is an end to all good things, however, and finally
the two brothers concerted action together, rose, and
then side-stepped toward the door, dripping the mop-
water at every step. Obviously they were bound for the
blacksmith's to lose their collar; and everyone in the saloon knew that the blacksmith was not in town.

The old man who had done the hoe-down hobbled to
the end of the barroom and before the table of Mac
Strann made a speech to the effect that Elkhead had

everything it needed except laughter, that Mac Strann had come to their assistance in that respect, and that if he, the old man, had the power, he would pension such an efficient jester and keep him permanently in the town. To all of this Mac Strann paid not the slightest heed, but with his fleshy brow puckered considered the infinite distance. Even the drink which Pale Annie, grateful for the averted riot, placed on the table befor him, Mac Strann allowed to stand untasted. And it was private stock!

It was at this time that Haw-Haw Langley made his way back to the table and occupied the contested seat.

"That was a bum play," he said solemnly to Mac Strann. "When Barry hears about what you done here to two men, d'you think he'll ever hit your trail?"

The other started.

"I never thought about it," he murmured, his thick lips, as always, framing speech with difficulty. "D'you s'pose I'd ought to go back to the Cumberland place for him?"

A yell rose at the farther end of the room.

"A wolf! Hey! Shoot the damn wolf!"

"You fool!" cried another. "He ain't skinny enough to be a wolf. Besides, whoever heard of a tame wolf comin' into a barroom?"

Nevertheless many a gun was held in readiness, and the men, even the most drunken, fell back to one side and allowed a free passage for the animal. It seemed, indeed, to be a wolf, and a giant of its kind, and it slunk now with soundless step through the silence of the barroom, glancing neither to right nor to left, until it came before the table of Mac Strann. There it halted and slunk back a little, the upper lip lifted away from the long fangs, its eyes glittered upon the face of the giant, and then it swung about and slipped out of the barroom as it had come, in utter silence.

In the utter silence Mac Strann leaned across the table to Haw-Haw Langley.

"He's come alone this time," he said, "but the next time he'll bring his master with him. We'll wait!"

The Adam's apple rose and fell in the throat of Haw-Haw.

"We'll wait," he nodded, and he burst into the harsh, unhuman laughter which had given him his name.

36 · The Discovery of Life

THIS is the letter which Swinnerton Loughburne received over the signature of Doctor Randall Byrne. It was such a strange letter that between paragraphs Swinnerton Loughburne paced up and down his Gramercy Park studio and stared, baffled, at the heights of the Metropolitan Tower.

"Dear Swinnerton,

"I'll be with you in good old Manhattan about as soon as you get this letter. I'm sending this ahead because I want you to do me a favor. If I have to go back to those bare, blank rooms of mine with the smell of chemicals drifting in from the laboratory, I'll—get drunk. That's all!"

Here Swinnerton Loughburne lowered the letter to his knees and grasped his head in both hands. Next he turned to the end of the letter and made sure that the signature was "Randall Byrne." He stared again at the handwriting. It was not the usual script of the young doctor. It was bolder, freer, and twice as large as usual; there was a total lack of regard for the amount of stationery consumed.

Shaking his head in bewilderment, Swinnerton Loughburne shook his fine gray head and read on: "What I want you to do, is to stir about and find me a new apartment. Mind you, I don't want the loft of some infernal Arcade building in the Sixties. Get me a place somewhere between Thirtieth and Fifty-eighth. *Two* bedrooms. I want a place to put some of the boys when they drop around my way. And at least one servant's room. Also at least one large room where I can stir about and wave my arms without hitting the chandelier. Are you with me?"

Here Swinnerton Loughburne seized his head between both hands again and groaned: "Dementia! Plain and simple dementia! And at his age, poor boy!"

He continued: "Find an interior decorator. Not one of these fuzzy-haired women-in-pants, but a he-man who knows what a he-man needs. Tell him I want that place furnished regardless of expense. I want some deep chairs that will hit me under the knees. I want some pictures on the wall—but *nothing out of the Eighteenth Century* —no impressionistic landscapes—no girls dolled up in fluffy stuff. I want some pictures I can enjoy, even if my maiden aunt can't. There you are. Tell him to go ahead on those lines.

"In a word, Swinnerton, old top, I want to live. For about thirty years I've *thought,* and now I know that there's nothing in it. All the thinking in the world won't make one more blade of grass grow; put one extra pound on the ribs of a long-horn; and in a word, thinking is the bunk, pure and simple!"

At this point Swinnerton Loughburne staggered to the window, threw it open, and leaned out into the cold night. After a time he had strength enough to return to his chair and read through the rest of the epistle without interruption.

"You wonder how I've reached the new viewpoint? Simply by seeing some concentrated life here at the Cumberland ranch. My theories are blasted and knocked in the head—praise God!—and I've brushed a million cobwebs out of my brain. Chemistry? Rot! There's another sort of chemistry that works on the inside of a man. That's what I want to study. There are three great preliminary essentials to the study:

1st: How to box with a man.

2nd: How to talk with a girl.

3rd: How to drink old wine.

"Try the three, Swinnerton; they aren't half bad. At first they may give you a sore jaw, an aching heart, and a spinning head, but in the end they teach you how to keep your feet and *fight!*

"This is how my eyes were opened.

"When I came out to this ranch it was hard for me to ride a horse. So I've been studying how it should be done. Among other things, you should keep your toes turned in, you know. And there are many other things to learn.

"When I had mastered them one by one I went out the other day and asked to have a horse saddled. It was done, and a lantern-jawed cowpuncher brought out a piebald gelding with long ears and sleepy eyes. Not a lovely beast, but a mild one. So I went into the saddle according to theory—with some slight hesitations here and there, planted my feet in the stirrups, and told the lantern-jawed fellow to turn loose the head of the piebald. This was done. I shook the reins. The horse did not move. I called to the brute by name. One ear wagged back to listen to me.

"I kicked the beast in the ribs. Unfortunately I had forgotten that long spurs were on my heels. The horse was instantly aware of that fact, however. He leaped into a full gallop. A very jolty process. Then he stopped— but I kept on going. A fence was in the way, so I was halted. Afterward the lantern-jawed man picked me up and offered to carry me back to the house or at least get a wheelbarrow for me. I refused with some dignity. I remarked that I preferred walking, really, and so I started out across the hills and away from the house. My head was sore; so were my shoulders where I hit the fence; I began to think of the joy of facing that horse again, armed with a club.

"It was evening—after supper, you see—and the light of the moon was already brighter than the sunlight. And by the time I had crossed the first range of hills, it was quite dark. As I walked I brooded upon many things. There were enough to disturb me.

"There was old Joe Cumberland, at death's door and beyond the reach of my knowledge; and he had been taken away from death by the wild man, Dan Barry. There was the girl with the bright hair—Kate Cumberland. In education, nothing; in brain, nothing; in experience, nothing; and yet I was attracted. But she was not attracted in the least until along came the wild man again, and then she fell into his arms—actually fought for him! Why? I could not tell. My name and the things I have done and even my money, meant nothing to her. But when he came it was only a glance, a word, a smile, and she was in his arms. I felt like Caligula. I wished the world had only one neck, and I an axe. But why should I have felt depressed because of failures in the eyes of these silly yokels? Not one of them could read the simplest chemical formula!

"All very absurd, you will agree, and you may get some inkling as to my state of mind while I walked over those same dark hills. I seemed a part of that darkness. I looked up to the stars. They were merely like the pages of a book. I named them off hand, one after the other, and thought of their characteristics, their distances, their composition, and meditated on the marvels the spectrum has made known to us. But no sooner did such a train of thoughts start in my brain, than I again recurred to the girl, Kate Cumberland, and all I was aware of was a pain at heart—something like homesickness. Very strange.

"She and the man are together constantly. The other day I was in Joseph Cumberland's room and we heard whistling outside. The face of the old man lighted. "They are together again,' he said. 'How do you guess at that?' I asked. 'By the sound of his whistling,' he answered. 'For he whistles as if he expected an answer—as if he were talking with someone.' And by the Lord, the old man was right. It would never have occurred to me!

"Now as I started down the farther slope of a hill a whistling sound ran upon me through the wind, and looking back I saw a horseman galloping with great swiftness along the line of the crest, very plainly outlined by the sky, and by something of smoothness in the running of the horse I knew that it was Barry and his black stallion. But the whistling—the music! Dear God, man, have you read of the pipes of Pan? That night I heard them and it made a riot in my heart.

"He was gone, suddenly, and the whistling went out like a light, but something had happened inside me— the first beginning of this process of internal change. The ground no longer seemed so dark. There were earth smells—very friendly—I heard some little creature chirruping contentedly to itself. Something hummed—a grasshopper, perhaps. And then I looked up to the stars. There was not a name I could think of—I forgot them all, and for the first time I was contented to look at them and wonder at their beauty without an attempt at analysis or labeling.

"If I say that I went back to the ranchhouse with my feet on the ground and my heart up there among the stars, will you understand?

"I found the girl sewing in front of the fire in the living room. Simply looked up to me with a smile, and a certain dimness about the eyes—well, my breath stopped.

" 'Kate,' said I, 'I am going away tomorrow morning!'

" 'And leave Dad? said she.

" 'To tell you the truth," I answered, 'there is nothing I can do for him. There has never been anything I could do for him.'

" 'I am sorry,' said she, and lifted up her eyes to me.

"Now, I had begun by being stiff with her, but the ringing of that whistling—pipes of Pan, you know—was in my ears. I took a chair beside her. Something overflowed in my heart. For the first time in whole days I could look on her beauty without pain.

" 'Do you know why I'm going?' I asked.

"She waited.

" 'Because,' said I, and smiled right into her face, 'I love you, Kate, most infernally; and I know perfectly well that I will get never the devil a bit of good out of it.'

"She peered at me. 'You aren't jesting?' says she. 'No, you're serious. I'm very sorry, Doctor Byrne.'

" 'And I,' I answered, 'am glad. I wouldn't change it for the world. For once in my life—tonight—I've forgotten myself. No, I won't go away and nurse a broken heart, but I'll think of you as a man should think of something bright and above him. You'll keep my heart warm, Kate, till I'm a very old man. Because of you, I'll be able to love some other girl—and a fine one, by the Lord!'

"Something in the nature of an outburst, eh? But it

was the music which had done it. All the time it rang and echoed through my ears. My words were only an echo of it. I was in tune with the universe. I was living for the first time. The girl dropped her sewing—tossed it aside. She came over to me and took my hands in a way that would have warmed even the icicles of your heart, Swinnerton.

" 'Doctor,' says she, 'I know that you are going to be very happy.'

" 'Happiness,' said I, 'is a trick, like riding a horse. And I think I've learned the trick. I've caught it from you and from Barry.'

"At that, she let go my hands and stepped back. The very devil is in these women, Swinnerton. You never can place them for a minute at a time.

" 'I am trying to learn myself,' she said, and there was a shadow of wistfulness in her eyes.

"In another moment I should have made a complete fool of myself, but I remembered in time and got out of the room. Tomorrow I start back for the old world but I warn you beforehand, my dear fellow, that I'm bringing something of the new world with me.

"What has it all brought to me? I am sad one day and gay the next. But at least I know that thinking is not life and now I'm ready to fight.

RANDALL BYRNE."

37 · The Piebald

THE morning of the doctor's departure witnessed quite a ceremony at the Cumberland ranch, for old Joe Cumberland insisted that he be brought down from his room to his old place in the living room. When he attempted to rise from his bed, however, he found that he could not stand; and big Buck Daniels lifted the old man like a child and carried him down the stairs. Once ensconced on the sofa in the living room Joe Cumberland beckoned his daughter close to him, and whispered with a smile as she leaned over: "Here's what comes of pretendin', Kate. I been pretending to be too sick to walk, and now I *can't* walk; and if I'd pretended to be well, I'd be ridin' Satan right now!"

He looked about him.

"Where's Dan?" he asked.

"Upstairs getting ready for the trip."

"Trip?"

"He's riding with Doctor Byrne to town and he'll bring back Doctor Byrne's horse."

The old man grew instantly anxious.

"They's a lot of things can happen on a long trip like that, Kate."

She nodded gravely.

"But we have to try him," she said. "We can't keep him here at the ranch all the time. And if he really cares, Dad, he'll come back."

"And you let him go of your own free will?" asked Joe Cumberland, wonderingly.

"I asked him to go," she answered quietly, but some of the color left her face.

"Of course it's going to come out all right," nodded her father.

"I asked him when he'd be back, and he said he would be here by dark tonight."

The old man sighed with relief.

"He don't never slip up on promises," he said. "But oh, lass, I'll be glad when he's back again! Buck, how'd you and Dan come along together?"

"We don't come," answered Buck gloomily. "I tried to shake hands with him yesterday and call it quits. But he wouldn't touch me. He jest leaned back and smiled at me and hated me with his eyes, that way he has. He don't even look at me except when he has to, and when he does I feel like someone was sneaking up behind me with a knife ready. And he ain't said ten words to me since I come back." He paused and considered Kate with the same dark, lowering glance. "Tomorrow I leave."

"You'll think better of that," nodded Joe Cumberland. "Here's the doctor now."

He came in with Dan Barry behind him. A changed

man was the doctor. He was a good two inches taller because he stood so much more erect, and there was a little spring in his step which gave aspiration and spirit to his carriage. He bade them good-bye one by one, and by Joe Cumberland he sat down for an instant and wished him luck. The old ranchman drew the other down closer.

"They's no luck for me," he whispered, "but don't tell none of 'em. I'm about to take a longer trip than you'll ride today. But first I'll see 'em settled down here—Dan quiet and both of 'em happy. S'long doc—thanks for takin' care of me. But this here is something that can't be beat no way. Too many years'll break the back of any man, doc. Luck to ye!"

"If you'll step to the door," said the doctor, smiling upon the rest, "you'll have some fun to watch. I'm going to ride on the piebald."

"Him that throwed you yesterday?" grinned Buck Daniels.

"The same," said the doctor. "I think I can come to a gentleman's understanding with him. A gentleman from the piebald's point of view is one who is never unintentionally rude. He may change his mind this morning—or he may break my back. One of the two is sure to happen."

In front of the house Dan Barry already sat on Satan with Black Bart sitting nearby watching the face of his master. And beside them the lantern-jawed cowpuncher held the bridle of the piebald mustang. Never in the world was there a lazier appearing beast. His lower lip hung pendulous, a full inch and a half below the upper. His eyes were rolled so that hardly more than the whites showed. He seemed to stand asleep, dreaming of some Nirvana for equine souls. And the only signs of life were the long ears, which wobbled, occasionally, back and forth.

When the doctor mounted, the piebald limited all signs of interest to opening one eye.

The doctor clucked. The piebald switched his tail. Satan, at a word from Dan Barry, moved gracefully into a soft trot away from the house. The doctor slapped his mount on the neck. An ear flicked back and forth. The

doctor stretched out both legs, and then he dug both
spurs deep into the flanks of the mustang.

It was a perfectly successful maneuver. The back of
the piebald changed from an ugly humped line to a
decidedly sharp parabola and the horse left the ground
with all four feet. He hit it again, almost in the identical
hoof-marks, and with all legs stiff. The doctor sagged
drunkenly in the saddle, and his head first swung far
back, and then snapped over so that the chin banged
against his chest. Nevertheless he clung to the saddle
with both hands, and stayed in his seat. The piebald
swung his head around sufficiently to make sure of the
surprising fact, and then he commenced to buck in earnest.

It was a lovely exhibition. He bucked with his head
up and his head between his knees. He bucked in a
circle and in a straight line and then mixed both styles
for variety. He made little spurts at full speed, leaped
into the air, and came down stiff-legged at the end of
the run, his head between his braced forefeet, and then
he whirled as if on a peg and darted back the other
way. He bucked criss-cross, jumping from side to side,
and he interspersed this with samples of all his other
kinds of bucking thrown in. That the doctor stuck on the
saddle was a miracle beyond belief. Of course he pulled
leather shamelessly throughout the contest, but riding
straight up is a good deal of a myth. Fancy riding is
reserved for circus men. The mountain-desert is a place
where men stick close to utility and let style go hang.

And the doctor stuck in the saddle. He had set his
teeth, and he was a seasick greenish-white. His hat was
a-jog over one ear—his shirt tails flew out behind. And
still he remained to battle. Aye, for he ceased the passive clinging to the saddle. He gathered up the long
quirt which had hitherto dangled idly from his wrist,
and at the very moment when the piebald had let out
another notch in his feats, the doctor, holding on desperately with one hand, with the other brandished the
quirt around his head and brought it down with a crack
along the flanks of the piebald.

The effect was a little short of a miracle. The mustang
snorted and leaped once into the air, but he forgot to

come down stiff-legged, and then, instantly, he broke a little, soft dog trot, and followed humbly in the trail of the black stallion. The laughter and cheers from the house were the sweetest of music in the ears of Doctor Randall Byrne; the most resounding sentences of praise from the lips of the most learned of professors after this, would be the most shabby of anticlimaxes. He waved his arm back to a group standing in front of the house—Buck Daniels, Kate, the lantern-jawed cowboy, and Wung Lu waving his kitchen apron. In another moment he was beside the rider of the stallion, and the man was whistling one of those melodies which defied repetition. It simply ran on and on, smoothly, sweeping through transition after transition, soaring and falling in the most effortless manner. Now it paused, now it began again. It was never loud, but it carried like the music of a bird on wing, blown by the wind. There was about it, also, something which escaped from the personal. He began to forget that it was a man who whistled, and such a man! He began to look about to the hills and the sky and the rocks—for these, it might be said, were set to music—they, too, had the sweep of line, and the broken rhythms, the sense of spaciousness, the far horizons.

That day was a climax of the unusual weather. For a long time the sky had been periodically blanketed with thick mists, but today the wind had freshened and it tore the mists into a thousand mighty fragments. There was never blue sky in sight—only, far up, a diminishing and lighter gray to testify that above it the yellow sun might be shining; but all the lower heavens were a-sweep with vast cloud masses, irregular, huge, hurtling across the sky. They hung so low that one could follow the speed of their motion and almost gauge it by miles per hour. And in the distance they seemed to brush the tops of the hills. Seeing this, the doctor remembered what he had heard of rain in this region. It would come, they said, in sheets and masses—literally waterfalls. Dry arroyos suddenly filled and became swift torrents, rolling big boulders down their courses. There were tales of men fording rivers who were suddenly overwhelmed by terrific walls of water which rushed down from the higher

mountains in masses four and eight feet high. In coming
they made a thundering among the hills and they
plucked up full grown trees like twigs thrust into wet
mud. Indeed, that was the sort of rain one would expect in such a country, so whipped and naked of life.
Even the reviving rainfall was sent in the form of a
scourge; and that which should make the grass grow
might tear it up by the roots.

That was a time of change and of portent, and a
day well fitted to the mood of Randall Byrne. He, also,
had altered, and there was about to break upon him
the rain of life, and whether it would destroy him or
make him live, and richly, he could not guess. But he was
naked to the skies of chance—naked as this landscape.

Far past the midday they reached the streets of Elkhead and stopped at the hotel. As the doctor swung
down from his saddle, cramped and sore from the long
ride, thunder rattled over the distant hills and a patter
of rain splashed in the dust and sent up a pungent odor
to his nostrils. It was like the voice of the earth proclaim-
ing its thirst. And a blast of wind leaped down the street
and lifted the brim of Barry's hat and set the bandana
at his throat fluttering. He looked away into the teeth of
the wind and smiled.

There was something so curious about him at the instant that Randall Byrne wanted to ask him into the
hotel—wanted to have him knee to knee for a long talk.
But he remembered an old poem—the seashell needs the
waves of the sea—the bird will not sing in the cage. And
the yellow light in the eyes of Barry, phosphorescent,
almost—a thing that might be nearly seen by night—that,
surely, would not shine under any roof. It was the wind
which made him smile. These things he understood, without fear.

So he said good-bye, and the rider waved carelessly
and took the reins of the piebald and turned the stallion
back. He noted the catlike grace of the horse in moving,
as if his muscles were steel springs; and he noted also
that the long ride had scarcely stained the glossy hide
with sweat—while the piebald reeked with the labor. Randall Byrne drew thoughtfully back onto the porch of

the hotel and followed the rider with his eyes. In a moment a great cloud of dust poured down the street, covered the rider, and when it was gone he had passed around a corner and out of the life of the doctor.

38 · The Challenge

ALL this time Black Bart had trotted contentedly ahead of Satan, never having to glance back but apparently knowing the intended direction; save that when Dan Barry turned to the road leading out of the little town, the wolf dog had turned in an opposite direction. The rider turned in the saddle and sent a sharp whistle toward the animal, but he was answered by a short howl of woe that made him check Satan and swing around. Black Bart stood in the center of the street facing in the opposite direction, and he looked back over his shoulder toward his master.

There was apparently a perfect understanding between them, and the master first glanced up and made sure of the position of the sun and the length of time he might allow for the trip home, before he decided to follow the whim of the wolf dog. Then he turned Satan and cantered, with the piebald trailing, back toward Black Bart.

At this the wolf dog began to trot down the street, turned the next corner, and drew up at the door of a rambling building above which hung a dirty, cracked sign: "GILEAD SALOON" and underneath in smaller letters was painted the legend: "Here's where you get it!"

Black Bart strolled up to the swinging doors of the emporium and then turned to look back at his master; clearly he wished Dan to enter the place. But the rider shook his head and would certainly have ridden on had not, at that moment, the rain which had hitherto fallen only in rattling bursts, now burst over the roofs of the town with a loud roaring as of wind through a forest.

It was possible that the shower might soon pass over, so Dan rode under the long shelter which stretched in front of the saloon, dismounted, and entered behind Black Bart.

It was occupied by a scattering of people, for the busy time of the day had not yet commenced and Pale Annie was merely idling behind the bar—working at half-speed, as it were. To this group Black Bart paid not the slightest heed but glided smoothly down the center of the long room until he approached the tables at the end, where, in a corner, sat a squat, thick-chested man, and opposite him the most cadaverously lean fellow that Whistling Dan had ever seen. Before these two Black Bart paused and then cast a glance over his shoulder toward the master; Whistling Dan frowned in wonder; he knew neither of the pair.

But Black Bart apparently did. He slouched a pace closer, crouched, and bared his fangs with a tremendous snarl. At this the lean man left his chair and sprang back to a distance. Terror convulsed his face; but his eyes glittered with a fascinated interest and he glanced first at his companion and then at the great wolf dog, as if he were making a comparison between them. It was the broad shouldered man who first spoke.

"Partner," he said in a thick voice, in which the articulation was almost lost, "maybe you better take your dog out before he gets hurt. He don't like me and I don't like him none too much."

"Bart!" called Dan Barry.

But Black Bart gave no heed. There had been a slight flexing of his muscles as he crouched, and now he leaped—a black bolt of fighting weight—squarely in the face of the giant. He was met and checked midway in his spring. For the two long arms darted out, two great hands fastened in the throat of the beast, and Black Bart fell back upon the floor, with Mac Strann following, his grip never broken by the fall.

A scurry of many feet running toward the scene; a shouting of twenty voices around him; but all that Whistling Dan saw were the fangs of Bart as they gnashed fruitlessly at the wrists of Mac Strann, and then the great red tongue lolling out and the eyes bulging from their sockets—all he heard was the snarling of the wolf and the peculiar whine of rage which came from the throat of the man-beast fighting the wolf. Then he acted. His hands darted between the thick forearms of Mac Strann—his elbows jerked out and snapped the grip; next he dragged Black Bart away from the danger.

The wolf was instantly on his feet and lunging again, but a sharp "Heel!" from Dan checked him mid-leap. He came to a shuddering halt behind the legs of his master. Whistling Dan slipped a little closer to the giant.

"I should have knowed you before," he said in a voice which carried only to the ears of Strann. "You're the brother of Jerry Strann. And they's a reason why Bart hates you, partner!"

The thick upper lip of Strann lifted slightly as he spoke.

"Him or you—you and your wolf together or one by one—it don't make no difference to me. I've come for you, Barry!"

The other straightened a little, and his eyes traveled slowly up and down the form of Strann.

"I been hungering to meet a man like you," he said. "Hungerin', partner."

"North of town they's the old McDuffy place, all in ruins and nobody ever near it. I'll be there in an hour, m'frien'."

"I'll be waiting for you there," nodded Mac Strann, and so saying, he turned back to his table as if he had been interrupted by nothing more than a casual greeting. Still Dan Barry remained a moment with his eyes on the face of Mac Strann. And when he turned and walked with his light, soundless step down the length of the silent barroom, the wolf dog slunk at his heels, ever and anon swinging his head over his shoulder and glancing back at the giant at the end of the room. As the door closed on man and dog, the saloon broke once more into murmur, and then into an excited clamoring. Pale Annie stepped from behind the bar and leaned upon the table beside Mac Strann. Even while leaning in this manner the bartender was as tall as the average man; he waved back the others with a gesture of his tremendous arm. Then he reached out and took the hand of Mac Strann in his clammy fingers.

"My friend," said the ex-undertaker in his careful manner, "I seen a man once California a husky two-year old —which nobody said could be done, and I've seen some other things, but I've never seen anything to touch the way you handled Black Bart. D'you know anything about that dog?"

Mac Strann shook his ponderous head and his dull eyes considered Pale Annie with an expression of almost living curiosity.

"Black Bart has a record behind him that an old time gunman would have heard with envy. There are dead men in the record of that dog, sir!"

All this he had spoken in a comparatively loud voice, but now, noting that the others had heeded his gesture and had made back toward the bar to drink on the strength of that strange fight between man and beast, the bartender approached his lips close to the ear of the giant.

He said in a rapid murmur: "I watched you talking with Dan Barry and I saw Barry's face when he went out. You and he are to meet somewhere again today. My friend don't throw yourself away."

Here Mac Strann stared down at his mighty hand— a significant answer, but Pale Annie went on swiftly: "Yes, you're strong, but strength won't save you from Dan Barry. We know him here in Elkhead. Do you know that if he had pulled his gun and shot you down right here where you sit, that he could have walked out of this room without a hand raised to stop him? Yes, sir! And why? Because we know his record; and I'd rather go against a wolf with my bare hands—as you did —than stand up against Dan Barry with guns. I could tell you how he fought Jim Silent's gang, one to six. I could tell you a lot of other things. My friend, I *will* tell you about 'em if you'll listen."

But Mac Strann considered the speaker with his dull eyes.

"I never was much on talkin'," he observed mildly. "I don't understand talkin' very well."

Pale Annie started to speak again, but he checked

himself, stared earnestly at Mac Strann, and then hurried back behind his bar. His face was even graver than usual; but business was business with Pale Annie—and all men have to die in their time! Haw-Haw Langley took the place which Pale Annie had left vacant opposite Mac Strann.

He cast a frightened glance upward, where the rain roared steadily on the roof of the building; then his eyes fluttered back until they rested on the face of his companion. He had to moisten his thin lips before he could speak and even then it was a convulsive effort, like a man swallowing too large a morsel.

"Well?" said Haw-Haw. "Is it fixed?"

"It's fixed," said Mac Strann. "Maybe you'd get the hosses, Haw-Haw. If you're coming with me?"

A dark shadow swept over the face of Haw-Haw Langley.

"You're going to beat it?" he sneered. "After you come all this way you're going to run away from Barry? And him not half your size?"

"I'm going out to meet him," answered Mac Strann.

Haw-Haw Langley started up as if he feared Mac Strann would change his mind if there were any delay. His long fingers twisted together, as if to bring the blood into circulation about the purple knuckles.

"I'll have the hosses right around to the front," he said. "By the time you got your slicker on, Mac, I'll have 'em around in front!"

And he stalked swiftly from the room.

39 · The Storm

WHEN they rode out of the town the wet sand squashed under the feet of their horses and splashed up on their riding boots and their slickers. It even spotted their faces here and there, and a light brown spray darted out to right and left of the falling hoofs. For all the streets of Elkhead were running shallow rivers, with dark, swift currents, and when they left the little town the landscape was shut out by the falling torrents. It made a strange and shifting panorama, for the rain varied in its density now and again, and as it changed hills which had been quite blotted out leaped close upon them, like living things, and then sprang back again into the mist.

So heavy was that tropical fall of water that the horses were bothered by the beating of the big drops, and shook their heads and stamped fretfully under the ceaseless bombardment. Indeed, when one stretched out his hand the drops stung him as if with lashes of tiny whips. There was no wind, no thunder, no flash of lightning, only the tremendous downpour which blended earth and sky in a drab, swift river.

The air was filled with parallel lines, as in some pencil drawings—not like ordinary rain, but as if the sky had changed into a vast watering-spout and was sending down a continuous flood from a myriad holes. It was hard to look up through the terrific downpour, for it blinded one and whipped the face and made one breathless, but now and again a puff of the rare wind would lift the sodden brim of the sombrero and then one caught a glimpse of the low-hanging clouds, with the nearest whiffs of black mist dragging across the top of a hill. Without noticeable currents of wind, that mass of clouds was shifting slowly—with a sort of rolling motion, across the sky. And the weight of the rain forced the two to bend their heads and stare down to where the face of the earth was alive with the gliding, brown waters, whose surface was threshed into a continual foam. To speak to each other through the uproar, they had to cup their hands about their lips and shout. Then again the rainfall around them fell away to a drizzling mist and the beating of the downpour sounded far away, and they were surrounded by distant walls of noise. So they came to the McDuffy place.

It was a helpless ruin, long abandoned. Not an iota of the roof remained. The sheds for the horses had dropped to the earth; but the walls of the house still remained standing, in part, with the empty windows looking out with a mocking promise of the shelter which was not within. Upon this hollow shack the rain beat with redoubled fury, and even before they could make out the place through the blankets of rain, they heard the hollow drumming. For there were times, oddly enough, when any sound would carry a great distance through the crashing of the rain.

A wind now sprung up and at once veered the rain from its perpendicular fall. It slashed them in the face under the drooping brims of their sombreros, so they drew into the shelter of the highest part of the standing wall. Still some of the rain struck them, but the major part of it was shunted over their heads. Moreover, the wall acted as a sort of sounding board, catching up every odd noise from the storm-beaten plain beyond. They could speak to each other now without effort.

"D'you think," asked Haw-Haw Langley, pressing his reeking horse a little closer to Mac Strann, "that he'll come out after us in a rain like this?"

But simple-minded Mac Strann lifted his head and peered through the thick curtains of rain.

"D'you think," he parried, "that Jerry could maybe look through all this and see what I'm doin' today?"

It made Haw-Haw Langley grin, but peering more closely and observing that there was no mockery in the face of the giant, he wiped out his grin with a scrubbing motion of his wet hand and peered closely into the face of his companion.

"They ain't any doubt of it," he said reassuringly. "He'll know what you do, Mac. What was it that Pale Annie said to you?"

"Wanted me not to meet Barry. Said that Barry had once cleaned up a gang of six."

"And here we are only two."

"You ain't to fight!" warned Mac Strann sharply. "It'll be man to man, Haw-Haw."

"But he might not notice that," cried Haw-Haw, and he caressed his scrawny neck as though he already felt fingers closing about his windpipe. "Him bein' used to fight crowds, Mac. Did you think of that?"

"I never asked you to come," responded Mac Strann.

"Mac," cried Haw-Haw in a sudden alarm, "s'pose you

wasn't to win. S'pose you wasn't able to keep him away from me?"

The numb lips of Mac Strann sprawled in an ugly smile, but he made no other answer.

"*You* don't think you'll lose," hurried on Haw-Haw, "but neither did them six that Pale Annie was tellin' about, most like. But they did! They lost; but if you lose what'll happen to me?"

"They ain't no call for you to stay here," said Mac Strann with utter indifference.

Haw-Haw answered quickly: "I wouldn't go—I wouldn't miss it for nothin' Ain't I come all this way to see it—I mean to help? Would I fall down on you now, Mac? No, I wouldn't!"

And twisting those bony fingers together he burst once more into that rattling, unhuman laughter which all the Three B's knew so well and dreaded as the dying dread the sight of the circling buzzard above.

"Stop laughin'!" cried Mac Strann with sudden anger. "Damn you, stop laughin'!"

The other peered upon Mac Strann with incredulous delight, his broad mouth gaping to that thirsted grin of enjoyment.

"You ain't gettin' nervous, Mac?" he queried, and thrust his face closer to make sure. "You ain't bothered, Mac? You ain't doubtin' how this'll turn out?" There was no answer and so he replied to himself: "I know what done it to you. I seen it myself. It was that yaller light in his eyes, Mac. My God, it come up there out of nothin' and it wasn't a light that ought to come in no man's eyes. It was like I'd woke up at night with a cold weight on my chest and found two snakes' eyes glitterin' close to my face. Makes me shivery, like, jest to think of it now. D'you notice that, Mac?"

"I'm tired of talkin'," said Mac Strann hoarsely, "damned tired!"

And so saying he swung his great head slowly around and glared at Haw-Haw. The latter shrank away with an undulatory motion in his saddle. And when the head of Mac Strann turned away again the broad mouth began gibbering: "It's gettin' him like it done me. He's scared, scared, scared—even Mac Strann!"

He broke off, for Mac Strann had jerked up his head and said in a strangely muffled voice: "What was that?"

The bullet head of Haw-Haw Langley leaned to one side, and his glittering eyes rolled up while he listened.

"Nothin'!" he said, "I don't hear nothin'!"

"Listen again!" cried Mac Strann in that same cautious voice, as of one whispering in the night in the house of the enemy. "It's like a voice in the wind. It comes down the wind. D'ye hear now—now—now?"

It was, indeed, the faintest of faint sounds when Haw-Haw caught it. It was, in the roar of the rain, as indistinct as some distant light on the horizon which may come either from a rising star or from the window of a house. But it had a peculiar quality of its own, even as the house-light would be tinged with yellow when the stars are cold and white. A small and distant sound, and yet it cut through the crashing of the storm more and more clearly; someone rode through the rain whistling.

"It's him!" gasped Haw-Haw Langley. "My God A'Mighty, Mac, he's whistlin'! It ain't possible!"

He reined his horse closer to the wall, listening with mouth agape.

He shrilled suddenly: "What if he should hit us both, seein' us together? They ain't no heart in a feller that can whistle in a storm like this!"

But Mac Strann had lowered his head, bulldog-like, and now he listened and thrust out his blunt jaw farther and farther and returned no answer.

"God gimme the grit to stick it out," begged Haw-Haw Langley in an agony of desire. "God lemme see how it comes out. God lemme watch 'em fight. One of 'em is goin' to die—may be two of 'em—nothin' like it has ever been seen!"

The rain shifted, and the heart of the storm rolled far away. For the moment they could look far out across the shadow-swept hills, and out of the heart of the desolate landscape the whistling ran thrilling upon them. It was so loud and close that of one accord the two listeners jerked their heads about and stared at each other, and then turned their eyes as hastily away, as though terrified by what they had seen—each in the face

of the other. It was no idle tune which they heard whistled. This was a rising, soaring pean of delight. It rang
down upon the wind—it cut into their faces like the
drops of the rain; it branded itself like freezing cold into their foreheads.

And then, upon the crest of the nearest hill, Haw-Haw
Langley saw a dim figure through the mist, a man on
a horse and something else running in front; and they
came swiftly.

"It's the wolf that's runnin' us down!" screamed Haw-
Haw Langley. "Oh, God A'mighty, even if we was to
want to run, the wolf would come and pull us down.
Mac, will you save me? Will you keep the wolf away?"

He clung to the arm of his companion, but the other
brushed him back with a violence which almost unseated
Haw-Haw.

"Keep off'n me," growled Mac Strann, "because when
you touch me, it feels like somethin' dead was next to
my skin. Keep off'n me!"

Haw-Haw dragged himself back into the saddle with
effort, for it was slippery with rain. His face convulsed
with something black as hate.

"It ain't long you'll do the orderin' and be so free with
your hands. He's comin'—soon! Mac, I'd like to stay—
I'd like to see the finish——" he stopped, his buzzard eyes
glittering against the face of the giant.

The rain blotted out the figure of the coming horseman, and at the same instant the whistling leaped close
upon them. It was as if the whistling man had disappeared at the place where the rain swallowed his form,
and had taken body again at their very side. Mac
Strann shrank back against the wall, bracing his shoulders, and gripped the butts of his guns. But Haw-Haw
Langley cast a frightened glance on either side; his head
making birdlike, pecking motions, and then he leaned over
the pommel of his saddle with a wail of despair and
spurred off into the rain.

40 · The Arroyo

HE disappeared, instantly, in that shivering curtain of grayness. Mac Strann sat by the ruined house alone.

Now, in a time of danger a child will give courage to the strong man. There is a wonderful communion between any two in time of crisis; and when Haw-Haw Langley disappeared through the rain it was to Mac Strann as it was to Patroclus when Apollo struck the base of his neck and his armor of proof fell from him. Not only was there a singular sense of nakedness, but it seemed to him also that the roaring of the rain became a hostile voice of threatening at the same instant.

He had never in his life feared any living thing. But now there was a certain hollowness in the region of his stomach, and his heart fluttered like a bird in the air, with appalling lightness. And he wished to be far away.

With a clear heaven above him—ay, that would be different, but God had arranged this day and had set the earth like a stage in readiness for a death. And that was why the rain lashed the earth so fiercely. He looked down. After his death the wind would still continue to beat that muddy water to foam. Ay, in that very place all would be as it was at this moment. He would be gone, but the sky and the senseless earth would remain unchanged. A sudden yearning seized him for the cabin among the mountains, with the singing of the coffee pot over the fire—the good, warm, yellow fire that smoked between the rocks. And the skins he had left leaning against the walls of the cabin to dry—he remembered them all in one glance of memory.

Why was he here, then, when he should have been so far away, making his roof snug against this torrent of rain? Now, there would be no rain, surely, in those kindly mountains. Their tall peaks would shut out the

238

storm clouds. Only this plain, these low hills, were the place of hell!

He swung the head of his horse to one side, drove deep the spurs, and leaning his head to the volleying of the rain he raced in a direction opposite to that in which Haw-Haw Langley had disappeared, in a direction that led as straight as the line of a flying bird toward that cabin in the mountains.

Now and then the forefeet of his great horse smashed into a pool and sent a muddy shower of rain flying up. It crackled against his slicker; it beat like hands against his face. Everything was striving—all the elements of wind and rain—to hold him back.

Yet flight brought a blessed sense of relief and of safety. He eased the pace of his horse to a moderate gallop, and no longer driving blindly through the hills, he made out, by peering into the blast of rain, some of the pools which lay in his path, and swung aside to avoid them.

The rain lightened again about him; he caught a view of the kindly, sheltering hills on all sides; but as he urged his horse on toward them a shrill flight of whistling fell upon his ears from behind. He drew his horse at once to a halt and listened with his heart knocking at his teeth.

It was impossible, manifestly, that the fellow could have followed his track through the rain. For that matter, if the wolf-fiend could follow traces over a plain awash with water, why might they not as well follow the tracks of Haw-Haw Langley? There was no good reason.

The whistling? Well, the whistler was far away in the heart of the storm, and the sound was merely blown against the wind by a chance echo. Yet he remained holding his rein taut, and listening with all his might.

It came again, suddenly as before, sharp, and keen as a shaft of light in the blackest heart of night, and Mac Strann leaned over the pommel of his saddle with a groan, and drove the spurs home. At the same instant the rain shut in over the hills again; a fresher wind sprang up and drove the downpour into his face. Also its roar shut out the possibility of any sound reaching him from behind.

He was worse for that. As long as the whistling might reach him he could tell how near the pursuer rode; but in this common roar of the rain the man might be at any distance behind him—on his very heels, indeed. Ay, Dan Barry might rush upon him from behind. He had seen that black stallion and he would never forget—those graceful, agile lines, that generous breast, wide for infinite wind and the great heart. If the stallion were exerted, it could overtake his own mount as if he were standing still. Not on good footing, perhaps, but in this mucky ground the weight of his horse was terribly against him. He drove the spurs home again; he looked back again and again, piercing the driving mist of rain with starting eyes. He was safe still; the destroyer was not in sight; yet he might be riding close behind that wall of rain.

His horse came to a sudden halt, sliding on all four feet and driving up a rush of dirty water before him; even then he had stopped barely in time, for his forefeet were buried to the knees in water. Before Mac Strann lay a wide arroyo. In ordinary weather it was dry as all the desert around, but now it had cupped the water from miles around and ran bank full, a roaring torrent. On its surface the rain beat with a continual crashing, like axes falling on brittle glass; and the downpour was now so fearful that Mac Strann, for all his peering, could not look to the other side.

He judged the current to see if he might swim his horse across. But even while he stared the stump of a cottonwood went whirling down the stream, struck a rock, perhaps, on the bottom, flung its entire bulk out of the water with the impact, and then floundered back into the stream again and whirled instantly out of sight in the sheeted rain.

No horse in the world could live through such a current. But the arroyo might turn. He swung his horse and spurred desperately along the bank, keeping his eye upon the bank. No, the stream cut back in a sharp curve and headed him farther and farther in the direction of the pursuer. He brought the mighty horse to another sliding halt and swung about in the opposite direction, for surely there must lie the point of escape. Desperately he rode, for the detour had cost him priceless time, yet it might be made up. Ay, the stream sloped sharply into the direction in which he wished to ride. For a distance he could not judge, since seconds were longer than minutes to Mac Strann now.

And then—the edge of the stream curved back again. He thought it must be a short twist in the line of the arroyo, but following it a little further he came to realize the truth. The arroyo described a wide curve, and a sharp one, and to ride down its banks on either side was merely to throw himself into the arms of Whistling Dan.

Once he struck his fleshy forehead, and then turned with gritting teeth and galloped back for the point at which he had first arrived. To his maddened brain it occurred that the current of the arroyo might by this have somewhat abated. He might now make his way across it. So he halted once more on the bank at the point where the stream doubled back on its course and once more, in an agony, studied the force of the current. It seemed so placid at the first glance that he was on the verge of spurring the horse into the wide, brown stream, but even as he loosened the reins a gap opened in the middle of the water, widened, whirling at the brim, and drew swiftly into a fierce vortex with a black, deep bottom. Mac Strann tightened his reins again, and then turned his horse, and waited.

Back the veriest coward against the wall and he becomes formidable, and Mac Strann was one who had never feared before either man or beast or the powers of the storm. Even now he dreaded no reality, but there dwelt in his mind the memory of how Dan Barry had glared at him in the Gilead Saloon, and how a flicker of yellow light had glowed in the man's eyes— a strange and phosphorescent glimmer that might be seen in the darkness of night. When he turned the head of his horse away from the arroyo, he waited as one waits for the coming of a ghost. There was the same chill tingling in his blood.

Now the blanket of rain lifted and shook away to

comparative clearness—lifted, and for the first time he could look far away across the plains. Nothing but gray, rain-washed desert met his eyes, and then the whistling broke once more upon him at the crest of a thrilling run. Mac Strann strained his eyes through the mist of the storm and then he saw, vaguely as a phantom, the form of a horseman rushing swiftly into the very teeth of the wind. The whistle wavered, ended, and in its place the long yell of a wolf cut the air. Mac Strann brandished a ponderous fist in defiance that was half hysterical. Man or beast alone he would meet—but a wolf-man!—he whirled the horse again and urged him heedlessly into the water.

The whirlpool no longer opened before him—it had passed on down the arroyo and left in its wake a comparative calm. So that when the horse took the water he made good progress for some distance, until Mac Strann could see, clearly, the farther bank of the stream. In his joy he shouted to his horse, and swung himself clear from his saddle to lighten the burden. At the same time they struck a heavier current and it struck them down like a blow from above until the water closed over their heads.

It was only for a moment, however; then they emerged, the horse with courageously pricking ears and snorting nostrils just above the flood. Mac Strann swung clear, gripping the horn of the saddle with one hand while with the other he hastily divested himself of all superfluous weight. His slicker went first, ripped away from throat and shoulders and whipped off his body by one tug of the current. Next he fumbled at his belt and tossed this also, guns and all, away; striking out with his legs and his free arm to aid the progress that now forged ahead with noticeable speed.

The current, to be sure, was carrying them farther down the stream, but they were now almost to the center of the arroyo and, though the water boiled furiously over the back of the horse, they forged steadily closer and closer to the safe shore.

It was chance that defeated Mac Strann. It came shooting down the river and he saw it only an instant too late—a log whipping through the surface of the stream as though impelled by a living force. And with arrowy straightness it lunged at them. Mac Strann heaved himself high—he screamed at the horse as though the poor brute could understand his warning, and then the tree trunk was upon them. Fair and square it struck the head of the horse with a thud audible even through the rushing of the stream. The horse went down like lead, and Mac Strann was dragged down beneath the surface.

He came up fighting grimly and hopelessly for life. For he was in the very center of the stream, now, and the current swept him relentlessly down. There seemed to be hands in the middle of the arroyo, and when he strove to battle his way to the edge of the water the current tangled at his legs and pulled him back. Yet even then he did not fear. It was death, he knew, but at least it was death fighting against a force of nature rather than destruction at the hands of some weird and unhuman agency. His arms began to grow numb. He raised his head to pick out the nearest point on the shore and make his last struggle for life.

What he saw was a black head cutting the water just above him, and beside the horse, one hand upon the beast's mane, swam a man. At the same instant a hand fastened on his collar and he was drawn slowly against the force of the river.

In the stunning surprise of the first moment he could make no effort to save himself, and as a result, all three were washed hopelessly down the current, but a shrill warning from his rescuer set him fighting again with all the power of his great limbs. After that they forged steadily toward the shore. The black horse swam with amazing strength, and breaking the force of the current for the men, they soon passed from the full grip of the torrent and forged into the smoother shallows at the side of the stream. In a moment firm land was beneath the feet of Mac Strann, and he turned his dull eyes of amazement upon Dan Barry. The latter stood beside the panting black horse. He had not even thrown off his slicker in the fording of the stream—there had been no time for even that small delay if he wished to save Strann. And now he was throwing back the folds of the garment to leave free play for his arms. He panted from the fierce effort of the fording, but his head was high, a singular smile lingered about the corners of his mouth, and in his eyes Mac Strann saw the gleam of yellow, a signal of unfathomable danger.

From his holsters Barry drew two revolvers. One he retained; the other he tossed toward Mac Strann, and the latter caught it automatically.

"Now," said the soft voice of Barry, "we're equally armed.—Down, Bart!————" (for the wolf dog was slinking with ominous intent toward the giant) "and there's the dog you shot. If you drop me, you can send your next shot into Bart. If I drop you, the teeth of Bart will be in your throat. Make your own terms; fight in the way you want; knives, if you like 'em better than guns, or——and here the yellow flamed terribly in Barry's eyes—"bare hand to hand!"

The grim truth sank slowly home in the dull mind of Mac Strann. The man had saved him from the water to kill him on dry land.

"Barry," he said slowly, "it was your bullet that brung down Jerry; but you've paid me back here. They's nothin' left on earth worth fightin' for. There's your gun."

And he threw the revolver into the mud at Barry's feet, turned on his heel, and lumbered off into the rain. There was no voice of answer behind him, except a shrill whine of rage from Black Bart and then a sharp command: "Down!" from the master. As the blanket of rain shut over him, Mac Strann looked back. There stood the strange man with the wolf crouched at his feet, and the teeth of Bart were bared, and the hum of his horrible snarling carried to Strann through the beat of the rain. Mac Strann turned again, and plodded slowly through the storm.

And Dan Barry? Twice men had stood before him, armed, and twice he had failed to kill. Wonder rose in him; wonder and a great fear. Was he losing the desert, and was the desert losing him? Were the chains of humanity falling about him to drag him down to a tamed and sordid life? A sudden hatred for all men, Mac Strann, Daniels, Kate, and even poor Joe Cumberland, welled hot in the breast of Whistling Dan. The strength of men could not conquer him; but how could their very weakness disarm him? He leaped again on the back of Satan, and rode furiously back into the storm.

41 · The Falling of Night

IT had been hard to gauge the falling of night on this day, and even the careful eyes of the watchers on the Cumberland Ranch could not tell when the grayness of the sky was being darkened by the coming of the evening. All day there had been swift alterations of light and shadow, comparatively speaking, as the clouds grew thin or thick before the wind. But at length, indubitably, the night was there. Little by little the sky was overcast, and even the lines of the falling rain were no longer visible. Before the gloom of the darkness had fully settled over the earth, moreover, there came a change in the wind, and the watchers at the rain-beaten windows of the ranch house saw the clouds roll apart and split into fragments that were driven from the face of the sky; and from the clean washed face of heaven the stars shone down bright and serene. And still Dan Barry had not come.

After the tumult of that long day the sudden silence of that windless night had more ill omen in it than thunder and lightning. For there was something watching and waiting in silence. In the living room the three did not speak.

Now that the storm was gone they had allowed the fire to fall away until the hearth showed merely fragmentary dances of flame and a wide bed of dull red coals growing dimmer from moment to moment. Wung Lu had brought in a lamp—a large lamp with a circular wick that cast a bright, white light—but Kate had turned down the wick, and now it made only a brief circle of yellow in one corner of the room. The main illumination came from the fireplace and struck on the faces of Kate and Buck Daniels, while Joe Cumberland, on the couch at the end of the room, was only plainly visible when there was an extraordinarily high leap of the dying flames; but usually his face was merely a glimmering hint in the darkness—his face and the long hands which were folded upon his breast. Often when the flames leapt there was a crackling of the embers and the last of the log, and then the two nearer the fire would start and flash a glance, of one accord, toward the prostrate figure on the couch.

That silence had lasted so long that when at length the dull voice of Joe Cumberland broke in, there was a ring of a most prophetic solemnity about it.

"He ain't come," said the old man. "Dan ain't here."

The others exchanged glances, but the eyes of Kate dropped sadly and fastened again upon the hearth.

Buck Daniels cleared his throat like an orator.

"Nobody but a fool," he said, "would have started out of Elkhead in a storm like this."

"Weather makes no difference to Dan," said Joe Cumberland.

"But he'd think of his hoss——"

"Weather makes no difference to Satan," answered the faint, oracular voice of Joe Cumberland. "Kate!"

"Yes?"

"Is he comin'?"

She did not answer. Instead, she got up slowly from her place by the fire and took another chair, far away in the gloom, where hardly a glimmer of light reached to her and there she let her head rest, as if exhausted, against the back of the seat.

"He promised," said Buck Daniels, striving desperately to keep his voice cheerful, "and he never busts his promises."

"Ay," said the old man, "he promised to be back— but he ain't here."

"If he started after the storm," said Buck Daniels.

"He didn't start after the storm," announced the oracle. "He was out in it."

"What was that!" cried Buck Daniels sharply.

"The wind," said Kate, "for it's rising. It will be a cold night, tonight."

"And he ain't here," said the old man monotonously.

"Ain't there things that might hold him up?" asked Buck, with a touch of irritation.

"Ay," said the old rancher, "they's things that'll hold him up. They's things that'll turn a dog wild, too, and the taste of blood is one of 'em!"

The silence fell again.

There was an old clock standing against the wall. It was one of those tall, wooden frames in which, behind the glass, the heavy, polished disk of the pendulum alternated slowly back and forth with wearisome precision. And with every stroke of the seconds there was a faint, metallic clangor in the clock—a falter like that which comes in the voice of a very old man. And the sound of this clock took possession of every silence until it seemed like the voice of a doomsman counting off the seconds. Ay, everyone in the room, again and again, took up the tale of those seconds and would count them slowly—fifty, fifty-one, fifty-two, fifty-three—and on and on, waiting for the next speech, or for the next popping of the wood upon the hearth, or for the next wail of the wind that would break upon the deadly expectancy of that count. And while they counted each looked straight before him with wide and widening eyes.

Into one of these pauses the voice of Buck Daniels broke at length; and it was a cheerless and lonely voice in that large room, in the dull darkness, and the duller lights.

"D'you remember Shorty Martin, Kate?"

"I remember him."

He turned in his chair and hitched it a little closer to her until he could make out her face, dimly, among the shadows. The flames jumped on the hearth, and he saw a picture that knocked at his heart.

"The little bow-legged feller, I mean."

"Yes, I remember him very well."

Once more the flames sputtered and he saw how she looked wistfully before her and above. She had never seemed so lovely to Buck Daniels. She was pale, indeed, but there was no ugly pinching of her face, and if there were shadows beneath her eyes, they only served to make her eyes seem marvelously large and bright. She was pallid, and the firelight stained her skin with touches of tropic gold, and cast a halo of the golden hair about her face. She seemed like one of those statues wrought in the glory and the rich days of Athens in ivory and in gold—some goddess who has heard the tidings of the coming fall, the change of the old order, and sits passive on her throne waiting the doom from which there is no escape. Something of this filtered through to the sad heart of Buck Daniels. He, too, had no hope—nay, he had not even her small hope, but somehow he was able to pity her and cherish the picture of her in that gloomy place. It seemed to Buck Daniels that he would give ten years from the best of his life to see her smile as he had once seen her in those old, bright days. He went on with his tale.

"You would have busted laughin' if you'd seen him at the Circle Y Bar roundup the way I seen him. Shorty ain't so bad with a rope. He's always talkin' about what he can do and how he can daub a rope on anything that's got horns. He ain't so bad, but then he ain't so good, either. Specially, he ain't so good at ridin'—you know what bowed legs he's got, Kate?"

"I remember, Buck."

She was looking at him, at last, and he talked eagerly to turn that look into a smile.

"Well, they was the three of us got after one two year old—a bull and a bad 'un. Shorty was on one side and me and Cuttle was on the other side. Shorty daubed his rope and made a fair catch, but when his hoss set back the rope busted plumb in two. Now, Shorty, he had an idea that he could ease the work of his hoss a whole pile if he laid holts on the rope whenever his hoss set down to flop a cow. So Shorty, he had holt on this rope and was pulling back hard when the rope busted, and Shorty, he spilled backwards out'n that saddle like he'd been kicked out.

"Whilst he was lyin' there, the bull, that had took a header when the rope busted, come up on his feet agin, and I'll tell a man he was rarin' mad! He seen Shorty lyin' on the ground, and he took a run for Shorty. Me and Cuttle was laughin' so hard we couldn't barely swing out ropes, but I made a throw and managed to get that bull around both horns. So my Betty sits down and braces herself for the tug.

"In the meantime little Shorty, he sits up and lays a hand to his head, and same time he sees that bull come tarin' for him. Up he jumps. And jest then the bull come to the end of the line and wonk!—down he goes, head over heels, and hits the sand with a bang that must of jostled his liver some, I'll be sayin'!

"Well, Shorty, he seen that bull fly up into the air and he lets out a yell like the world was comin' to an end, and starts runnin'. If he'd run straight back the other way the bull couldn't of run a step, because I had him fast with my rope, but Shorty seen me, and he come tarin' for my hoss to get behind him.

"That bull was like a cat gettin' to his feet, and he sights Shorty tarin' and lights out after him. There they went lickety-split. That bull was puffin' on the seat of Shorty's trousers and tossin' his horns and jest missin' Shorty by inches; and Shorty had his mouth so wide open hollerin' that you could have throwed a side of beef down his throat; and his eyes was buggin' out. Them bow-legs of his was stretchin' ten yards at a clip, most like, and the boys says they could hear him hollerin' a mile away. But that bull, stretch himself all he could; couldn't gain an inch on Shorty, and Shorty couldn't gain an inch on the bull, till the bull come to the other end of the forty-foot rope, and then, whang! up goes the heels of the bull and down goes his head, and his heels comes over—wonk! and hits Shorty right square on the head.

"Been an ordinary feller, and he wouldn't of lived to talk about it afterward, but seein' it was Shorty, he jest goes up in the air and lands about ten yards away, and rolls over and hits his feet without once gettin' off his stride—and then he *did* start runnin', and he didn't stop runnin' nor hollerin' till he got plumb back to the house!"

Buck Daniels sat back in his chair and guffawed at the memory. In the excitement of the tale he had quite forgotten Kate, but when he remembered her, she sat with her head craned a little to one side, her hand raised for silence, and a smile, indeed, upon her lips, but never a glance for Buck Daniels. He knew at once.

"Is it him?" he whispered. "D'you hear him?"

"Hush!" commanded two voices, and then he saw that old Joe Cumberland also was listening.

"No," said the girl suddenly, "it was only the wind."

As if in answer, a far, faint whistling broke upon them. She drew her hands slowly toward her breast, as if, indeed, she drew the sound in with them.

"He's coming!" she cried. "Oh, Dad, listen! Don't you hear?"

"I do," answered the rancher, "but what I'm hearin' don't warm my blood none. Kate, if you're wise you'll get up and go to your room and don't pay no heed to anything you might be hearin' tonight."

42 • The Journey into Night

THERE was no doubting the meaning of Joe Cumberland. It grew upon them with amazing swiftness, as if the black stallion were racing upon the house at a swift gallop, and the whistling rose and rang and soared in a wild outburst. Give the eagle the throat of the lark, and after he has struck down his prey in the center of the sky and sent the ragged feathers and the slain body falling down to earth, what would be the song of the eagle rising again and dwindling out of sight in the heart of the sky? What terrible pean would he send whistling down to the dull earth far below? And such was the music that came before the coming of Dan Barry. It did not cease, as usual, at a distance, but it came closer and closer, and it swelled around them. Buck Daniels had risen from his chair and stolen to a corner of the room where not a solitary shaft of light could possibly reach him; and Kate Cumberland slipped farther into the depths of the big chair.

So that, in their utter silence, in spite of the whistling that blew in upon them, they could hear the dull ticking of the tall clock, and by a wretched freak of fate the ticking fell exactly in with the soaring rhythm of the whistle and each had a part in the deadliness of the other.

Very near upon them the music ceased abruptly. A footfall swept down the hall, a weight struck the door and cast it wide, and Black Bart glided into the room. He cast not a glance on either side. He turned his head neither to right nor to left. But he held straight on until he came to Kate Cumberland and there he stood before her.

She leaned forward.

"Bart!" she said softly and stretched out her hands to him.

A deep snarl stopped the gesture, and at the flash of the long fangs she sank into the chair. Old Joe Cumberland, with fearful labor, dragged himself to a sitting position upon the couch, and sitting up in this fashion the light fell fully upon his white face and his white hair and his white beard, so that he made a ghostly picture.

Then an outer door slammed and a light step, at an almost running pace speeded down the hall, the door was swung wide again, and Dan was before them. He seemed to bring with him the keen, fresh air of the night, and at the opening of the door the flame in the lamp jumped in its chimney, shook, and fell slowly back to its original dimness; but by that glow of light they saw that the sombrero upon Dan Barry's head was a shapeless mass—his bandana had been torn away, leaving his throat bare—his slicker was a mass of rents and at the neck had been crumpled and torn in a thousand places as though strong teeth had worried it to a rag. Spots of mud were everywhere on his boots, even on his sombrero with its sagging brim, and on one side of his face there was a darker stain. He had ceased his whistling, indeed, but now he stood at the door and hummed as he gazed about the room. Straight to Kate Cumberland he walked, took her hands, and raised her from the chair.

He said, and there was a fiber and ring in his voice

that made them catch their breaths: "There's something outside that I'm following tonight. I don't know what it is. It is the taste of the wind and the feel of the air and the smell of the ground. And I've got to be ridin'. I'm saying good-bye for a bit, Kate."

"Dan," she cried, "what's happened? What's on your face?"

"The mark of the night," he answered. "I don't know what else. Will you come with me, Kate?"

"For how long? Where are you going, Dan!"

"'I don't know where or how long. All I know is I've got to be going. Come to the window. Take the air on your face. You'll understand!"

He drew her after him and cast up the window.

"Do you feel it in the wind" he called to her, turning with a transfigured face. "Do you hear it?"

She could not speak but stood with her face lifted, trembling.

"Look at me!" he commanded, and turned her roughly toward him. There he stood leaning close to her, and the yellow light flickered and waned and burned again in his eyes.

He had held her hands while he stared. Now he dropped them with an exclamation.

"You're blank," he said angrily. "You've seen nothing and heard nothing."

He turned on his heel.

"Bart!" he called, and walked from the room, and they heard the padding of his soft step down the hall and on the porch and then—silence.

Black Bart slunk to the door and into the hall, but instantly he was back and peering into the gloom of the silent place like an evil-eyed specter.

A sharp whistle rang from outside, and Black Bart started. Still he glided on until he stood before Kate then turned and stalked slowly toward the door, looking back after her. She did not move, and with a snarl the wolf dog whirled again and trotted back to her. This time he caught a fold of her skirt in his teeth and pulled on it. And under the pressure she made a step.

"Kate!" called Joe Cumberland. "Are you mad, girl to dream of goin' out in a night like this?"

"I'm not going!" she answered hurriedly. "I'm afraid—and I won't leave you, Dad!"

She had stopped as she spoke, but Black Bart, snarling terribly, threw his weight back, and dragged her a step forward.

"Buck," cried old Joe Cumberland and he dragged himself up and stood tottering. "Shoot the damned wolf—for God's sake—for my sake!"

Still the wolf dog drew the girl in that snarling progress toward the door.

"Kate!" cried her father, and the agony in his voice made it young and sent it ringing through the room. "Will you go out to wander between heaven and hell—on a night like this?"

"I'm not going!" she answered, "I won't leave you—but oh—Dad!——"

He opened his lips for a fresh appeal, but the chorus of the wild geese swept in upon the wind, blown loud and clear and jangling as distant bells out of tune. And Kate Cumberland buried her face in her hands and stumbled blindly out of the room and down the hall—and then they heard the wild neighing of a horse outside.

"Buck!" commanded Joe Cumberland. "He's stealin' my girl—my Kate—go out! call up the boys—tell 'em to stop Dan from saddlin' a horse for Kate——"

"Wait and listen!" cut in Buck Daniels. "D'you hear that?"

On the wet ground outside they heard a patter of galloping hoofs, and then a wild whistling, sweet and keen and high, came ringing back to them. It diminished rapidly with the distance.

"He's carryin' her off on Satan!" groaned Joe Cumberland, staggering as he tried to step forward. "Buck, call out the boys. Even Satan can't beat my hosses when he's carryin' double—call 'em out—if you bring her back——"

His voice choked and he stumbled and would have fallen to his knees had not Buck Daniels sprung forward and caught him and carried him back to the couch.

"What's happened there ain't no man can stop," said

Buck hoarsely. "God's work or devil's work—I dunno—but I know there ain't no place for a man between Dan and Kate."

"Turn up the lights," commanded Joe Cumberland sharply. "Got to see; I got to think. D'you hear?"

Buck Daniels ran to the big lamp and turned up the wick. At once a clear light flooded every nook of the big room and showed all its emptiness.

"Can't you make the lamp work?" asked the old ranchman angrily. "Ain't they any oil in it? Why, Buck, they ain't enough light for me to see your face, hardly. But I'll do without the light. Buck, how far will they go? Kate's a good girl! She won't leave me, lad!"

"She won't," agreed Buck Daniels. "Jest gone with Dan for a bit of a canter."

"The devil was come back in his eyes," muttered the old man. "God knows where he's headin' for! Buck, I brought him in off'n the range and made him a part of my house. I took him into my heart; and now he's gone out again and taken everything that I love along with him. Buck, why did he go?"

"He'll come back," said the big cowpuncher softly.

"It's gettin' darker and darker," said Joe Cumberland, "and they's a kind of ringing in my ears. Talk louder. I don't hear you none too well."

"I said they was comin' back," said Buck Daniels.

Something like a light showed on the face of Joe Cumberland.

"Ay, lad," he said eagerly, "I can hear Dan's whistlin' comin' back—nearer and nearer. Most like he was jest playin' a joke on me, eh, Buck?"

"Most like," said Buck, brokenly.

"Ay, there it's ringin' at the door of the house! Was that a footstep in the hall?"

"It was," said Buck. "They's comin' down the hall!"

But far, far away he heard the whistling of Dan Barry dying among the hills.

"You let the lamp go out," said Joe Cumberland, "and now I can't see nothing. Are they in the room?"

"They're here," said Buck Daniels, "comin' toward you now."

"Dan!" cried the old man, shading his eyes and peering anxiously—"no, I can't see a thing. Can you find me, lad?"

And Buck Daniels, softening his voice as much as he could, answered. "I can find you."

"Then gimme your hand."

Buck Daniels slipped his own large hand into the cold fingers of the dying cattleman. An expression of surpassing joy lay on the face of Joe Cumberland.

"Whistlin' Dan, my Dan," he murmured faintly, "I'm kind of sleepy, but before I go to sleep, tonight, I got to tell you that I forgive you for your joke—pretendin' to take Kate away.

"They's nothin' but sleep worth while—and goin' to sleep, holdin' your hand, lad——"

Buck Daniels dropped upon his knees and stared into the wide, dead eyes. Through the open window a sound of whistling blew to him. It was a sweet, faint music, and being so light it seemed like a chorus of singing voices among the mountains, for it was as pure and as sharp as the starlight.

Buck Daniels lifted his head to listen, but the sound faded, and the murmur of the night-wind came between.